To all of my readers, this one is for you.

You make me smile, you make me laugh, and above all else, you make me love what I do.

Thank you. ~Nic~

Chapter One

♂♀

"Are you fucking kidding?" Kaleb could barely make out his youngest brothers words as Zane doubled over in laughter.

"Hell, no. I'm dead serious. Sawyer was standing on the side of the road, holding up a sign that said 'will work for sex'. I shit you not." Kaleb finished pouring his coffee before taking his mug back to his desk, dodging Zane in the process.

Hello? This was Sawyer Walker they were talking about, so Kaleb shouldn't have been all that surprised really. But, he'd been hard pressed to keep his jaw out of his lap as he drove past his brother standing shirtless, wearing jeans and shit kickers while standing on the side of the road holding up the damn sign. To top it off, there was a truck full of women pulled over talking to him.

"You know Dad's gonna be pissed when he sees it." Zane doubled over in another fit of laughter.

Kaleb wasn't all that worried about their father and what he thought about Sawyer's wild and crazy antics. It was their mother they actually had to worry about. Curtis Walker would laugh right along with Zane, but Lorrie Walker would be fit to be tied.

But that was Sawyer for you. At thirty three, he wasn't supposed to be the wildest of the seven of them, but he even gave Zane a run for his money.

The screen door slammed and Zane sat upright, immediately choking on his laughter. As Travis made his way into the small kitchen, Kaleb barely suppressed a groan.

"What's going on?" The oldest of the seven Walker brothers wasn't smiling, and Kaleb had a feeling he wouldn't find Sawyer's antics all that funny anyway, so Kaleb kept his mouth shut.

"Sawyer's down on Main and 1st half-dressed holding up a sign."

"Fuck." Kaleb muttered and pinned his brother with a death glare. "Seriously, Zane?"

He was met with a shrug.

Telling Travis anything that didn't pertain to Walker Demolition was like telling their mother as far as Kaleb was concerned. The oldest of the Walker boys at thirty five, Travis had turned into an old man in recent years – at least as far as his mood was concerned.

"Fuck." Travis groaned as he turned to the coffee pot sitting on the counter. "When will he ever grow up?"

Today, just like any other day, Kaleb was going to give Travis a wide berth, not to mention, knock Zane upside his head for telling on Sawyer. "Likely never if I had to guess." Kaleb chimed in, knowing that was the only sufficient answer.

"Did you hear back from Carl Stranford?" Travis glanced over his shoulder at Kaleb before returning his attention to pouring his coffee. "You were going by his house yesterday?"

Suddenly wishing he'd had more coffee, Kaleb rubbed his hand over the back of his neck trying to squeeze some of the tension out. Not that there ever was a good time to have this conversation with Travis, but now certainly wasn't it.

"Yeah." He definitely stopped by Carl's, just like he had several times that week, but his brief conversation hadn't resulted in anything other than the expected *'Let me think about it, Kaleb, and get back with you.'*

"Shit." Travis groaned, obviously knowing what that response had been before Kaleb even had to say it out loud. "That man keeps stalling, and I don't know what the hell for. You'd think he'd be ready to sell off a portion of that land by now. He's all but lost every one of his crops and to tell you the truth, I'm getting damn tired of waiting."

And if Carl didn't do something soon, he'd lose a lot more than just his crops, but Kaleb wasn't going to share that with Travis just yet. Until he had the chance to talk to Zoey about it, he wasn't ready to spread the devastating news.

Not to mention, it wouldn't matter what he told Travis because until he had a firm agreement from Carl, none of it mattered. His oldest brother would just get even more pissed off than he already was.

Walker Demolition – the company Kaleb and his brothers had built from the ground up – had grown leaps and bounds over the last few years, and instead of being content with what they'd built, Travis was ready to venture in another direction, expand their horizon's he'd said.

Instead of focusing solely on tearing shit up, Travis had come up with the idea to build a resort. Not that Kaleb didn't think it was a brilliant idea because he did. He was just content with the tearing shit up part.

The plans he'd seen for a mega resort the likes of which their small town had never seen, were underway. They'd received the necessary approvals, and now the only thing left to do was to secure the land. Travis had already bought out two of their adjacent neighbors, acquiring a good three hundred acres of decrepit old farmland, but he hadn't been satisfied with that. Now he was looking for another hundred that backed up to what they'd already purchased. Only this land belonged to Carl Stranford, an ornery old farmer who had been giving them the runaround for the better part of the last six months.

"Call him." Zane's tone was laced with sarcasm. "Or better yet, go see him. Maybe some of your macho intimidation will make him come to a decision."

Kaleb groaned.

Zane was the youngest of seven and considering the age difference between him and Travis, he didn't remember much of the Travis they had all grown up with. The fun loving, hang on by the seat of your pants guy they'd all wanted to be like. But that man never returned from the four year stint in the Army. In his place was the grouchy, unsmiling man that sat before them now.

"I might just do that." Travis snapped, before turning and walking out of the room.

When the screen door slammed behind their brother, Zane turned to Kaleb. "Why don't you go talk to Carl? Or better yet, Zoey?"

"What does Zoey have to do with this?"

Zane liked to give Kaleb shit about Carl Stranford's only daughter. Not only had she been Kaleb's closest female friend for the better part of the last decade, she was also the woman Kaleb had always wanted, but never had. Despite the ever present physical attraction, he'd somehow managed to be friends with her without ever trying to push it any further, although he'd wanted to.

More than wanted to.

Since she'd never shown even an inkling of interest in him other than friendship, Kaleb had opted to take what he could get and they'd established a very solid friendship. Hell, the woman knew everything there was to know about him and most of his brothers, yet she still chose to associate with him, so he considered himself lucky.

They were infamous in their little town, but that was mostly due to their wild and crazy behavior since about the time each of them could walk. They were a rowdy bunch, and there was a long list of rumors associated with them – some true, some not entirely true. For whatever reason, Zoey chose to ignore them, and for that, he was grateful.

Not that Zoey Stranford wasn't as wild as they came. That was partly what he found so damn attractive about the woman. She didn't care what other people thought about her, and it seemed her one goal was to have fun and not hurt anyone in the process.

So, he'd mastered the art of pretending when it came to Zoey. First and foremost, he was her friend, but that wasn't the problem. His issue was in learning to hide the unbridled lust burning deep and hot for as long as he'd known her.

And since his brothers had dubbed her the one woman who wouldn't give him the time of day, they loved to give him a hard time about her.

It certainly wasn't a hardship being friends with Zoey, but it had gotten increasingly more difficult in the last few years. Ever since she and that jackass Jason Tribbons divorced, Kaleb did everything he possibly could to make sure he kept his feelings for her hidden. But hell, he wasn't a saint and he wasn't sure how much longer he could pull off the charade.

"Zoey doesn't have any say in what her father does with that land." Kaleb added as he watched the wheels turn in Zane's head. His little brother was going to piss him off, he could feel it.

"Yeah, but she likes you." Zane goaded. "I'm sure if she goes running to daddy, telling him her boy toy wants to buy the land, he'd sell it in a heartbeat."

Boy toy? "I know you've got something better than that."
Kaleb pushed.

Kaleb had grown quite fond of his own dick over the years, and he didn't have any intentions of losing it, thank you very much. Carl Stranford would just as soon cut off Kaleb's dick than let him date his daughter.

Carl was an overprotective son of a bitch when it came to his one and only daughter, and he and Zoey had had to clarify their friendship on more than one occasion over the years. Granted, Carl was close to eighty now, and Zoey was very much a grown woman who didn't let her daddy tell her whom she could see, but still...

Hell, he'd expected Carl to answer the damn door with a shotgun in his hand the night he had taken Zoey to her senior prom. Thankfully Carl hadn't, but that was probably due to Zoey's mother who had liked Kaleb. Not that Kaleb could blame the man. If a nineteen year old man had the balls to show up on his doorstep asking to take his seventeen year old daughter to the prom, Kaleb knew damn well that young man would know how acquainted he was with his gun collection.

But true to his word, even back then when he was ruled by hormones alone, Kaleb never laid a finger on Zoey, no matter how badly he wanted to. And to this day, he'd never so much as kissed her, and his dick knew it all too well.

Shaking off the thought, Kaleb pushed himself out of his chair. "I'll go talk to Carl. Until we get that land, Travis won't let it go."

"Nope, he won't." Zane agreed as he stood. "Tell Zoey hello for me."

"Fuck off." Kaleb grinned as he walked out the back door.

Not fifteen minutes later, Kaleb was pulling up to Carl Stranford's house, wishing like hell he didn't have to do this again today. Thankfully Zoey's truck wasn't in the driveway, which meant she was probably working – something Kaleb should've been doing. Instead, he'd get the pleasure of explaining to Carl yet again what he wanted and why he was there.

He pulled around to the back of the house, put the truck in Park and climbed out. Stealing himself for the conversation to come, Kaleb took a deep breath and looked around. With the sun shining bright and not a single cloud in the sky, Kaleb took in the vast landscape, looking off to the south as he tried to picture the entrance to the resort as Travis envisioned it.

He could see the massive wrought iron gates in his mind, the ones that would be manned twenty four hours a day by security, allowing only those invited to come inside. Kaleb had seen the artwork for the gates design, including the large "A" and "I" that would be welded into the intricate iron design. *Alluring Indulgence*, the name he and his brothers all agreed on.

Given the type of resort they were looking at creating, the name suited it. The goal had been to come up with a name to reflect the carnal temptation they fully intended it to be. So, thanks to an online dictionary and a case of beer, Alluring Indulgence was born.

He wouldn't lie, he was anxiously waiting for the day they opened their doors, but in order for that to happen, Kaleb had to convince Carl to sell him the land. With a resigned sigh, Kaleb shut the truck door and made his way to the side door of the house.

Rapping his knuckles on the wood frame, Kaleb waited like he always did until Carl's gruff voice instructed him to "Come in." The man never bothered to get up, nor did he bother locking any of his doors so Kaleb let himself into the large, typical farmhouse kitchen.

"Mr. Stranford." Kaleb greeted Zoey's father as he stepped into the living room.

Instead of a greeting, Kaleb was met with a muted "Hmmphh".

Figures.

"How are you today?" When Carl pointed to the couch, Kaleb took a seat, keeping a smile on his face and his eyes on the old man sitting in the chair.

Just like in recent days, Kaleb felt an overwhelming sense of nostalgia sitting on the couch in the Stranford's dated living room. With the dark wood paneling, well-worn hardwood floors and a ceiling fan that had to have been produced in the 1980's, he was hit with flashbacks from his teenage years. There was even the faint smell of cigarette smoke still lingering, although Kaleb knew Carl had quit smoking long ago.

He and Zoey spent many days sitting right there on the very same maroon and green, flowery couch Kaleb sat on now, talking, laughing and avoiding the glares of one ornery old man who continuously traipsed back and forth through the room, making sure the up-to-no-good teenage boy in his living room wasn't somehow taking advantage of his sweet little girl.

"Was doing fine until you showed up."

That was definitely the Carl he'd grown accustomed to. He much preferred the ornery old man to the fragile, forgetful one he'd spent hours with, as well. Carl had been diagnosed with Alzheimer's within the last year, and as each day passed, Kaleb recognized more and more symptoms. At times, he was positive Carl didn't know who he was, even though he pretended to.

"If you're looking for Zoey, she's not here."

Kaleb barely heard him over the television turned up loud enough for Carl to hear without the hearing aids he refused to wear. Glancing over at the TV and then back at Carl, he bit back a laugh when Carl sighed dramatically before turning the volume down with the remote on the arm of his chair.

"I'm not here to see Zoey, Mr. Stranford. I'm here to see you."

"Ahhh." Carl didn't look any happier than he sounded by the news. "Out to try and steal my land again, are you?"

"No, sir." Kaleb said, forcing back a smile. He was, of course, looking to *acquire* some of Carl's land, but in his opinion, the offer was more than fair. So, no, he was not looking to steal anything.

"So, why is it that you can come over to talk to me about my land, but you aren't here trying to woo my daughter?"

Kaleb couldn't tell whether Carl was serious or trying to jack with him. *Woo? Seriously?* Who said woo anymore?

He couldn't very well tell Carl that he'd been thinking about "wooing" his daughter for some time now, but had never gotten up enough nerve to do so. No matter how Carl sounded, Kaleb wasn't convinced he'd take any man's intentions toward his daughter as a good thing. Not after her devastating divorce.

Shaking off that train of thought, Kaleb focused his attention on Carl once more. "Mr. Stranford, I wanted to stop by to see if you'd come to a decision about the land."

"What are you planning to do with my land again?"

Kaleb's hands balled into fists, but he kept them hidden. He was fairly certain Carl knew exactly what he and his brothers intended to do with it, but he figured he had no choice but to oblige him.

"Sir, we're looking to build a hotel." Well, it was more of a resort, but he didn't want to go into the details.

"A hotel? Like what? A La Quinta?"

Fighting the urge to laugh, Kaleb shook his head. "No, sir. Not a La Quinta." Not by a long shot, he thought to himself.

"What do you plan to do with my house if you build this hotel?" Carl asked, sincerely, his forehead creased with worry.

"We don't have any plans for your house, Mr. Stranford. We aren't looking to buy the land that your house sits on. We're only looking to acquire the one hundred acres that sit adjacent to my father's land."

"One hundred acres, huh?"

Oh, brother.

"Yes, sir."

The amount that Kaleb and his brothers were looking to purchase was about half of what Carl owned in total. Even though he was certain Carl didn't have any intentions of using the land in the future, they didn't want to go overboard. In Kaleb's opinion, Travis was riding a fine line as it was.

Since Travis was insistent that the entrance face the south, for a number of reasons he'd been told, this had been their only option.

"And how much are you offering me?"

Kaleb was pretty sure he saw a twinkle in Carl's eye, and if he wasn't mistaken, the man was trying to catch him in a lie. Well, that was one thing the Walker's didn't do. They didn't lie, and they didn't try and cheat someone out of what was rightfully theirs.

Taking a deep breath, Kaleb settled in for the long haul. For the next half hour, he repeated the same conversation he'd had with Mr. Stranford for the umpteenth time.

♀♂

To say Zoey was tired was an understatement.

She and V were going on hour number three of their weekly visit to the Wilson's gi-freaking-normous house in which they scoured the five thousand square foot monstrosity from top to bottom. Sometimes she wished she wasn't quite so gullible because when Victoria Wilson had bragged about how well kept her house was, Zoey had actually believed her.

Ummm... That was *so* not the case.

"V?" Zoey called out, her voice echoing off of the Travertine floors and twenty feet tall ceilings. "Where are you?"

Making her way to the master bedroom downstairs, Zoey had a good idea where V was, and she smiled at the thought.

Noticing that the master bedroom was in tip top shape, Zoey continued toward the master bathroom and the sound of V sighing. Loudly.

"Are you almost done?" Zoey asked when she found V on her hands and knees near the toilet – the one thing V absolutely detested about cleaning houses. For a while, she had tried to convince Zoey that she was allergic to toilets, and some of her excuses had bordered on insane, but knowing V, Zoey had never given in.

"Does it look like I'm almost done?" V snarled. "If someone," *cough, cough,* "understood how much I truly hate this part of the job," *cough, cough,* "they might've agreed to handle the bathrooms all by herself."

"Ummm... In case you didn't know, I've already cleaned the other four. And you're just lucky I volunteered to clean the kid's bathroom." Zoey snarled back, remembering all too vividly what the Wilson's son's bathroom had looked like before she went in there.

Unfortunately, the bathroom hadn't been the worst of it this time. She wasn't sure what it was the Wilson's did to make this much of a mess in a seven day period, yet each week it seemed to get worse. With six children – Zoey had no idea how they kept up with six kids – it was a wonder the house was even still standing.

"Well, what's one more?" V asked, still scrubbing away before flushing the toilet and standing. With a little wiggle of her hips, V managed to straighten her skirt before tossing her hair back over her shoulder.

How the woman could come to work – cleaning houses, mind you – looking impeccable day in and day out was beyond her. If she didn't know better, Zoey would've thought V worked in the corporate world for all of the trouble she went through to get dressed up each day.

Not Zoey. No way. Her outfit for the day consisted of her soft, faded jeans and an oversized t-shirt that had clearly seen better days. But, neither her shirt nor her jeans had holes in them, and that was about as good as it got for her.

Staring back at her friend, Zoey realized they looked like polar opposites, what with V wearing wedge heels and a flouncy skirt. V was also tall and curvy in all the right places while Zoey was on the short side. Like day and night, Zoey smiled to herself.

After V stripped the latex gloves off, tossing them into the sink, she turned her attention to Zoey. "What's left?"

"I think we're done." Zoey smiled. "As long as you're done in here, that is."

"Oh, I'm done." V said feigning exasperation.

"What do you say I buy you a drink then?" Zoey asked, turning toward the kitchen to pack up the rest of their things.

"Throw in dinner, and you've got a date." V stated, tossing the last of her supplies into the bucket they used to haul them back and forth from the truck.

"Can't do dinner tonight." Zoey grinned. "I'm meeting Kaleb."

"Ohhhh... That's right. I almost forgot. You're weekly date." V pretended to be offended, but Zoey knew better. "I'm being shunned for that sexy, hot neighbor of yours."

"It's not a date." Zoey realized how defensive she sounded as soon as the words were out of her mouth.

"When are you going to give in and sleep with him?"

Hefting her bucket of cleaners, Zoey managed to lock the front door and roll her eyes at her friend while pretending not to have heard the question.

It wasn't the first time V had asked that particular question, and she knew it wouldn't be the last, so Zoey wasn't even going to dignify it with a response. Best friend or not, V had an uncanny ability to get on Zoey's last nerve with her constant pestering when it came to her friendship with Kaleb Walker.

It seemed as though once a week V would go off on a tangent about how Zoey and Kaleb were dancing around one another and should just give in and admit they wanted to sleep together. For the most part, Zoey managed to ignore her. The rest of the time she just made it worse by arguing.

There was possibly a smidgeon of truth to V's assessment of the situation, but Zoey wouldn't admit it. Ever since Zoey's marriage came crashing down around her, she and Kaleb had managed to rekindle the friendship they'd shared since middle school. Only this time, her best buddy managed to spark an irritating amount of lust that Zoey refused to acknowledge.

Considering there weren't many days that passed in which they didn't meet up for dinner or drinks, or just to hang out with a group of friends, Zoey was having a hard time ignoring this little infatuation she'd apparently developed for him.

As far as she could tell, there wasn't an ounce of reciprocation from Kaleb's side, so it made it a little easier to pretend he was just her friend. And she could've lived with that if her warped and twisted mind hadn't gone and conjured up a plethora of images that consisted of all of the things Zoey wanted to do to the man.

She had a feeling V's comments were to blame for that carnal slide show playing over and over again in her mind.

Ten minutes later, Zoey was pulling her truck into the gravel parking lot of Moonshiner's – the one and only bar in their very small town. For a Thursday afternoon, it was packed, but the more the merrier, Zoey thought to herself.

It took a little persuading – or flirting, whatever you wanted to call it – to commandeer two bar stools, but they finally managed. Ordering their usual – mango margaritas – Zoey glanced around the dimly lit room, scoping out the familiar faces.

Most of the Thursday crowd was younger, getting a jump start on the weekend and choosing to battle it out at the pool tables. The dance floor was empty, but that wasn't unusual for this time of day. It usually livened up quite a bit after dark, but they were still a few hours off from that.

Feeling a tad surly after V's pestering from earlier, Zoey turned to her friend and threw out the one question she knew would get V riled up. "So, when are you going to focus on your own Walker man and lay off my nonexistent sex life?"

"*My* Walker man?" V almost sounded as though she had no idea what Zoey was talking about. Almost. "Who the hell are you talking about?"

Remembering the way V had all but jumped on Zane Walker the last time they'd all gotten together, Zoey arched an eyebrow in challenge. "Don't deny it. I saw the way you were eye fucking Zane the last time we were here."

"Zane? *Zane Walker* – Zane?" Vanessa laughed, and the sultry sound had half the bar turning to look at them.

"Do you know another one?"

The best defense is a good offense – the phrase suddenly rang through Zoey's mind when she saw the look in Vanessa's eyes. It was about to be a free for all.

"Wait." V held up a hand, taking a sip of her drink. "You first."

"Me first, what?" Zoey was confused.

"You admit to crushing on Kaleb, and then I'll tell you my story."

"Oh, whatever." Zoey laughed. "I am not crushing on Kaleb or anyone else for that matter. But you, my beautiful friend have a bad case of the hots for one Zane Walker."

V blushed immediately, but turned her head and avoided Zoey's knowing stare. It was obvious the woman had been lusting after Kaleb's younger brother, but Zoey had no idea for how long. Not that age mattered, but there was a six year age gap between V and Zane, which was surprising because her friend had never been the type to go for younger men.

"You can't deny it, V."

When Vanessa's ears flamed red, Zoey knew she'd hit her mark. But, they both knew it was all in good fun because yes if either of them were to own up to it, both of them had the hots for one of the Walker brothers.

"Maybe not, but what about you and Kaleb?"

"What about me and Kaleb?" Zoey asked, forcing a smile. She did not like where this conversation was going, regardless of whether this was her best friend or not. She was not willing to admit whatever these strange feelings were that she'd developed for Kaleb.

"You have to admit he's hot." V grinned.

"Well, of course, he's hot." That wasn't a secret.

"Have you ever fantasized about what it would be like to kiss him?" V asked, getting pushy as always.

What was this? Eighth grade?

Hoping like hell the heat that suddenly infused her face wasn't visible, Zoey smarted off. "Hasn't everyone?"

The smile that beamed on V's face had Zoey stilling in her chair.

Oh God.

She was suddenly enveloped in strong, muscled arms and overwhelmed by the all too familiar, highly intoxicating scent of the one man she wished hadn't just heard that comment.

"So, what would it be like?" Kaleb's sexy voice whispered in her ear, his warm breath tickling her cheek seconds before his lips landed in a chaste, friendly kiss.

Shoving him off of her, Zoey laughed because if she didn't, she might just cry. "Oooh, gross! Boy cooties." *Yep, definitely eighth grade.*

"Boy cooties?" V asked, laughing. "That's what you scream when Kaleb Walker plants a kiss on you? Mercy, woman. I'm beginning to seriously worry about you."

Zoey felt the heat flood her face as she purposely ignored Vanessa, all the while trying to pretend Kaleb hadn't actually heard their conversation.

"You're early." She told him when she finally managed to compose herself.

"I'm starving." He waved off the bartender when he strolled over. "Take me to dinner."

"Nuh uh, buddy. It's your turn to pick up the tab." Zoey reminded him.

Before Kaleb could argue, Zane walked up and Zoey watched as V's entire demeanor changed. If she wasn't mistaken, it just got a lot warmer in the bar, despite the blast of cold air from the air conditioner.

Zoey smiled. Right. Nothing there.

"Ok, I'll take you to dinner." Zoey stood abruptly. "Here, Zane. Take my seat." Throwing a knowing grin at Vanessa and watching as her friend tried to shoot daggers from her eyeballs, Zoey laughed.

"You are so dead," V mouthed before Zoey turned away.

Truer words had never been spoken because as Zoey turned to walk out of the bar with Kaleb, she was hammered with a sudden, overwhelming urge to... kiss him.

Chapter Two

♀♂

Five minutes later, Zoey was pulling her truck into a vacant parking space beside Kaleb's. She'd insisted on following him to the restaurant because she had needed a minute to get a grip. As she shut the truck door, turning to face him, she realized she probably could've used a few more minutes. Damn it.

Walking through the parking lot, Zoey tried to distract herself by figuring out what she was going to have for dinner. She had to reminder herself not to let him choose the restaurant in the future because although the food was decent at this particular establishment, the service was well...

"You thought about trading that truck in lately?" Kaleb interrupted her thoughts as he held the door open for her.

Trading it in? What on earth was the man talking about? She loved her old Chevy and couldn't imagine ever trading it in. "No, why?"

"Because it's too damn slow." He goaded her before throwing his arm around her shoulder in a friendly gesture.

Zoey took the opportunity and elbowed him in the ribs for his comment. "It's not my fault I don't drive like a bat out of hell. If you and that monster of a truck would obey the law, you wouldn't be worried about my driving."

"Where's the fun in that?" He asked as they approached the hostess stand which was as usual lacking a hostess.

Zoey's senses were assaulted by the delightful smells of home cooking, mixed with the low hum of conversations as they waited for someone to seat them. The place was packed, but that was normal for any day of the week but especially on Thursday when fried chicken was the specialty.

"Hey, Kaleb." Rachel Talbott, the hostess slash waitress, swooned.

"Hey. You got a table for two?"

"I do, sugar. Anything for you."

Yuck.

Zoey had spent more than one night watching as one woman or another lusted after Kaleb, more than obvious in their pursuit of him, regardless of her presence. Since she and Kaleb were only friends, and the entire town knew it, she'd come to expect it, but it still grossed her out.

"Yeah, *sugar*. *Anything for you.*" Zoey muttered, and Kaleb squeezed her shoulder as they followed the overly flirty hostess through the restaurant.

Once seated, Rachel took their order – their frequent visits made them regulars and they always got the same thing. Two of the specials, salad with ranch dressing, mashed potatoes and iced tea. Two peas in a pod they were.

"So, tell me more about this kissing fantasy of yours." Kaleb said, trying to hide a grin. He didn't fool her.

"Oh, shut it." Zoey laughed, but the telltale heat was back in her face. "There is no fantasizing going on here." She lied.

"Awww, well, that's too bad. I was going to share some of my fantasies with you, but noooo. I get it."

Zoey smirked. "I have no desire to hear what goes on in that warped brain of yours." *Unless of course your fantasies include me.*

"Now you're lying."

Zoey was mesmerized by that signature Walker grin – just a little crooked, just a little wicked, and just a lot sexy.

"I heard you myself. You've fantasized about kissing me. What if I said I've fantasized about kissing you, too?"

The sudden desire to wish he were telling the truth was overwhelming as was the increasing awareness of him as way more than just her buddy. "Cool it, cowboy. So, what'd you do today?"

"Not nearly enough." Kaleb stated, sounding serious.

"Something wrong?"

"Not necessarily, no."

Zoey could tell Kaleb was holding something back, and she had an idea of what it was. "You went to talk to my dad, didn't you?"

Purchasing some of her father's land was one of the main priorities of Kaleb's for several months now, and yet, he hadn't spoken to her much about it. Figuring he was trying to avoid an argument – not that she would've argued – Zoey never broached the subject either.

"I did." Glancing down at his hands, then back up at her, Kaleb continued, "I just don't get it."

"Get what?" Ok, so now she was curious what they'd discussed.

"From the past conversations I've had with him, he seemed interested, yet for the last few days, he's given me the run around as soon as I walk in the door."

Watching his mouth, Zoey did her best to listen to what he was saying, but she was becoming way too distracted. "With the economy the way it is, I figured he'd be all for getting rid of it." She told him.

"That's what I thought, but I'm beginning to wonder if he's hesitant because of the family connection. You said the land had been in your family for generations, right?"

"Yes. My great great grandfather purchased the land back when the town wasn't even a town. And it's been handed down generation after generation to the men in the family."

"Which makes sense, but..."

Zoey was pretty sure Kaleb continued to speak because she saw his lips move, but she was suddenly flooded with a wave of desire so strong the roaring in her ears drowned him out. It seemed that whatever this condition was, she was growing more aware of the man every time they were together. From his adorable, unkempt hair, those scorching blue gray eyes that every single one of the Walker boys had inherited, to his sinfully delicious body, the man made her dormant libido come to life.

Not a good thing.

Especially not while she was trying to have a casual, friendly dinner with the man.

"Earth to Zoey."

Shit.

"Sorry, what?"

"Where'd you go?" That stunning grin of his damn near blinded her. "Off to fantasy land again?"

This time the blush suffused her face, and she was unable to hide her embarrassment.

Good Lord.

What the hell was wrong with her?

♂♀

Ok. Something was seriously off here.

Call him crazy, but there was a remarkably different feel to this so called casual dinner with Zoey. Not only was he having a damn hard time focusing, but apparently he wasn't the only one. Since the second he walked up on Zoey and Vanessa having a conversation not meant for him to overhear, he'd been fighting a mad case of the *what the fucks.*

Didn't she know that he'd laughed off her comment and was only teasing when he brought it up? If he thought there was a chance in hell that Zoey had actually fantasized about him...

Ok, so his dick knew exactly what to do with that thought, unfortunately, now was not the time, and this was certainly not the place.

As much as he wanted to think that Zoey had actually fantasized about him once or twice – God knows she'd played a starring role in some of his more erotic thoughts – Kaleb knew she had just been joking.

Hadn't she?

For a second, he wasn't so sure.

The woman sitting across from him – the one wringing her hands together, blushing, and avoiding eye contact – was not the same woman Kaleb had known for so long. His best friend would be giving him a rash of shit about anything and everything, going off about Rachel's incessant flirting no matter when they came in, or better yet, telling him to dream on as far as fantasies went. That's the exact opposite of what was going on between them right now.

They were no longer acting like best buds. Instead, they were acting like... a man and a woman.

On a date.

Fuck.

What the hell was he supposed to do about this? Truth be told, this was exactly what he'd hoped for, but not exactly the circumstance in which he envisioned it happening. Call him a romantic, but he'd thought of a much more appealing place for them to come to terms with any sort of physical attraction than Mama's Diner.

On the other hand, he hadn't actually expected it to happen at all.

"So, what did my dad say?" Zoey asked, interrupting his thoughts.

"Same as last time. He knew what I was talking about, but he wanted me to clarify it for him all over again. Still no decision."

He hadn't talked much about their plans with Zoey because quite frankly, she didn't seem all that interested. Supportive? Yes. Oddly enough. She just didn't care to talk about it, which was interesting because it had turned into a hot topic for her at the moment.

"Who knows with him," Zoey penetrated him with those beautiful blue eyes.

It was clear they needed to find a much safer topic.

"So, how'd it go at the Wilson's? You get Vanessa to work today?"

Zoey laughed, and her husky voice sent a shiver down his spine. He tried like hell to ignore it.

"V always works. She just likes to complain about it when she does."

Rachel interrupted them, setting their tea glasses on the table and standing oddly close to Kaleb which was just a little awkward. Normally, he wouldn't have thought much of it, shrugging it off like he usually did. Without ego, Kaleb was acutely aware of the heads that turned when he and his brothers were in a room, generally of the female persuasion. Yet, when he was sitting across from the one woman whose head he didn't seem to be able to turn, it didn't do a whole lot for him.

"Did you get her to clean the bathrooms?" Without trying to be rude, Kaleb continued his conversation with Zoey and Rachel finally took the hint.

"One. I consider that progress." Zoey laughed again. "There for a while she was seriously trying to convince me that she was allergic to toilets. Not bleach or cleaner, but to the actual toilet. She's nuts."

"What's up with her and my brother?" Until Zane had shown up at Moonshiner's Kaleb would've never guessed that there might be something going on between his brother and Zoey's friend, but even he felt the sexual tension sparking between the two of them.

"I was wondering the same thing." Zoey sipped her tea, sat the glass back on the coaster before sliding her hands down the glass to wipe the condensation away. Kaleb had a sudden longing to be that fucking glass.

Maybe it was in the air, whatever the hell it was.

"So, have you decided on whether you're coming to my parent's fiftieth wedding anniversary party?" Kaleb asked after a few moments of silence.

"Next weekend, right?" Zoey asked, still fondling that damn glass and still not looking at him.

"Yes. And since you owe me, I know you'll be there, right?"

That got her attention.

"I owe you?" A sexy little grin tugged at the corners of Zoey's mouth and just like every time he was around her, Kaleb felt a throb begin between his legs.

"You do." He confirmed, smiling back. He had no idea what she owed him for, but it sounded good.

Before he had to answer, Rachel approached their table with two plates overflowing with food, setting them down in front of them while smiling at Kaleb. When she didn't turn away immediately, Kaleb looked up at her.

"So, I was wondering..." Rachel let the sentence hang, looking just a tad bit nervous.

Oh hell.

Kaleb liked Rachel; she was a sweet girl, always flirting with him and all of his brothers when they came into her parents' restaurant, but that was also the downside to eating there once a week.

"You know, Kaleb," Zoey began, trying to appear serious, yet Kaleb could see a devilish gleam in her eyes, "I'd really like to go out with you next weekend."

Kaleb fought the urge to laugh and choke all at the same time.

"Well!" Rachel said before stomping off.

Kaleb watched Zoey while Zoey watched Rachel leave.

"You know, I get it that you're a sexy guy, but shit, do they have to swarm all over you whenever we go out together?" Zoey stated, clearly exasperated as she picked up her fork and began digging into her food.

Kaleb mirrored her, grabbing his fork, trying to focus on the food in front of him, but having a damn hard time. Did she seriously just call him sexy?

He found himself staring at her, watching while she pushed her food around on her plate.

"What?" She asked when she finally acknowledged him.

"I'm beginning to worry about you, Zoey." He had to do something to ease the tension coursing between them because honestly, the throb that had started between his legs had turned into a full blown ache, and he damn sure wasn't going to be able to sit there much longer with a hard on. So he decided to tease her. "First you tell Vanessa that you fantasize about kissing me and now you call me sexy."

"Oh, get over yourself, Kaleb Walker." Zoey laughed, but there was another pink tinge to her cheeks. She was even more beautiful when she blushed.

He'd always thought of her as being pretty, ever since he'd been in the eighth grade. But sitting here with her, it was like seeing her for the first time. She was stunning. Even in her oversized t-shirt and sexy as hell tight jeans, the woman made him want things.

What he didn't understand was what was different now. Tonight specifically.

They had been friends for years, going out at least twice a week, hanging out on the weekends most of the time with his friends or hers, or both. Ever since he had taken her to her senior prom, they'd been close friends, but although he'd always been attracted to her, Kaleb had never considered anything more. Tonight, looking at her, he couldn't get his mind off of what she would look like naked, beneath him...

And yes, if truth be known, he'd fantasized about that on more than one occasion. But never had he felt as though something might be reciprocated on her side. It wasn't like they had ever hinted around about any possible attraction to one another.

Kaleb tried to eat the food in front of him, but he was having a damned hard time thinking, much less eating. Instead, he continued to steal glances of the beautiful woman across from him.

Thankfully, neither of them spoke much for the rest of the meal, finishing quickly and not lingering the way they normally did. Kaleb managed to track down Rachel, having to go find her just so he could pay the bill, and once that was taken care of he found Zoey halfway to her truck, not even waiting for him.

"Hey!" He called out to her when her legs began moving faster.

"Sorry." Zoey mumbled. "I need to... get home... to my dad."

Well, if that didn't sound like a lie, Kaleb didn't know what did. Something was going on because the Zoey standing before him was not the same woman he'd seen when he walked into Moonshiner's earlier.

Reaching out, he took her hand, and it was then and there that Kaleb knew exactly what was going on between them. When she flinched like she had been burned, he was pretty damned sure she felt it, too. That spark of electricity that had nothing to do with static, and everything to do with something much more intimate.

She pulled away immediately, and Kaleb let her go.

"Are you all right?" He asked, taking another step closer.

The difference in their heights was significant. Since Kaleb topped out at six feet four inches, and Zoey couldn't possibly be more than five feet two if that, he had to look down at her and she up at him. He'd never paid much attention to it until now. Until he thought of nothing more than kissing her and in order for that to happen, he was going to have to lean down, or she was going to have to go up on her toes. Either way, it wasn't going to happen, and he knew that, but his brain still entertained the idea.

"So, if I don't see you next week, I will see you at my parents' party, right?" Kaleb had no doubt he would see Zoey several times before then, but for now he was going to give her the illusion of space.

Whatever this was – the shift in the atmosphere – they'd both been affected by it obviously. Zoey might want to ignore it, or pretend it didn't happen, but Kaleb knew this was just the opportunity he'd been looking for.

Zoey nodded her head in agreement before she bolted for her truck, leaving Kaleb standing in the parking lot. He watched her tail lights as they disappeared into the darkness, a smile on his face. This was going to get interesting.

Chapter Three

♀♂

Zoey heard the truck as it pulled up the drive, and she glanced out the window in her father's kitchen just in time to see Kaleb's truck barreling up the long narrow driveway.

Shit.

She hadn't seen him since their awkward as hell dinner, and she had purposely put him off the last time she talked to him. Not because she didn't want to see him, but because she did.

In a bad way.

In a way that she wasn't sure he'd be comfortable with. Knowing Kaleb and his flirting ways, he'd probably think she had lost her mind if she gave in to what she was suddenly feeling for him. Granted, it wasn't a foreign feeling by any means. It's just that she denied herself that one little desire for so long it felt a little awkward to be around him at the moment.

"Who's out there?" Her dad called from the living room, interrupting Zoey's wayward thoughts.

The man had superhuman hearing apparently, or maybe he just had a sixth sense when it came to the Walker boys.

"Kaleb." She called out, drying the last dish before sitting it in the dish drainer.

"Damn boy." Carl grunted and Zoey smiled.

She knew why he was there, which was the only reason she wasn't sneaking out the back door. Kaleb wasn't there to see her, but rather her father. According to Carl, Kaleb had stopped by twice during the week to speak with him and yet again, he was giving poor Kaleb the runaround. Her father didn't tell her that last part, but Zoey knew him all too well.

A gentle knock sounded on the side door, the main entrance everyone used when they stopped by. In the last few months, it had been Grand Central Station at the Stranford house, what with the various Walker men coming and going to talk to her father.

"Come in." Zoey called out, drying her hands on a dish towel. "What brings you by?" She asked, pretending there wasn't some weird nervous tension between them after the last time they saw one another.

"Is your dad here?" Kaleb asked now standing just inside the doorway in the oversized kitchen. His deep, rich baritone sent a chill racing down her spine, and she ignored it. Or tried to anyway.

"In the living room." She said, tilting her head in that direction. "Go on in."

The smile Kaleb shot back at her was pure sin and Zoey had to turn away just to keep her reaction to herself.

At twenty nine years old, one would think she'd figured out how to control her overheated libido, but, unfortunately for her, that had never happened when it came to Kaleb; no matter how much she pretended otherwise. Good thing he never seemed to notice, or he just didn't care.

"Hey." Kaleb called to her, forcing her to turn his way again. "Don't run off. I want to talk to you when I'm done here."

"Umm... ok."

Talk to *her*? Zoey watched as Kaleb disappeared into the living room and for a brief moment, she considered disappearing. If her damn curiosity hadn't won out, she would have too. Instead, she busied herself with the laundry she had put off for the last two days.

It had been a busy week for her and Vanessa, having acquired two new clients whose houses were almost as big as the Wilson's and had just as many kids to boot. Her little cleaning company was growing, and she and Vanessa were beginning to feel the pain of working so many hours just to get it all done. Not for the first time, she wondered whether she should hire a few more people to help make it easier.

Admittedly, she had a hard time committing to sharing her business with anyone else except for V. It had been a long road to get to this point in her life, and the independence she'd established had come at a high price. Even if she was living at home, Zoey knew she was making it on her own. And she knew the hard work wasn't going to kill her.

Ever since her mom had passed away, almost four years before, Zoey had returned home to live with her father. It was actually a series of events that played out during that time which convinced her to stay, but she hated to think about the rest, so she did what she did best. She ignored it.

Initially, she hadn't planned to move back home, just wanted to stay for a little while to make sure her father was taken care of, considering he was getting up there in age. Her mother hadn't been young when she finally conceived Zoey, and her father was a good decade and a half older than her mother. That put him just a few months shy of eighty, and he was showing every single minute.

Which meant Zoey was back home full time, living in the guest house and trying to help out with the remedial chores. After the first couple of weeks of being back at home, finding herself divorced, and just a little distraught, Zoey had come up with a plan. Instead of moping around the house, because that definitely wasn't in her nature, she had decided to clean houses for a living.

Her father found the decision amusing considering she'd gone to college and all, but Zoey had been going through a period where she didn't want to be around people. Ok, so yes, she'd been moping.

It didn't take long for her to establish a regular clientele and found herself with more work than she could handle, which was when she turned to Vanessa Carmichael, her best friend since grade school and now her one and only full time employee. Since that day, they hadn't slowed down. Not that Zoey was complaining – work was good. Especially in the small ranching community they lived in.

When Zoey sought V to help her, she'd been working as a dog groomer and decided what the hell – Zoey still laughed at the idea because V was certainly not the kind to get dirty, especially cleaning other people's messes. But, the two of them worked like clockwork and V had the same strong work ethic as Zoey, so it all worked out.

Now she struggled to find the time to clean her father's house on a weekly basis, hence the reason she was there on a Friday afternoon folding laundry and doing dishes when she would much rather be out with Vanessa or Kaleb. Well, maybe not Kaleb, but that was only because she was still freaked out by whatever chemistry had sparked between them the week before. She still wasn't completely sure she hadn't imagined it.

Standing in the laundry room, Zoey heard Kaleb's booming voice as he talked to her father, having to talk louder than normal due to Carl's hearing loss – and the volume of the television. Come to think of it, Zoey had to wonder how he knew every time someone pulled down the main drive to the house.

Filling a plastic basket with towels, she went to work folding them quickly, before moving on to toss another load of clothes in the washer. There always seemed to be extras to wash thanks to the rags they used to clean houses. Today was no exception.

"Hey."

Zoey jumped at the sound, turning and nearly stumbling head first into Kaleb who was standing only a foot or so behind her. Putting her hands out to stop herself, she ended up damn near face planting into his chest.

"I'm so sorry." She whispered; her hands suddenly glued to his massive chest. God he smelled good - something woodsy and fresh and far too appealing. And why the hell were her hands still on his chest because *holy shit*, no matter how many years she'd seen him without a shirt on, Zoey had never expected him to feel quite as hard as he looked.

"No. *I'm* sorry." Kaleb stated, putting one large hand over hers which were, yes, still planted on his chest.

The warmth of his callused fingers as they brushed against the back of her hand had her nearly stumbling yet again. For all the time she had known the man, never once did his touch have the impact it did right then.

Looking up into those intense blue gray eyes, Zoey felt more than saw the heat reflected there. Taking a quick step back, she pulled her hands from underneath his and shoved them into the pockets of her jeans. "What's up?" She asked, going for unaffected, but probably sounding like an idiot.

"Can we take a walk?" Kaleb asked, glancing back toward the living room where her father sat watching television.

"Sure." Zoey didn't know why she was committing herself to this endeavor because, after that little electric jolt, she wasn't so sure her legs would hold her up.

Being close to Kaleb was doing strange things to her insides.

Chapter Four

♂♀

Kaleb wasn't sure what the hell had just happened, but he was certain that whatever it was that sparked between him and Zoey, she had felt it too. From the second her hands touched him, an electric current jarred his entire body to attention. This wasn't necessarily a good thing right now.

He had asked Zoey to go for a walk with him, only now he had a fucking hard on that was making it damned difficult to stand, much less move. That single touch had his cock raring to go, harder than granite and throbbing like a mother fucker.

Letting her walk in front of him, he attempted to situate himself so that he didn't do any damage because his jeans were suddenly way too tight. Stepping out into the bright Texas sunshine, the warm August breeze wasn't helping cool him down either.

"What did you want to talk about?" She asked, stopping suddenly and turning to look at him.

Kaleb nearly skidded to a stop, wary of touching her again because he wasn't sure he'd be able to keep from pulling her against him the next time. And he was fairly certain there would be a next time. That was exactly the reason he was there, he just hadn't intended it to be this soon.

Ever since that night at the diner, Kaleb hadn't been able to think of much else other than the way Zoey had reacted to him.

Since he fully intended to take advantage of the opportunity, he'd decided to pursue her, rather than to sit back and wait. Zoey was stubborn, and if he had to wait around for her, well, hell, he might be waiting forever.

"Let's walk." With a tilt of his head, he directed her toward the tree line separating the Stranford land from the Walker's.

"Have you talked to your dad today? He doing ok?" He just spoke to Carl, but today seemed worse than the last time he stopped by just a couple of days before. His memory seemed to be failing him. Either that or the man was pretending with the best of them. Kaleb didn't quite believe that though.

"He seems fine to me. Most of the time." Zoey said, not looking at him. "I asked him about the land."

Kaleb contemplated what to say next. That was only part of his reason for coming over today, or maybe it had just been his excuse. Either way, he was still interested in purchasing the land and anything that would help get Travis off his ass would be worth it. "And?"

"I think he's interested." She admitted, stopping just short of the tall oak trees and turning to look up at him. "I think you were right. I think he's leery of letting go of this land because it's been in our family for so long."

It was a valid concern. From where Kaleb stood if the shoe had been on the other foot, he wasn't so sure his family would be able to part with what had become part of their heritage, even if it meant they might lose it all.

He just happened to believe that buying the land would help alleviate some of the financial strain on Carl and Zoey. Telling her that might just get him in a world of hurt, because if Zoey was anything, she was independent, and knowing others were aware of her financial struggles wouldn't sit well with her.

"Scared, maybe." Kaleb said, looking down at Zoey standing only a few inches away from him. He wasn't sure if she realized how close they were to one another but he damn sure did. "Ornery, definitely."

The way she stared at him, as though she expected him to pounce on her at the first chance he got was somewhat amusing. If she only knew how long he'd been fighting this attraction, and how many times he considered pulling her close and kissing her until neither of them knew their own names.

Standing next to her now, Kaleb again felt the significant difference in their height and their size. Zoey was a petite little thing, proven when he'd been able to cover both of her small hands with just one of his. But her size didn't fool him. Small in stature, big in spirit, Zoey was.

"You're still coming to the party tomorrow, right?" Ok, so that was his other reason for coming over.

Zoey looked down at the ground before turning her beautiful blue eyes back on him. She didn't look nearly as confident as she normally did.

"I don't know." If he didn't know her better, Kaleb might've been worried about her answer, but the look in her eyes told him everything he needed to know. Zoey could never hide anything from him, not even when she tried.

His brain was suddenly sidetracked, his eyes riveted on her mouth and the way she chewed her bottom lip. He wanted to lick her lips, to taste her sweetness, to hold her in his arms and show her exactly what he'd been holding back for more years than he cared to think about.

So what was holding him back?

When her tongue slid out, running over her bottom lip, he barely restrained a groan. She was killing him here, and a quick look into her eyes said she knew it.

"You owe me, remember?" She didn't owe him a damned thing, but if she was going to tease him like this, even if she wasn't aware she was doing it, he wasn't responsible for what might happen next.

"So are you asking me to go to the party as your friend?" Zoey asked; those intense eyes boring a hole into him.

"Yes. No. Fuck." He was back to watching her mouth, desperate to touch her, taste her. "What would you say if I said that I wanted you to go with me as more than friends?"

Zoey looked like he just spoke in a foreign language and she was trying to translate, but he could see a glimmer of interest in her eyes. He just wanted her to say yes, and at this point, he was ready to kiss the answer out of her.

"I'm still pretty sure I don't owe you," Zoey smiled a real smile for the first time since they'd walked outside, "but I'd still say yes."

It took him a second to comprehend what she was telling him, but when it hit him, his entire body tensed. Although, he hoped she might hedge a little because the idea of kissing her was damned appealing.

He managed a small smile at the same time he put one hand on her cheek, feeling the soft, smooth skin beneath his fingers. When she leaned into his touch, he knew the moment couldn't have been better. Taking one step closer, he hesitated, waiting to see what she would do. When she didn't take a step back, he took that as a good sign.

"Zoey." He growled her name, unable to control the hunger that had been building in intensity over the years any longer. She was still looking up at him when he closed the gap between them. "I'm not sure I can stay away from you much longer."

Aside from the wind rustling the branches of the trees, they were hidden behind and a couple of birds braving the Texas heat, the only other sound was Zoey's sharp intake of breath. Looking down at her, he could see the rise and fall of her breasts with every ragged breath and that was all the assurance he needed.

Cupping her jaw, trying to keep his hands from groping every luscious curve of her body, he bent his head until his lips hovered just above hers. Before he could get closer, she took the decision away from him when she pushed up on her toes and planted her warm lips to his.

The kiss started out sweet, just her mouth pressed to his, but the sweet scent of her hair sent a rush of adrenaline flooding his system and he was past the point of no return. Pulling her flush against him, Kaleb kept his hands on her face, not willing to push her too far too fast, but Lord have mercy, he had to taste more of her.

Thrusting his tongue between her lips, he locked his knees to keep him from falling over as soon as her little pink tongue surged forward to meet his. Then the world tilted, exploded, and the only thing remaining was the feel of Zoey's delicious taste overwhelming his senses.

He growled when she whimpered, pressing her tight little body against his, grinding her hips into his, her fingers slipping into his hair, pulling him closer until he knew that, at any moment, he was going to take it too far. The image of being buried inside of her, both of them naked and sweating flashed through his brain and his dick throbbed behind the irritating zipper of his jeans.

The only thing that slowed them down was their need for oxygen, and when their lips parted, he pushed his forehead to hers, but didn't let her go.

"It seems like I've waited my whole life for you to do that." Zoey whispered.

Her admission made Kaleb's head spin. He *had* waited his whole life. Since junior high school when he had fallen head over heels in love with her, he'd ached to kiss her. For years, he'd spent many a session with his own hand, dreaming about what it would feel like to have her mouth on him – everywhere – or to bury his tongue into the warm depths of her pussy. And all the ways he intended to pleasure her.

"Trust me, baby. I *have* waited my whole life for that."

Having been friends for so long, he worried that this little derailment of their friendship might just be leading down a road better left untraveled, but hell, the woman was so fucking tempting.

Wild fantasies and some of the hottest dreams he'd ever had starred Zoey, but Kaleb never figured any of it would come to fruition, but right here, right now, in the small copse of trees, shielded from the rest of the world, he wanted to do just that.

Not that he would.

Not yet anyway.

She knew some of the darker sides of Kaleb, but in all the years they'd known each other, never had they talked about it. And no matter what she thought she knew about him, Kaleb knew she didn't understand the beast that prowled beneath his skin. The one that wanted more than her innocence could possibly fathom.

"We should go back." He said reluctantly, not wanting to move from her embrace, not wanting to lose the warmth of her tender touch, but terrified that he might just do what he'd wanted to do for the last week. Hell, for the last *fifteen years*.

♀♂

Zoey nodded her agreement, but neither of them pulled away for long minutes. The feel of Kaleb's work roughened fingers against her cheek was unlike any touch she had ever felt before, and for as long as she had waited, she didn't feel as though she'd gotten enough of him yet.

When she told him that she'd waited her whole life, she hadn't been lying. And after years of anticipation, she certainly hadn't been disappointed. At least not by his kiss. Boy, could he kiss. The way his tongue expertly stroked hers, Zoey knew she'd wait another lifetime for just a promise of another.

Never had she been kissed like that.

She wasn't a prude by any means, but no other man had invoked her desire the way Kaleb's lips did when they touched hers, or the spicy scent of the man as it infused her senses, making her want, making her ache.

If only they weren't outside... If only they weren't standing yards away from her father's house. Zoey didn't want to let the moment end because she feared it would never happen again and going another minute without his touch would be too much. Not to mention, she feared she would never get up the nerve to do it again.

This, whatever this was, could very well destroy the friendship they'd developed over the years, and if either of them thought about it long enough, they might just come to their senses.

When Kaleb pulled away, despite the heat from the early August day, Zoey still felt the warmth being drawn away. She would've wrapped her arms around herself just to hold in the lingering heat if Kaleb hadn't taken her hand.

Looking down to where he now laced their fingers, their arms hanging between them, she felt like a teenager all over again. The one who had pretended that being friends with Kaleb Walker was all she ever wanted, but knew deep down she'd wanted so much more from him. But they weren't teenagers, they were adults, and Kaleb was all man. One that she wanted to explore in ways she'd only dreamed about. And yes, maybe that categorized her as slightly crazy.

"What time is the party?" She asked, trying to make conversation and ignore the fact that she would much rather sneak deeper into the trees and experience the wonder of Kaleb's mouth on every inch of her skin.

"Seven." Kaleb responded, his voice still a little gruff.

Zoey liked the rasp in his voice, liked the way he growled his pleasure because it was sexy as hell. But she expected that from him. With Kaleb, there was an intensity about him, a measure of control that he didn't let slip. Of all the Walker brothers, he was the laid back, gentle giant, but Zoey knew beneath that nonchalant exterior, there was a demanding creature that wanted to break free.

"So I should be there then?" She asked, trying to get her mind out of the gutter.

"No. I'll pick you up at six forty five." Kaleb said, turning to face her. His voice lowered, and those sparkling blue eyes lit up with something dark and possessive.

Good grief. If he only knew what that sexy tone of his did to her insides, or how her pussy throbbed from the sensuality she detected in the smoky blue depths of his eyes... She was pretty sure if he knew, they wouldn't be standing there right now. They'd find the nearest place to get horizontal and get to know each other on a much more intimate level.

Lowering his head closer to hers, Kaleb brushed his lips against hers once more. "Zoey..." He growled, "woman, you don't know what you do to me."

No, she didn't, and she had the sudden urge for him to tell her because she was so tired of waiting for this man, so tired of aching for his touch, his kiss. And now that this – she still had no clue what it was – was happening between them, she didn't want to waste another second.

Instead of telling him that, she pressed her lips to his gently, then took a step back. She needed to go home and take an ice cold shower. "Tomorrow night. Six forty five," she said. "I'll see you then."

Kaleb nodded and watched as she walked inside. Zoey felt the heat of his gaze on her skin and once again, she knew tomorrow was going to be the longest damn day, and it had nothing to do with work.

An hour later, Zoey had managed to calm her hormones by way of a shower, although it hadn't been all that cold. She'd quickly made her father some dinner, finished the few remaining chores before hurrying back to the guest house.

When she walked in the door, she glanced around, wondering what was different.

"Hey, V." That's what she got for leaving her door unlocked. She wasn't sure how she hadn't noticed V's car parked out front, but somehow she'd missed it. Sitting on her couch, her feet propped up on the coffee table, V looked right at home.

"I was hoping we could hang out for a while. You know, talk." V smiled, and Zoey immediately knew something was up.

"About?" As she listened for her friend's response, she detoured to the kitchen and pulled out a bottle of wine and two glasses. Based on the twinkle in V's eyes, this was going to be one of those nights. Hopefully one bottle would be enough.

"Oh, I don't know." V hollered from the living room. "Maybe we can start with you abandoning me the other night."

Zoey smiled to herself as she poured the wine. "Don't even pretend you weren't happy about that."

"I wasn't!" Vanessa was extremely animated, and she was showing it now. Sitting up, she tried to act as though she were truly upset.

Zoey knew better.

"So, how'd it go with Zane?" Handing one of the glasses to V, Zoey toed off her boots and then sat on the couch beside her friend, pulling her feet up beneath her.

V didn't answer in words, but her face lit up like Rudolph's nose.

"Oh. My. God." Now it was Zoey's turn to get animated. "You didn't!"

"Oh, honey, we did. And holy fucking shit!" V's smile lit up the entire living room.

"If you even think about leaving out a single detail, I'll kill you." Zoey exclaimed.

Vanessa and Zane? *Holy crap.*

"Well, he is a Walker, and you've heard the rumors about them."

Which one, Zoey thought to herself. There were too many to recall. The Walkers were celebrities in town, and there were so many stories and rumors Zoey had never been able to keep up.

"Let's just say we were lucky the sheets didn't go up in flames." V said, no longer blushing but still grinning like a fool.

"So, it wasn't good?" Zoey threw in some sarcasm, although she smiled at her friend's happiness.

"Good isn't nearly the word to describe Zane Walker naked, honey. But, I seriously don't want to sit here and talk about that."

"Like hell." There was no way Zoey was going to let her friend get away with not sharing the details. "Did you go back to his house or yours?"

"Mine of course. There is no man out there going to get me to do the walk of shame. No way. Uh-uh." V smirked. "And let's just say, it was nearly dawn before he went home."

Zoey felt a smidgeon of jealousy listening to V and, had she not just experienced the hottest kiss of her lifetime just that day with Kaleb, she might actually tell her so. Instead, Zoey smiled. "Well, you know I'm happy for you," Zoey took a sip of her wine before continuing, "but you also know I'm going to tell you to be careful."

V was one who fell in love easily and often. Although most of the time she didn't get hurt in the end, there was always that chance that her heart would get broken and Zoey didn't want to see it happen. Because Zane Walker was a heartbreaker.

"You don't have to worry about me." V stated, not sounding nearly as confident as she normally did.

"Are you gonna see him again?"

"I don't know. I'll leave that up to him. I refuse to add my name to the long list of women who flaunt themselves at the Walker brothers and chase them down. If Zane thinks I'm one of them, he's got another thing coming."

"I seriously doubt it's like that." Zoey said, downing the last of her wine and reaching for the bottle. "So how's your mom?"

V didn't answer immediately, but Zoey knew she would eventually. It wasn't a secret that Vanessa had had a tough life growing up. But the woman was more determined than anyone Zoey had ever met, and she'd insisted on making a better life for herself than her mother had. It didn't stop V from worrying about her mother, and because she was her friend, Zoey worried, as well.

"She's fine." Her tone was clipped, but V half-smiled before she said, "I *really* didn't come over to talk about that. So, how'd it go with Kaleb the other night?"

Should she tell V about what happened then or even today? Zoey wasn't quite sure what was going on, but sometime in the last week there had been a shift in her relationship with Kaleb and the incredible friendship they'd established had morphed into something intensely complicated. At least in the way Zoey felt for the man.

"It was weird." Zoey said, watching V pour more wine into her own glass. Apparently her statement startled V because she nearly knocked her glass over. With quick reflexes, V saved Zoey's carpet from a disaster before turning her attention on her once more.

"Weird how?" There was a sincere interest in V's eyes, and Zoey decided she had to share with someone.

"I don't know. We went to dinner, but something seemed off that night. Maybe it was your fault with the whole fantasizing about kissing him bit, but for some reason, that's all I could think about."

V laughed before leaning back into the couch, getting comfortable. "I don't think I'm the one who put that idea in your head. You know as well as I do that you've been fantasizing about that man for as long as you've known him."

"Not like that." Zoey would admit to fantasies, but never had they consumed her like that. She'd been overwhelmed by his intensity that night, as well as his sexy good looks and his scrumptious smell, and well... him. "He kissed me."

"Holy hell!" V leaned forward, this time not nearly as lucky because she sloshed red wine on the carpet. "No, don't get up." V exclaimed as she sat her glass on the table and rushed to the kitchen. Her voice came from the other room, "You better tell me about that kiss, you hear me?"

Zoey chuckled. She still relived that kiss and the way it felt to have Kaleb's hands on her, even if he kept them on her face, never venturing to where she would've preferred to have them. In the past, they might've danced a time or two when they went out with others, but she'd never felt the possessiveness in his touch the way she did today.

"Ummm... Still here. Waiting." V rattled as she wiped up the spill with cleaner and a towel.

"It was the best kiss I've ever had." Zoey blurted. "There, is that what you wanted to hear?"

"Of course it is." V beamed. "And I know you're not lying because you still haven't wiped that damn goofy grin off your face."

No. No, she hadn't. And Zoey was beginning to think that grin was permanent.

Chapter Five

♀♂

The next morning, Zoey crawled out of bed wishing like hell she hadn't scheduled any house cleanings on a Saturday. Unfortunately, she and V were so overloaded, they hadn't had a choice, and now she had about fifteen minutes to get ready, grab her coffee, and head out the door, or she'd be late.

Without a second to spare, Zoey rushed through the house, pulling on her clothes while waiting for her coffee to brew, then brushing her teeth and running a brush through her unruly curly hair. Pulling it back in a ponytail, she managed to look presentable enough to clean houses for the day. After one last stop at the medicine cabinet for a couple of aspirin to ward off the wine hangover she could feel looming, Zoey was on her way.

By the time she was in her truck, she was feeling somewhat more human, and that damn grin from the night before had returned. With the music up loud, she rolled down the windows and drove as fast as she dared to Vanessa's to pick her up.

Thankfully V was one of those women who insisted on being early. Sometimes that grated on Zoey's nerves, but that was only because she always found herself running late.

"Are you glowing?" V laughed when she climbed into the truck. "You are! Oh my goodness. Are you still thinking about kissing Kaleb?"

Yes, damn it, Zoey was still thinking about it. Kaleb Walker had scorched her brain cells with his soul stealing kisses, and she'd thought of little else ever since.

"You're in love, aren't you?" Vanessa crooned. "Zoey and Kaleb sittin' in a tree..."

Zoey turned up the radio, hoping to drown V out, grinning as she did. There was no stopping Vanessa when she got started, and by the end of the day Zoey would likely be on the verge of throttling her closest friend.

Figuring there was no stopping her, Zoey didn't even try. She had to focus on getting the two appointments out of the way so she could get home. She had a party to get ready for, and unlike any other party she had been invited to, Zoey was a little nervous about this one. After what transpired yesterday, there was a very real chance something might just happen between her and Kaleb. Despite her fantasies, Zoey never seriously considered the real possibility, but now... Well, now she had her fingers crossed.

In fact, at twenty two, she'd all but given up hope that anything would happen between her and her best friend Kaleb, and ended up marrying Jason Tribbons. Their marriage lasted for five not so long years until one day Jason decided he'd had enough.

Just like that.

That was an incredibly difficult time for Zoey because yes, she had been in love with Jason. Yes, she thought she would spend the rest of her life with him, having babies and growing old together. According to Jason, that wasn't his plan. He wanted to get out of their little town, explore the world, live life to its fullest.

Without her.

So, she'd done what Zoey was famous for. She conceded; never arguing, never begging him to stay.

He had packed up his things and disappeared from her life for good. She hadn't heard from him again. At all. As though the five years they'd spent together never actually happened. Not hearing from him was strange, but probably a good thing, as well. Rumors in their small town ran rampant, and if he'd have stayed, Zoey wasn't so sure she could've lived each day hearing how great his life was without her.

That was five years ago. Since then, Zoey lost her mother and was now taking care of her ailing father while managing her booming cleaning service. After the first year or so after her and Jason divorced and after the pain from losing her beloved mother eased, Zoey had set forth on a new path.

No longer was she the passive woman expecting life to come to her. She was making her own path, exploring her own interests, and loving every minute of it. Her business was thriving, and she was enjoying what time she had with her ornery, yet loveable, father. With no expectations, she found each day was much more promising by the fact that she didn't expect anything from anyone. She'd become independently successful and opposite from Jason, Zoey loved her small town.

The only thing lacking was her sex life, but if she was lucky, that might all be changing with Kaleb Walker. And at her age, rumored to be nearing her sexual prime, Zoey wasn't going to put any limits on what might happen between them either.

For the first time in her life, she wasn't going to take a backseat. She was going to go after what she wanted, and now, more than ever, she knew exactly what that was.

♂♀

It was six o'clock on Saturday evening when Kaleb finally managed to sneak out of the office and head to his small cabin located on the Walker ranch. Each of his brothers had their own except Brendon and Braydon, who shared the largest of the six.

Lorrie Walker, their very overprotective mother, insisted years ago that her boys needed to stay close to home. Despite the fact that the main house was large enough to hold every one of them comfortably, she knew very well her boys weren't at all excited about living at home. It wasn't easy living in a house with nine people, no matter how spacious it was.

Kaleb had been the first to insist on moving out, which prompted Lorrie and Curtis Walker to come up with a plan if they expected the boys to stay close to home. That's when Lorrie told her husband that it was time to start building. And that they did.

Six decent sized cabins were built on the Walker Ranch, scattered randomly about on various sections so her boys would be close, but still have the privacy they needed. That was his mother for you. If she had a say in the matter, they would all live right there on the ranch for the rest of their lives.

Kaleb didn't see that happening, but for now, none of his brothers had an issue with it. Well, except maybe Sawyer. But then again, Sawyer was rarely home, apparently spending more time with his various women than he did anywhere else.

Since their old man wasn't the type to let them sit by and have things handed to them, he insisted they were going to put in some blood, sweat and tears. Which they did.

Bucket loads.

Their hard work resulted in six remarkably different structures, varying from the typical log cabin, to the eclectic glass monstrosity that Ethan had designed himself. Thankfully Kaleb didn't have to see Ethan's place from his.

Kaleb's tastes were the opposite of Ethan's, running more toward the typical western with strong oak and rustic iron as the main decor. It was home, plain and simple. He slept there, he ate there from time to time, but most of all, it was his place to get away when it all became too much to handle.

Spending days on end with one's brothers tended to wear on you after a while. Especially when there were a total of seven, each very different from the other. When they had decided to go into business together, they'd sealed their fate and invariably cemented the fact that they would rarely get a moments peace.

It was all worth it though. With Walker Demolition taking off, each of them was immersed in what they loved to do the most. Thankfully a company as complex as theirs required each of their different talents, so no one had been pushed into doing anything they didn't want to do. With more changes in the works, thanks to Travis' resort, they were all going to be just as busy doing more than one job at a time.

Travis, the oldest at thirty five was the money man for Walker Demolition and the man behind the resort dream. He was moody and cranky most of the time, but he was the sole reason they were making money. He guarded the accounts with his life, ensuring every penny was accounted for and governing exactly how they spent it. He was also the man who had found some investors from Dallas interested in backing the resort.

Then there was Sawyer, the second oldest at thirty three, although he didn't act a day over twenty one. When it came to his job – sales – he was top notch and no one held a candle to the man when it came to wheeling and dealing and spewing loads of bullshit.

Kaleb was the third oldest, and at thirty two, he knew the best was yet to come as far as he was concerned. Walker Demolition had been his brain child, his baby, and even though they all contributed one hundred percent, most of the time his brothers still looked to him as their leader. Being in charge of demolition design and a few unwanted tasks, Kaleb loved what he did and wouldn't have changed a thing.

Next were Braydon and Brendon, twenty nine year old identical twins, who managed the construction sites as the head foremen on each job. They were also known as the lovers, not the fighters in the family. They were inseparable, doing everything together. And when Kaleb said everything, he meant *everything*. Including women. They were known to share their women between them.

Ethan, the second youngest at twenty seven was solely responsible for their commercial equipment. He purchased and maintained every single piece they owned. Of course, Zane was the youngest at twenty four, and he worked alongside Ethan, but he was responsible for their vehicle maintenance. Both of his youngest brothers were brilliant when it came to machinery, which had gotten them through many a bind.

Kaleb wasn't sure whether his parents ever intended to have enough boys to maintain such an intricate company, but they'd started out eight years earlier and hadn't slowed down since.

When he reached his house, Kaleb parked his truck haphazardly near the front porch before hurrying to get inside. He was quickly running out of time to get ready, so it was a good thing he didn't need much. He had to be at Zoey's in less than an hour, and he refused to be late.

Stripping his clothes off and tossing them in the laundry hamper, he quickly shaved before jumping in the shower. Just the thought of seeing Zoey again had his cock hard and in desperate need of release, but again, he didn't have time. Not to mention, it wouldn't help. His dick was in a constant state of awareness whenever he thought about her, so being around her was likely going to push his limits.

Fifteen minutes later he was dressed and quickly straightening the few things that were out of place. Not that he had any intentions of bringing Zoey back to his cabin, but he had to admit, if she was game, he couldn't make any promises.

Damn. He was in such a hurry, one would've thought this was his first date.

♀♂

Zoey was putting the finishing touches on her makeup, something she very rarely wore, when she heard the truck pull up in front of the small cottage that had acted as a guest house and until about four years ago, hadn't had a guest in quite some time.

When she originally came back home, Zoey hadn't lived too far away from her parents, but since the house she had been living in belonged to Jason before they got married, she opted to let him have it. For the first few weeks after she came home, she lived in the main house, but she felt like she was imposing on her father, and she was pretty sure he felt like he was stepping on her toes, as well. So, the two of them had worked to get the guest house ready for her and here she was.

It was a quaint little house, no more than a thousand square feet, but completely doable for just one person. With a bedroom, a lavish bathroom which she had paid to have remodeled, a living room and one small half bath off of the kitchen, Zoey had more than enough space for her and her things. And quite frankly, she'd grown comfortable there.

She was pretty sure her father liked the idea of having her close as well, but also not having to give up his privacy though he often complained about rummaging around in such a large house all by himself.

The rapping of knuckles on the screen door had her tossing her lip gloss back in the drawer before heading to the living room while gargantuan butterflies started up a ping pong match in her stomach.

There, standing on the wide front porch was the object of her wildest fantasies, looking striking in tight jeans and a short sleeve polo shirt that hugged him tight across the chest and arms, accentuating every hard plane and angle of his torso. The man made her mouth water.

"Hi." Zoey greeted when she came closer. "Come in." Years of friendship and a comfortable existence alongside this man disappeared entirely as she stood before him now. Never had Zoey cared what she looked like, or what he thought about her appearance until this moment.

"Damn." Kaleb whispered, "You look beautiful."

His words made her blush, but she didn't turn away. Zoey had destroyed her closet trying to find the perfect outfit to wear when she'd finally settled on one of her favorite sundresses. It was strapless and flirty and made her feel feminine so she'd figured it was just what this night warranted. Since she was more inclined to wear jeans and boots, she was self-conscious about it, but his reaction helped.

"Thank you." She said when she finally found her voice. "I just need a minute."

"Take your time."

She fought the urge to sigh like a damned school girl. His voice was rich and dark, sending chills over her skin while those beautiful eyes sparkled with heat. She clearly wasn't the only one who felt this attraction fizzling between them.

She couldn't help but wonder how this had come about. Maybe it was in the water. What with V and Zane hooking up and all – although Zoey was hoping what was going on between them was more than a hookup, but knowing Zane, she was a little concerned. Not that V couldn't handle herself.

Zoey rushed back to her bedroom, spritzed her favorite perfume behind her ears and on her neck, before taking one last look in the mirror. She was as ready as she'd ever be.

Once back in the living room, she found Kaleb still standing by the door, glancing out at the wide expanse of land encompassing what was left of the Stranford farm. There wasn't much left, other than the acres of land that sat barren after years of farming the rich soil and a large barn that had seen better days. The crops were all gone, as were the horses, which had Zoey still wondering why her father was hanging on to it.

She was fully aware of the Walker's desire to purchase a vast amount that straddled their own, and if it were up to her, she'd have done it by now. Only because her father needed the money more than he needed a couple hundred acres of dead grass. But that wasn't public information and Zoey was working double time trying to figure out what she could do to resolve the financial strain.

"Ready?" Zoey asked, interrupting Kaleb who looked to be far away as he peered out the screen door.

Turning his head back to her, he smiled and those piercing blue eyes lit up with promises left unspoken. She stepped out onto the porch, shutting the door behind her before following him to his truck. When he stopped to open her door, her heart melted just a little.

Kaleb Walker, as well as every other Walker man, was a gentleman to his very core. For as long as she could remember, he'd opened her door for her, although they were only friends. Their mother had raised them to value women, although Zoey happened to know that they sometimes valued them a little too much. The Walker boys might be gentleman, but they undoubtedly weren't saints.

Once inside the truck, Zoey put her seatbelt on, waiting for Kaleb to climb in. A minute later they were turning out of her father's driveway and onto the main road that would lead around to the entrance to the Walker ranch.

"Do your parents know about the party?" Zoey asked as they drove.

"It's a surprise, actually. Don't ask me how Travis and Sawyer pulled that one off." Kaleb laughed. "They've been working on it for at least two months, and it took some creative manipulation to get my folks out of town for the last couple of days so they could get everything set up."

"Are they home yet?"

"They should be back any minute now. Dad called and said they were on the road and running a little behind, which turned out to be a good thing." Kaleb turned the truck onto the dirt road that led to the Walker's house and Zoey found herself mesmerized by the muscles working in his arms. "They had a problem setting up one of the tents and that pushed all of the set up back. Everything seems to be back on schedule though."

Zoey turned away, glancing out the window as they approached the house and the various cars and trucks that were parked in several lines down the side of the house. There had to have been at least a hundred or so parked haphazardly along the main drive.

Kaleb pulled the truck a little farther out, probably to ensure he wouldn't get blocked in, before turning off the truck. "Don't move." He warned her as he exited and walked around.

Zoey sat patiently waiting for him to open her door, which she knew was what he insisted on doing. Again, her heart turned over. She loved that about Kaleb, how genuinely sweet he was, and it had been something she hated to see him dole out on other women over the years, but Zoey would've never mentioned it. Not to him, not to anyone. But it was a definite turn on.

She expected him to open the door, so when she turned to slide down, she wasn't expecting him to grip her waist and pull her closer, pressing his impressive body against hers. His cologne tickled her nostrils while his warm hands sent chills racing down her spine.

"I can't wait." The seductively dark voice slid around her, captivating her as she zeroed in on his mouth as he moved closer.

Zoey braced herself for the impact of his kiss, knowing if, like last time, she'd very well have to force herself not to fall into him. When his lips met hers, his brawny hands gripping her waist, she instinctively brushed her hands over his smooth cheeks before sliding her fingers into his silky hair.

Lost to the sensations, the rest of the world fell away, leaving them standing just outside of the truck, the open door blocking anyone else's view, but not providing nearly enough privacy for what she wanted. When he pressed his hips against hers, she felt the rigid length of his erection between her thighs, and she couldn't hold back the moan as she pulled him closer.

It was as if her body had come to life over the course of the last couple of days, a renewed hunger building inside of her, acknowledging there was something she'd been missing for five incredibly long years. The touch of a man should've been foreign, having gone so long without it, but with Kaleb, it felt... Well, it felt familiar.

A horn honked, stunning her and causing Kaleb to gently pull away. Zoey realized five years were a damn long time to go without a man's touch, to go without sex period, and she knew beyond a shadow of a doubt, she was putting an end to her abstinence just as soon as Kaleb was willing.

Friends with benefits, she thought to herself.

Why hadn't she ever thought about that before?

Chapter Six

♂♀

The party, Kaleb knew, would undoubtedly be classified as a success. An hour into it and he was still busy greeting people, some he hadn't seen in years, but had known all of his life, and others he had the pleasure of seeing nearly every day. The Walker's had a large extended family, with Curtis, their father, having four brothers and three sisters, and Lorrie, their mother, having five sisters and three brothers. And thanks to all of them, Kaleb had close to forty cousins. Yep, they were a veritable small town, all on their own.

And tonight, Kaleb was in charge of greeting all of those family members and friends as they poured in by the masses. Thankfully Zoey was acquainted with a lot of his cousins, having grown up in their small town, and she knew many of Kaleb's aunts and uncles thanks to the number of hours she'd spent around his house. Although he was pretty sure she was having a hard time putting names with faces, she was doing a phenomenal job keeping up.

For the last hour, Kaleb kissed so many cousins, hugged just as many more, and shook hands with more people than he could count, all while Zoey stayed close, reminding him exactly what he'd prefer to be doing. He tried not to dwell on how responsive she'd been to him by the truck because the all too familiar hard on she inspired was not appropriate with all these people around.

Had it not been for someone honking their horn, Kaleb wasn't sure how far he might've taken that little make out session by his truck, nor would he have guaranteed they'd be at the party right now.

For the life of him, he couldn't figure out how they'd managed to ignore the apparent chemical reaction that occurred when they touched. Not that he'd expected anything from her tonight, other than her company, but the way she kissed him spoke of salacious promises and he was having a hard time ignoring them.

"Kaleb!" A familiar voice sounded from somewhere behind him, and Kaleb turned. He slid his hand into Zoey's, linking their fingers and holding her close because that was the most natural thing to do.

The woman approaching them, aside from being the equivalent of ice water on his balls, looked so out of place, and Kaleb suddenly wondered why she was even there.

"Regina." He couldn't hide his distaste, but he didn't figure she cared.

When she went to reach in for a hug, Kaleb pulled Zoey closer, using her as a shield because the last thing he wanted was Regina touching him in any way. Immature? Maybe.

So fucking what.

"Why are you here?" He asked bluntly, taking in how she was dressed.

Wearing those spiked heels he'd thought intensely sexy at one time, he wondered how she didn't get stuck in the grass; the image of her fighting to get loose almost made him smile.

Almost.

The fact was, nothing Regina Hollingsworth did or said would ever make him smile again. Not after the hell she put him and his family through.

"Travis invited me." She said, glancing around as though she were looking for Kaleb's older brother.

"Bullshit." He barked, glaring back at her. He knew damn good and well Travis never would have invited the lying, scheming bitch, nor would any of them actually have wanted her there. It had been several years since he'd last seen her and as far as Kaleb was concerned, it could be several hundred more, and it wouldn't make a damn bit of difference to him.

Regina pretended not to notice how pissed off he was, when she turned her attention on Zoey.

"Who's your little friend?"

Kaleb hated the way Regina talked down to everyone she met and above all else, he couldn't fathom what he had ever seen in the woman. Aside from being attractive, she was as shallow as the water in their drought riddled stock tank.

"Cut the crap, Regina. You know damn well who I am." Zoey spoke up. Was it his imagination, or did she take a step closer to him?

"Oh, right, you're the little girl from next door. I didn't recognize you since you don't look like a *boy*." Regina said in the poorest excuse for nice that he'd ever seen. She was talking to Zoey as though she weren't twice the woman Regina could ever be.

Turning his attention on the woman beside him, he smiled down at her and then turned to go. He didn't have anything to say to the scheming, cheating bitch who once had Kaleb convinced they were going to get married one day. He'd never fully fallen into that trap until...

Realizing he didn't want to think about her deceit, he started to tell her as much, but Regina put her hand on his arm and smiled back at him.

"If you wouldn't mind, once you take Zoey home, I'd like to talk to you." Regina whispered, none too quietly. "In private." The seductive grin she sent him had the hair on the back of his neck standing up in warning. The woman just didn't quit.

If he knew Regina, which, unfortunately, he did, she was doing this just to get a rise out of Zoey. She would stoop to any level just to prove what a complete bitch she was. Regina knew as well as he did that he wouldn't give her the time of day, much less talk to her alone in private.

"Kaleb," Zoey interrupted, smiling up at him. "You might want to let her know that I don't plan on going home tonight. At least not alone."

Kaleb bit back a groan. Zoey might've just said that to bait Regina, or piss her off, but his body didn't know the difference. Smiling down at her, he pulled her close and pressed his lips to hers. "Don't worry, baby. I don't have any intentions of leaving you alone tonight."

Zoey kissed him back before smiling up at Regina. "Sorry." She smirked, sounding anything but.

Damn the woman drove him absolutely wild. But that was Zoey for you. All spunk.

"Regina, look." Kaleb turned back to her. "I'm not sure why you're here, but I promise, if I find out you're going after one of my brothers, you won't like the consequences."

Regina had already tried it once. Four years ago to be exact. After all but convincing Kaleb she was pregnant with his child, she had the audacity to try to sneak into Sawyer's bed one night after he'd had way too much to drink. As it turns out, most people, namely women didn't understand the true depth of their brotherly bond.

A Walker man didn't turn his back on his family, and sleeping with one another's women, unless with their explicit consent, would cross a line none of them were willing to cross. And yes, there were times when they had shared a woman, many times, in fact, but never unless everyone was in agreement.

Regina had never been one that any of them shared, and Kaleb had a sneaking suspicion she resented him for it. Among other things.

Regina narrowed her eyes on Kaleb and put her hands on her hips. "I don't care about your warnings, Kaleb. I never have. And you can't stop me from going after what I want."

"No, you're right. I can't stop you. But I can assure you, not a one of them is interested in yesterday's trash, especially not the likes of you." With that, Kaleb turned and would've walked away if the one person guaranteed to ensure Regina Hollingsworth wasn't allowed to get her claws into another Walker man didn't walk up.

"Why're you here?" Lorrie asked, coming to stand on Zoey's other side, glancing from Regina then to Kaleb and down to Zoey. "Hey there, sweetie. I'm so glad you could come tonight."

Kaleb's mother leaned in and hugged Zoey before taking a step back and pinning Regina with that *don't fuck with my family* glare they'd all seen on her face only a few times in their lives.

"Congratulations, Mrs. Walker." Regina smiled, apparently aiming for sweet.

Kaleb glanced down at his mother, seeing the tight line of her lips as she obviously fought back some pretty nasty comments.

"I admit I wasn't privy to the guest list, but I'd bet my last dollar you're not on it." Lorrie was fit to be tied, and Kaleb had to fight back a smile. Not that he wanted his mother's night to be ruined, but seeing her stand up to the deceitful bitch made him proud.

"Regina was just leaving, Ma." He assured her, looking back at Regina.

"I most certainly am not." She argued, cocking her hip and putting her hands down to her side. Her attempt to get all high and mighty, which she was known to do, was thwarted when one of those spiked heels got lodged into the moist earth beneath her feet sending her stumbling.

Zoey, bless her, didn't have the decency not to laugh, which only made Lorrie and Kaleb follow suit, which only pissed Regina off more. The laughter died the moment Kaleb's father approached, putting an arm around Kaleb's mother and shooting fire from his eyes. "I see my boys didn't think about security tonight."

Kaleb watched in utter fascination as Curtis took it upon himself to seek out the nearest person – his cousin Jaxson – to "assist the woman back to her vehicle", his gruff tone instructed. Jaxson looked more than happy to escort Regina from the property. Once they were on their way, Regina sending death glares at the four of them, the tension eased, and Zoey spoke first.

"Congratulations, Mr. and Mrs. Walker."

"Awww, thank you, honey." Lorrie smiled, her brilliant blue eyes sparkling. "I'm glad you could join us."

Kaleb was still holding Zoey's hand, and he saw the instant his father noticed, as well. The look in his dad's eyes was more of a warning than anything, and Kaleb nodded his head in silent agreement.

His parents had nothing to worry about, although he knew they would. They would worry for both Zoey and Kaleb, but as far as he was concerned, they were wasting their time. Whatever was going on between them, they were both grown up enough to handle it.

Thankfully another group of people stopped by and distracted his parents and Kaleb took the opportunity to sneak away, leading Zoey away from the throngs of people. When they were out of ear reach, Zoey turned and looked up at him. "That bitch definitely hasn't aged well."

Kaleb chuckled. Regina Hollingsworth was just as beautiful as always, at least in the physical sense, but once they had all realized her agenda, there wasn't a lick of makeup that could help her now. Zoey was right, Regina hadn't aged well.

Zoey turned and glared behind him, apparently looking to see if Regina was still around, but then turned her attention back on him. When he met her eyes, he expected to see something other than the warmth that radiated from the cobalt blue orbs. "Well, nobody's perfect." She teased him. "Maybe now you'll realize whose door you should've been knocking on all along."

Kaleb gripped Zoey's hand, pulling her around to the side of the house where they had a small measure of privacy before pressing her against the stone wall. "Are you teasing me, woman?" He asked, wanting to get lost in the warmth of her gaze.

"Maybe." She smiled, tracing his lip with her thumb.

"You better be careful." He warned her. "I've known for a long time that I don't have any control when it comes to you."

"Well, I've dreamt of a million ways to make you lose control, so we're even."

Kaleb crushed his mouth down on hers, needing her kiss, needing her touch, but trying to remember where they were. He didn't let it go nearly as far as he wanted to when he pulled back and glanced down at his watch. "How long's this damn thing going to last anyway?"

Zoey laughed, then slid her small fingers into his once again. "Come on. I think there's a dance floor calling your name."

He didn't hear a damn dance floor, but he could hear a bed calling his name. Or hell, the wall would suffice. Either way, Kaleb knew that they weren't going to make it through the night before he had her completely naked and he was using his tongue to explore a whole lot more than just her mouth.

♀♂

Regina Hollingsworth was a crazy, delusional bitch and Zoey couldn't stand the sight of her any more now than she could back then. It wasn't her snotty attitude or the too tight skirt or the too revealing shirt, or even the ugly ass heels she wore. It was the woman herself and her lack of any type of conscience.

Zoey remembered what had happened between Kaleb and Regina mainly because of how giddy she'd been to find out that Kaleb wouldn't be getting married. She'd been conflicted at the time because learning that Regina had wronged Kaleb in such a horrible way had broken her heart for him, but in turn, she was thankful that he hadn't gone through with any plans to marry her.

At the time, their friendship had been on the back burner, mainly because of her marriage and Kaleb's relationship with Regina. Rightfully so, they were both working on their own love lives and their significant others hadn't appreciated their close friendship. So, they had abandoned one another temporarily.

As if it wasn't unfortunate enough that Regina had lied to Kaleb, and the rest of the Walker family, convincing them all she was pregnant, but to have tried to sleep with Sawyer... That was an all-time low. It was evident the woman didn't know the Walker family all that well because she would have realized early on that they didn't swing that way.

With Kaleb pressed against her now, holding her close as they two stepped slowly across the makeshift dance floor, Zoey sent up a silent thank you.

Despite the fact that Kaleb had been hurt by such awful deceit, Zoey knew she wouldn't even have this chance now had Regina finally snagged him for good. She figured once a Walker man married, he married for always, and that would have been a long road for Kaleb.

Zoey remembered the story, knew Regina had gone so far as to try to convince everyone she actually lost the baby, and for a time, Kaleb and Lorrie had both been devastated. Only one night, when Regina was in a drunken rage down at Moonshiner's, she'd out and out admitted it was all a lie. Which was the reason Zoey was so damn surprised the woman actually had the audacity to show up tonight.

As it turned out, Regina tried to sneak into Sawyer's bed in an attempt to get the two brothers at one time. And that was another rumor that ran rampant through their small town. The Walker boys were known to be just a little wild, and there were some exceptionally hot stories by women who claimed to have been taken by more than one of them at a time.

Zoey and Kaleb had never talked about that side of him, although she knew, for a fact, the rumor was true. There were many nights Zoey fantasized about what it would be like to be the filling in such an intensely sexy Walker sandwich, but her friendships with the men made those exactly that. Fantasies.

The idea of being with one of the Walker boys, namely Kaleb, was so much more than Zoey could fathom, she couldn't even imagine being with two of them at one time. What would it even be like?

Oh God. Clearly her mind was wandering way too far from reality because that was something she could never imagine doing, although the idea of it, from time to time, made for some remarkably vivid fantasies.

Shaking off the thought, she turned to look up at Kaleb as the song ended and he stopped moving. When their eyes met, she felt the heat from the flame she saw burning there. It was almost as though he could read her thoughts.

"What were you thinking about?" He asked, dispelling her assumption and making her breathe a sigh of relief. Zoey wasn't the type of woman to engage in wild sexcapades, and thinking about something as hot as a threesome like that was only a fantasy. Nothing more.

"You." She said truthfully. At least a partial truth anyway.

"You're making this harder and harder on me, Zoey." Kaleb said, sounding almost remorseful.

Taking a step back, she looked deep into his eyes, trying to understand what he was telling her. Gone was the flirty, sexy grin and in its place, pure agony.

"Why? What's wrong?"

Kaleb took her hand and led her to one of the empty tables that lined the provisional wooden dance area. When he sat down on the bench, he pulled her down beside him, leaving barely enough room between them for air.

"You're making it entirely too difficult to keep my hands off of you."

He sounded as if that was a bad thing.

"I've waited so long for you, dreamed about you..." When he slid his finger down her cheek, she instinctively leaned into the touch, never breaking eye contact.

"And why have you never told me this?" Zoey asked, thinking about how close of a friendship they had developed over the years. They were inseparable most of the time, but never once had they talked about anything that could possibly occur between them, including sex. *Especially* sex.

"What was I going to tell you?" Kaleb asked, sounding dumbfounded. "I would've never thought to share some of the things I dreamt about doing to you. I know you, Zoey. You would've run for the hills."

True. Zoey wasn't one to have engaged in any sort of intimate relationship over the last few years. Not since Jason. Her heart had been broken, and she had no intentions of letting it get broken again. Not by any man. But this... this was different. Kaleb was her best friend, and if they were smart about it, there was no reason they couldn't incorporate a little sex into it. Neither of them were having it, and she knew that for a fact, so they wouldn't be hurting anyone else either.

"Ok, maybe you're right." She admitted. "But that doesn't mean we can't do the whole friends with benefits thing, right?"

"Friends with benefits?" Kaleb smiled, but Zoey realized immediately that it didn't quite reach his eyes. Did he not want to do this?

"Yes. You know, we get naked every now and again?"

"Hmmm. I like the idea of seeing you naked."

That was the Kaleb she knew. The man who flirted the panties right off of women everywhere.

When he leaned closer, Zoey smiled and then kissed him. For some reason, it felt natural to kiss Kaleb. Maybe that's because she'd dreamt about it for so long.

"This night has been a long time coming." Zoey whispered against his lips.

At least for her that was true.

When he pulled back, locking those smoky eyes with hers, one of those lingering embers deep in her core burst into flame. She suddenly wished they were alone, someplace where they could explore the firestorm that was brewing out of control between them.

He didn't say anything, but Zoey knew he was beginning to reconsider. The gentleman in him couldn't allow him to throw caution to the wind, likely from fear of hurting her. Zoey wasn't fragile, neither in heart or spirit, and she wanted to assure him that she could deal with the aftermath. She wasn't looking for strings, or attachments, or promises.

"I want to be with you tonight." Zoey said, willing him to see everything she was feeling as they stared at one another. "Even if that's all you've got to give me. Just give me tonight."

She wasn't sure where the words came from, or when she had started feeling that way, but there it was. Maybe it was the fact that she'd been in lust with this man for as long as she could remember, or maybe it was because she wanted to pursue something she felt might very well slip from her grasp if they waited too long.

This was exactly where she wanted to be; in Kaleb's arms for as long as he would have her. It didn't have to be forever, she wasn't sure she even believed in forever anymore. But for one night – this night – she knew exactly what she wanted.

♂♀

The sound of metal clinking on glass caught their attention, and Kaleb forced himself to look away from Zoey. He wasn't quite sure what he was feeling – definitely lust, maybe something more – but he was grateful for the distraction.

"First, I want to thank everyone for coming." Travis said, standing in the middle of the floor beneath the tent holding a microphone. "As you all know, on this day, fifty years ago, my parents vowed to love one another and, somehow, I'm not quite sure how, my mother has put up with my father through all of these years and here they are. Still together."

A rumble of laughter erupted from the crowd; exactly Travis' intention. The man might not be one to laugh easily, but he had a way with crowds.

"Mom, Dad, we came together to celebrate this day with you because you've been an inspiration to us all. The love and support you've provided us, your family and friends, through the years, hasn't gone unnoticed, nor has it been unappreciated.

"As the oldest of the seven of us, I can tell you that you've shown us what it means to love and be loved and for that, we will always be grateful."

Kaleb wasn't sure where his brother had come up with the words, but he'd easily expressed exactly what Kaleb felt. Glancing at his brothers, they were all riveted to the three people standing in the center of the floor, each of them smiling, endorsing every word Travis spoke.

Curtis tilted his head in his normal acknowledgement while Lorrie had tears streaming down her face. Granted, they were tears of joy, but the sight still tugged at Kaleb's heart as it did anytime his mother cried. Thankfully that wasn't often, unless, of course, she was getting mushy. They definitely tried to avoid those times.

"Dad, if you don't mind." Travis stated, handing him the microphone.

Curtis' voice boomed through the microphone, drifting across the humid August night, spilling out from the tent and washing over each of the guests who had come to celebrate the wondrous occasion. "I'd like to thank everyone for coming, and I'd like to thank my boys for thinking ahead and sending me on a wild goose chase across the state of Texas just so they could put this little shindig together." Again the crowd laughed. "But most importantly, I'd like to thank my beautiful bride for honoring me fifty short years ago." Looking down into Lorrie's eyes, Curtis continued. "I'd do it all over again. In a heartbeat."

To Kaleb's surprise, his sweet, demure mother, threw her arms around his father's neck and planted a scorching hot kiss right on his mouth. The crowd cheered. Then Curtis raised the microphone, glanced around at the hordes of people circling around them. "And that's all I've got. Time for everyone to clear out now because I've got somewhere I need to be."

Handing the microphone back to Travis, Curtis pulled Lorrie into his arms, lowered his mouth back to hers and again, the crowd cheered.

When Kaleb glanced down at Zoey, he noticed she was smiling, as well as wiping what appeared to be a tear from her eye. His heart turned over. Pulling her in close to him, he continued to focus on his parents, trying to give Zoey a little privacy.

When the band started up again, he turned back to the woman beside him, tilting her chin until she looked at him.

"I'm taking you to my place tonight." He warned her, the driving hunger roiling through him. "I just need you to know what you're getting yourself into."

Zoey nodded her head as though she understood what he was telling her. He continued anyway.

"I've waited too damn long to have you. I've kept my distance, kept my hands to myself, but I can't any longer." Her eyes darkened with the same overwhelming desire he felt every time he looked at her. "Do you understand what I'm telling you?"

She didn't answer, but she didn't look away.

"I can't promise gentle, and I can't promise I'll shower you with sweet words. As much as I want to, I'm not that man. I need you, Zoey."

This time she did nod her head, her fingers linking with his and squeezing her silent agreement.

Now if only the damn party would end. Kaleb wasn't sure how much longer he'd be able to wait.

Chapter Seven

♀♂

Zoey was a nervous wreck. Her hands were shaking, her palms sweating, and her heart was pounding like she'd just run a marathon. For the better part of the last hour, she and Kaleb had made their rounds, talking to the lingering guests, dancing, and finally saying their goodbyes to Lorrie and Curtis before walking out to the truck. Where they were now.

Kaleb reached the door before she did, and he eased it open, taking a step back so she could get in. When he crowded her between the truck door and the seat, similar to the way he had earlier, her blood pressure spiked, and she feared she might just pass out.

Never in her life had she felt like this. Never had her body throbbed with anticipation, an eagerness to touch and be touched. But that's what Kaleb did to her. He had always heightened her sensuality, made her want things she didn't figure she would want from a man.

It wasn't like she was a virgin. This wasn't her first time. She'd been with two men in her life, one being her husband, the other a man she dated before Jason. Both of those were serious relationships, both of which she knew what she was walking into. She knew Kaleb better than she knew either of them, but yet, she felt as though there was so much she didn't know.

And here she was about to alter the rest of her life because Zoey knew without a doubt that being with Kaleb would ruin her for any other man. She loved him. Had always loved him; although maybe that love was based more on friendship than anything else, but it was love nonetheless. There was no way to confuse lust with love when it came to Kaleb because, despite the fact that she was attracted to him, she deeply cared about him. Always had and always would.

That didn't mean she was *in love* with Kaleb, but she feared she was. She had always feared he could break her heart so easily if she had given him the chance. And maybe that's why she'd kept her distance for so many years. Their friendship was strong, always had been and why would she want to ruin that with one night of passion.

It was too late to think about that now because her body was committed, her heart might be a little hesitant, but she wasn't listening to her heart. Not tonight.

"You sure about this?" Kaleb asked, his masculine scent like a drug, infusing her body with a buzz that had her aching for more. Addicted. That's what she was. She was addicted to this man.

She dared a glance up into the gray-blue of his mesmerizing eyes and smiled. She was ready. "Yes, I'm sure."

If she wasn't mistaken, Kaleb's hands were shaking nearly as much as hers were. She doubted he was nervous, probably just anticipating what was to come. If the chemistry between them was anything to go by, then they were in for the ride of their life when their bodies came together as one.

Instead of lingering, she climbed up into the truck, aware of his penetrating eyes still raking over her, making her knees weak. If she wasn't careful, she'd be a puddle of hormones by the time they reached his house.

When Kaleb climbed into the driver's side, he didn't say a word, but he did link his fingers with hers again as they drove in silence down the dirt roads that bisected the Walker land. Her nerves were rioting, and she was pretty sure he could hear the pounding of her heart over the low hum of the engine and the radio that was playing softly through the cab of the truck.

When they pulled up to his house a minute or two later, she steeled herself. Choosing to preoccupy her mind by admiring his home, rather than dwell on what was about to happen, Zoey found herself reliving some of the times she'd been here.

They had hung out at his house a number of times in recent years, but almost every time someone else had been there too. Generally a group of people including Kaleb's friend Gage, who was currently out of state. He was another one of the men in town that the women lusted over, and it was no secret he too had been included in some of Kaleb's more infamous rendezvous.

Never had she been to Kaleb's house alone before now.

His house was the epitome of the man, and she knew he was proud of it. Dark wooden beams held up the cover over the front porch while river rock lined the bottom of the house. The cabin wasn't so much a cabin as it was a house, but because of its size and seclusion, she figured that's why they referred to them as such.

Instead of wood logs, the house was dark, chocolate brown stucco, with thick wooden beams for trim. The front of the house was mostly windows and a door, and during the day, with it positioned to face the sun rising in the east, there was a vast amount of sunlight peeking through the thick trees, bringing with it warmth and light.

Zoey's thoughts were interrupted when Kaleb opened her door, standing just outside looking sinfully sexy with his mussed hair and chiseled good looks. Although she figured he'd shaved when he had come to pick her up several hours before, he now had a line of stubble along his jaw, and she wanted to run her fingers over it, just to feel the sensual scrape against her skin.

Without further hesitation, she climbed out of the truck, joining him as he led her up the steps and onto the wide front porch, before opening the front door and allowing her to go in before him.

Once inside, Kaleb flipped on a small table lamp and the room filled with a soft yellow glow. It took every ounce of nerve she possessed to stand there, trying to ignore the tension that had grown to monumental proportions in the last few hours.

Taking a step forward, Zoey was in the living room, arranged exactly as it was the last time she'd been there. An oversized brown sofa, covered in buttery soft, distressed leather, and an equally large recliner sat facing a wall of river rock encasing a fireplace. The room had little else besides a table made of unfinished wood and wrought iron, holding a couple of coasters and a remote control for the massive flat panel television.

On the impressive wood beam mantle, a couple of pictures caught her eye and she ventured over to see them. She didn't remember seeing them before. One was a picture of the seven boys standing beside a sign for Walker Demolition. Every one of them smiled brightly and the sun reflected off of their exotic blue eyes, twinkling with mischief. They were a handsome bunch that was for sure.

Another framed picture was of his mother and father, neither of them expecting the camera, so they looked relaxed, gazing at one another like only two people truly in love ever did.

The third picture caught her eye and she almost stumbled as she moved closer. It was of the two of them from her senior prom. It was the cheesy pose they made you take for the photographer, but it was still overwhelming to see it sitting right there for the world to see. Glancing back at Kaleb, he looked shy, and so boyishly handsome, her heart swelled even bigger than it had when he'd held her hand for most of the night.

"I didn't expect to see this." She admitted truthfully.

Kaleb took a few steps closer, pulling her against him. When the warmth of his chest pressed into her back, her breath hitched in her throat. With his arms wrapped around her, Zoey felt a strange sense of comfort wash over her. As foreign as it felt to be in his arms, it was also incredibly familiar although Kaleb had never touched her like this. The closest they'd come had been when she had been grieving for her mother and Kaleb had been there for her, holding her while she broke down.

"You stole my breath that night." Kaleb admitted, his voice low and sexy.

When she looked at the photograph, she remembered that night like it was yesterday and not fifteen long years before. She hadn't intended to go, not really caring to, but he insisted it was a rite of passage and if she didn't have a date, he was going to take her. They'd been talking about it, and she was teasing him that she wasn't going to attend her senior prom. When he had asked her, she'd been pleasantly surprised, and although it was nothing more than two friends at a dance, she remembered that night fondly.

"Zoey." Kaleb whispered in her ear, his voice sounding gruff and strained. Almost as though he were trying to hold himself back.

Turning in the circle of his arms, she looked up and her breath caught. He looked stricken by some unnamed emotion, clearly trying to rein in what he was feeling. She knew how he felt because she'd been overwhelmed by a number of emotions since the first time he kissed her just the day before. Had it only been one day? It felt as though they'd been doing the dance leading up to this moment for ages, not just hours.

"You're so beautiful." This time Zoey whispered the compliment, using her fingers to trace the stubble on the hard line of his jaw. Her fingers trembled as she outlined his warm skin, brushing her thumb over his bottom lip.

Before she could think about what they were doing, what the next step was, Kaleb pressed his mouth to hers, stealing her soul with his kiss before he lifted her in his arms, throwing her off balance until she wrapped her legs around his waist, ringing her arms around his neck.

She half expected him to carry her to the bedroom, but he surprised her when he turned to the sofa, easing himself down until she was straddling his lap. One of his big hands cupped the back of her head, holding her to him, his tongue exploring her mouth as she devoured him, unable to hold back the hunger that had been building in her all night.

Or rather years.

♂♀

Kaleb knew he had to go slow, but it was so damn difficult when the only thing he wanted to do was strip Zoey of that frilly dress and bury his cock in her sweet warm depths until she was wrapped around him in every way possible. When she brushed her soft fingers along his jaw, it was all he could do to keep from grinding himself against her, desperate to get lost in the sensations.

He'd waited. Then and now.

It felt as though Kaleb had been waiting his entire life for this moment. For the chance to feel her, to touch, taste, explore every glorious inch of Zoey's sweet smelling skin.

One night stands, Kaleb was used to. Repeated sexual adventures, he'd been there, done that, as well. As much as he wanted to convince himself that they were in it for one night, or even a week or two, he knew he was lying to himself. This night was going to change his life forever, and how he proceeded would lay the path for whatever was to come.

When he told Zoey that he wasn't gentle, he hadn't been lying. He wasn't. There was a dark hunger that lived just beneath the surface and Zoey pushed every ounce of his control. If he let go, if he took her with the aggressive need he felt coursing underneath his skin, he'd risk scaring her, yet Kaleb feared he couldn't hold back.

Zoey broke the kiss, leaning back until she was staring down at him. She stole his breath, robbed him of every good intention because she was just so damn sweet.

When her palms glided down his chest, over his stomach until she reached the waistband of his jeans, he held his breath, anticipating her next move. Realizing her intentions, he pushed farther into the couch so she could pull the hem of his shirt out of his jeans. Without an ounce of finesse, he pulled his shirt up and over his head, throwing it somewhere in the near vicinity.

When her blue eyes darkened as they trailed over his chest, he had to bite his tongue to hold back. Then their eyes met again, and he waited with bated breath for her to tell him that she couldn't do this; to tell him that they were moving too damn fast. They were, he knew it. He should have taken her home, should have left her alone for at least this night until he could get his head on straight.

He hadn't done that though, and now she was straddling him, her hungry gaze trailing over his skin, leaving a raging inferno that would bloom into a wildfire the likes of which they'd both be consumed by.

What she did next had him praying for patience.

Zoey lifted the bottom of her strapless dress, raising it up and over her head, baring more of her smooth skin to his gaze. She wasn't wearing a bra and her breasts spilled free before him, begging for his touch.

"Fuck." He growled, knowing he was at the end of his rope. Either he was about to hang himself, or he would be freefalling.

"Kaleb." Her sweet voice caught his attention, and he forced his eyes back to hers.

"Don't hold back." She whispered. "Not tonight."

The growl that tore from his chest sounded more like an animal than anything human, and Kaleb slid his hands up her tiny waist, over her ribs until he was cupping each glorious mound, squeezing gently as she watched him.

"So fucking pretty." Leaning forward, Kaleb licked her nipple and Zoey gasped, her fingernails digging into his shoulders.

"God, yes." She moaned. "More, Kaleb. Please."

Squeezing more firmly, he pulled her closer until he could fill his mouth with one warm, soft breast, suckling like a starving man. He was lost in her taste, in her responsiveness, and when she pulled his head closer, he devoured her like the starving man he was.

He lavished each generous mound in turn, using his tongue to tease her nipples until they puckered so beautifully from his touch. She was going to kill him, the need building until he wasn't sure he could take anymore before he plunged into her pussy, seeking the relief that he knew he'd only ever find in her body.

Zoey didn't give him a chance to do more before she slid off of his lap, right to the floor in front of him. He knew right then and there that he would die and go to heaven before the night was over.

"Zoey." He warned, knowing he wouldn't be able to control himself if she did what he expected she would do next.

When her tiny fingers pulled the button on his jeans from the loop, then lowered his zipper, his stomach cramped tight as he anticipated the moment when she wrapped her soft hands around his cock.

She smiled up at him, and he damn near lost it.

He lifted his hips, assisting by pushing the denim down, allowing his steel hard shaft to spring free, begging for her glossy lips to put him out of his misery.

Kaleb was mesmerized by the sight of Zoey on her knees between his thighs, her small hand wrapped around his cock, slowly stroking as she licked her lips.

"Put your mouth on me, baby." He groaned, his words coming out none too gently.

When she sucked in a breath, he met her eyes, waiting to see whether she would run or if she would give in to the firestorm licking at them, ready to consume them in its fury.

"Fuck!" Kaleb damn near screamed the word when her warm tongue met the engorged head of his dick. He wasn't going to last, there was no way in hell he could hold back once she...

Holy fucking shit.

Kaleb gripped the cushions of the couch, holding himself back from gripping her head in his hands and thrusting hard and fast into the fiercely hot cavern of her mouth.

Throwing his head back, Kaleb closed his eyes, letting the moist heat lick at him, his balls drawing painfully tight against his body.

"Zoey. Baby. Fuck. It's too fucking good. Just like that." He was rambling, his brain overloaded with the pleasure of having her mouth wrapped around his cock, the heat encompassing him, robbing him entirely of all common sense, all good intention. There was nothing except the feel of Zoey's lips wrapped around the swollen head, her wicked tongue licking him, his cock threatening to explode.

When he went to move his hands, wanting to pull her closer, to control her movements, to push farther, deeper, faster, Zoey slowed, clasping her hands around his wrists, then holding them to the couch. He pulled his head forward, looking down at her and he saw stars. Watching as she bathed his cock with her little pink tongue was nearly his undoing.

She let the head of his cock slide from her mouth. "No hands." She said, a warning of her own. "I want to taste you."

How could he argue with that? He balled his hands into fists and pressed them into the cushion, his thigh muscles knotting, his back board straight as he tried to hang on.

"Fuck." Apparently she had reduced his vocabulary down to only one word with the intensity of her lush mouth, the soft vibration as she moaned around his cock. "It's too good."

Zoey proceeded to suck, lick, drive him absolutely fucking crazy with her explorations, and when she sucked him fully into the fiery recesses of her mouth, he bit his lip. He was going to come. His eyes were glued to where she was between his thighs, her small hand gripping the base of his cock, stroking in rhythm to her head bobbing up and down.

"Deeper." He insisted because he couldn't hold back. "Take me deeper, Zoey." Fuck, she was killing him with ecstasy. "That's it baby. All the way."

Kaleb's fingers were going numb from where he dug them into the palm of his hands as he tried to keep from touching her.

"I'm gonna come in your mouth, Zoey. Suck me, baby."

The world exploded in bright lights and the roar of his blood in his ears when she drove his cock deep into her mouth, the oversensitive head brushing the back of her throat. "Zoey!" Her name was ripped from his throat, sounding desperate as his release erupted, a sharp, sudden sensation tearing up from the base of his spine, racing outward in every direction.

Unable to control himself, he gripped her head, his fingers lacing into the fine silk of her hair as he held her to him, spilling his seed deep in her throat.

Chapter Eight

♀♂

Zoey sat completely still, Kaleb's salty taste flooding her mouth as he came, his hands gripping her head painfully hard as her body ignited in a rush of overwhelming sensation. He hadn't even touched her, but her body was burning, aflame from the power that coursed through her at the realization of what she'd just done. She'd brought him pleasure, and in turn, she had barely contained her own orgasm. It was unlike anything she'd ever done, anything she'd ever known.

When his still erect cock slid from her lips, Kaleb moved forward, falling to his knees on the floor before her as he shoved the coffee table out of the way with ruthless force. She didn't have a chance to do anything before he had her flat on her back, the coarse fibers of the rug tickling her skin as he came over her.

When his mouth met hers, she pulled him closer, although he managed to hold himself above her when she wanted nothing more than to feel his weight pressed into her, the warmth of his skin encompassing her.

"Baby, I don't know what I'm going to do with you." Kaleb said when he tore his mouth from hers.

She could think of a number of things she wanted him to do to her. Apparently he had some ideas of his own because he pushed her thighs apart, kneeling between her legs, staring down at her. His gaze was like a physical caress, her nerve endings reaching out for him, selfishly relishing in the admiration she saw in his eyes.

"Touch me, Kaleb." She moaned, unable to help herself. She needed his touch like she needed air to breathe, probably more so in that very moment.

"Baby, I fully intend to." Kaleb smiled down at her. "Trust me."

Oh, she trusted him all right. She trusted he would have her body screaming. So what was he waiting for?

"So pretty." He whispered as he trailed one finger down her neck, over her collar bone, then circling one painfully erect nipple.

She wanted him lower, between her thighs, easing the ache that had taken up residence since the first time she felt his incredible mouth on her lips. The rest of her body felt entirely too neglected, wanting to feel his mouth in ways she'd never been fond of.

When his tongue replaced his finger, swirling around her nipple, she bucked her hips upward, needing his touch lower. She was going to burn alive.

Thankfully he didn't tease for too long before he was easing lower, his broad shoulders sliding between her thighs, forcing her legs wider, the only thing between her sensitive pussy and his hungry gaze were her panties, and she was half tempted to rip them from her body just so he'd get on with it.

He obviously had other intentions because he eased her panties to the side, using one hand to open her lips while he trailed one thick finger through the folds, teasing her clit only briefly.

Zoey had never been into oral sex, never found enough pleasure in it to need it, but with Kaleb, just his heated stare was enough to have her pussy clenching, her juices preparing her for the invasion she ached for. When he used his tongue to separate her wet folds, she bucked off the floor.

Too much. Oh, God, it was too much.

"Easy, baby." Kaleb crooned. "Let me taste you."

She wanted to beg him to hurry, unsure how long she'd be able to last with him torturing her clit with the soft, warm flicks of his tongue. But she did as he instructed, she tried to relax, tried to enjoy the sensations that short circuited her body as he began to lick her, suckling her clit, before going lower, his tongue pushing through the sensitive flesh of her pussy. When he thrust his tongue inside, she cried out.

"You've got such a pretty pussy." His words lit her up like a pyrotechnics show, the glorious colors flashing behind her closed eye lids as she let the pleasure take over.

"So pink. So soft." He continued to mumble the words while she moved closer and closer to the brink, gripping the razor sharp edge as she tried to hold on.

With her eyes closed, her body begging for that little bit that would send her over, Zoey sucked her bottom lip into her mouth, trying not to beg. When he thrust one thick finger inside her pussy, using his mouth to suckle her clit, her orgasm detonated, her muscles locking painfully as the sudden, intense buzz raced through her.

"Kaleb!" Screaming his name, she mentally reached out to him, praying he would catch her if she didn't stop freefalling into the abyss.

"I've got you, baby."

Suddenly he was closer, his breath against her ear, his rich voice easing the fear that she wouldn't come back to herself. He kissed her softly, his warm lips a lifeline that she latched onto, wrapping her weary arms around his neck. Her body was so overcome with emotion; she fought back the tears, scared of what would happen if she opened herself up more to this man.

With her arms around Kaleb's neck, Zoey held on as he lifted her from the floor, wondering whether he was actually picking her up or if she was just floating because either way, it was a welcome relief from the onslaught of sensation that she was succumbing to.

"Zoey." Kaleb said her name and she forced her eyes open as he laid her on his bed, his immense body coming over her. "I need to be inside you. I need to feel you."

She needed to feel him too. She met his eyes and the smoky blue depths swirled with something she had never seen before, mirroring the emotions racing through her.

Oh, God. She was in trouble here.

♂♀

Kaleb wasn't exactly certain what was going on, but something had come over him, something stronger than even his need for this woman. Maybe it was possessiveness, an overwhelming urge to protect her, but he was swamped with emotion.

It might've started when they walked through his front door, or it might've started when he deposited her on his bed, either way, he couldn't fight it. Zoey was the only woman he'd brought back to his house since Regina, the only woman who had ever been in this bed, and the need to own her, to possess her – mind, body, and soul – was quickly becoming an obsession.

"Baby," Kaleb stared down into the rich, warm blue of her eyes, felt his heart swell to the point he wondered whether his chest could contain it. "I need to feel you."

He wasn't sure what he was getting at, but he had to be inside of her, had to become one with this woman because if he didn't, he didn't think he'd survive.

"Do I need a condom?" Kaleb knew the answer, knew he should have never asked her, but fuck, he didn't want anything between them. The need to feel her slick, warmth around his dick was more than he could bear.

"No." She said, and he wondered whether she knew what she was saying.

"Are you...?"

"I'm on birth control. But, what about..."

At least she was aware of what he was asking and what it actually meant. Kaleb had never been with a woman without a condom. Never. Not even with Regina so when she told him that she was pregnant, he'd battled to understand how that happened, never even remembering any mishaps with the condoms he religiously wore. With Zoey, he almost didn't care, but he would never make a decision for her.

"I'm clean. I've never had sex without a condom. Always been safe..." He began to mumble, unsure whether he was trying to convince her or him. Aligning their bodies, he tilted her chin, pressed a soft kiss on her lips. "Are you sure?"

Gripping his chin with her tiny fingers, she whispered, "I'm sure, Kaleb."

Kaleb gripped the base of his cock, sliding the head against her slick opening before pressing against her. Zoey's body opened for him, gripping the head of his cock as her muscles relaxed enough to push deeper. She was so fucking tight, so hot. Skin to skin, it was the most intense pleasure he had ever known.

"Awww, baby." Kaleb whispered, the sheen of tears in her eyes nearly his undoing. He had no idea when he'd become so emotional. When he told her that he wasn't gentle, that he couldn't give her sweet words, he'd apparently been lying because with Zoey, he wanted to do that and more. Making love to her was the closest to heaven he'd ever been.

"Please." Zoey begged. "Kaleb."

He knew what she was feeling because he was consumed by it. Pressing his hips against hers, he buried his cock to the hilt, sucking in air as the flames licked at his balls. The warmth of her body embraced him; the soft clamp of her muscles gripped him, pulling him deeper until they were one.

Brushing her hair back from her eyes, he pressed his mouth to hers as he began a gentle rocking of his hips. Her pussy enveloped him, like a velvet fist, squeezing until the pleasure mingled with pain. She was tight, warm and wet, and he was battling his own need to come.

Pushing up on his forearms, he was able to retreat from her body before pushing back in, deeper than he thought possible. Her legs wrapped around his hips, trying to pull him closer when he would have pulled back. The friction sent shards of pleasure bolting through his cock. Unable to keep his movements slow and sweet, Kaleb let the need take over.

Pumping his hips, he began a furious rhythm, thrusting harder, faster, deeper until Zoey was meeting his, their bodies slamming against one another.

"Harder." Zoey moaned, and Kaleb let go.

Pushing up onto his knees, he pulled her until her ass rested against his thighs, his cock angling deeper, her knees bent against his sides. He gripped her thighs, holding her to him as he slammed into her over and over until his brain became fuzzy, his orgasm threatening.

"Come for me, Zoey." He insisted, needing her to come before he wouldn't be able to hold out any longer.

Zoey's pussy clamped onto his cock when she screamed his name, her fingernails digging into his forearms and her head thrashing back onto the pillow. It was the sexiest fucking thing he'd ever seen, and it ripped his release from him, his cock pulsing deep inside the warm depths of her body.

It didn't take much to realize that this one woman, his best friend had just changed him in inconceivable ways. From this moment forward, Kaleb knew he'd never be the same.

If only he knew what to do about that, he might just be able to sleep.

Chapter Nine

♀♂

Zoey woke slowly, the warmth pressed against her back bringing her out of a deep, dreamless sleep. Kaleb. She could hear his soft breaths; feel them against her neck where he cuddled up against her. A graphic visual of the night before flashed in her mind and a heated blush crept over her skin. The way the man had played her body should've been illegal.

What she had thought would be rough and hungry had been gentle and sweet, though just as intense. Her body still burned for him, needing something she hadn't received the night before. The way he made love to her had been better than she even imagined, but the hunger still tore at her insides, the driving ache still throbbing between her thighs.

Rolling over, she turned so that she was facing him, trying not to wake him, but wanting nothing more than to touch him again. When his eyes opened, piercing her with the vivid blue glow that she'd remembered from the night before, Zoey's womb spasmed.

"Morning." He said gruffly.

Zoey merely smiled, using her hand to push the blankets down. It was getting warm, and she knew it didn't have anything to do with blankets and everything to do with the way this man heated her from the inside out.

"What's that look for?" Kaleb asked, a gleam in his bright eyes.

Still not speaking, Zoey pushed herself up, kneeling on the bed until she straddled his hips, grateful for his morning erection because she needed to feel him again. Stroking slowly, she kept her eyes trained on his face, watching as she sought to bring him to the edge.

Kaleb apparently wasn't having any of that because he slid his hands up her thighs before gripping her hips. "Ride me," he insisted, striking a chord deep in her womb.

Zoey caught something dark and possessive flash in those quicksilver smoky eyes as she lowered herself gently onto his cock, taking him fully inside of her in one quick thrust. There was initial pain as her body fought to accommodate the width of him, but it was quickly subdued by the increasing pleasure.

"Ride me, Zoey."

Zoey detected a different side of Kaleb lying beneath her. Gone was the sensitive lover from the night before, replaced by a man looking to force her to take what she wanted. There was no way she could resist, rocking her hips back and forth, letting the friction ignite the nerve endings in her clit as it brushed against his pelvis.

"Lift your hips." He stated, his lips a hard line.

Zoey could feel his tension, knew he was trying to hold back from her. Here she was reveling in this new side of him that she'd never known, and he was probably worried he'd scare her. She did exactly as he told her, but nothing more, waiting for his next instruction. This was new for her. New and erotic.

Last night, their first time, he'd been sweet and loving; exactly the opposite as he'd told her that he would be. But this morning, there was an intensity in his gaze and in his words that she could relate to. That she wanted more of.

"Tell me." Zoey stated, continuing to ride his cock as he lay perfectly still on the bed, giving her complete control. She didn't want control. She wanted to *be* controlled. Dominated. Taken with the lust and hunger she felt pulsing just beneath his warm skin.

There was a spark of recognition in his eyes, and Zoey was pretty sure Kaleb realized what she needed almost as much as she did. In a move that damn near stole her breath, Zoey found herself face first on the mattress, Kaleb kneeling behind her. Gripping her hips, he pulled her to her knees, thrusting his cock into her in one swift move that had her body spasming, her orgasm igniting, threatening to break loose.

With his fingers digging into her hips, Kaleb began ramming into her from behind, his cock filling her with every thrust, but there was no pain, only mind numbing bliss.

"Fuck." He groaned from behind her, and Zoey began rocking her hips, so she met each body slamming assault, her muscles involuntarily clamping down on him as she fought to stem the orgasm that was building.

She screamed, reveling in the way he'd lost control, taking her, claiming her, possessing her.

"Kaleb!" Oh, God. She was going to come, her body couldn't take any more, it was too sweet, too hot, too good. "I'm coming!"

And as she did, her body propelled itself into the ether, every nerve ending ablaze with the ferocity of the way he used her body.

There was an animalistic growl that shattered her mind at the same time her second orgasm tore through her. Kaleb stilled, his cock pulsing, filling her, igniting another mini explosion deep in her womb.

♂♀

Kaleb stilled, momentarily unable to do more than breathe. What the hell just happened?

Well, he wasn't stupid, he knew what happened, but how the hell had he let it go that far?

"Kaleb?" Zoey's sweet voice broke through his momentary trance, bringing him back to the present and the soft, female laying on his bed, looking back at him from over her shoulder.

"Are you ok?" He asked, ready to apologize profusely. After the way they made love the night before, for him to have taken her like a wild fucking animal was so uncalled for, he didn't know what to think.

"Better than ok." She said, her soft hand sliding over his thigh.

"I'm –" *Wait, what?* Kaleb looked at Zoey, really looked at her and noticed the smile tipping her lips.

Relief, warm and welcome washed over him as he eased himself back down on the bed, pulling Zoey against him. When she turned in his arms, her small, cool fingers trailing his neck, Kaleb closed his eyes.

"Promise we'll do that again."

She couldn't have surprised him more than she did in that moment. Although what they had just done was tame in comparison to what Kaleb had done in the past; to know that he hadn't sent Zoey running and screaming from his house made it easier to breathe.

Turning away from her, he still found it difficult to look her in the eye. If she'd only known the things going through his mind, all of the ways he wanted to pleasure her, to possess her, she'd probably blush fifty shades of crimson. In fact, if she knew the fantasies he wanted to live out with Zoey, she would probably never look at him again.

Pulling her against him, he held her close; wondering if now would be the time to insert some distance between them again. Maybe he was on to something all those years ago when he hadn't touched her, because what he wanted from her now bordered on raunchy and lascivious. To know that she was open to his more carnal urges, he was scared of what he might ask of her.

But he could sense it within her. She loved sex. She was open and eager, the complete opposite of the innocence he'd expected.

Figuring now was not the time to go into that, he forced his eyes closed, willing himself to sleep. For just a little while longer, he wanted to enjoy the feel of her in his arms.

□■□■

By the time Tuesday rolled around, Kaleb was feeling the whiplash from the emotional roller coaster he'd been strapped to since Saturday night when he brought Zoey back to his house. After their little encounter Sunday morning, Kaleb had battled with some internal demons where she was concerned.

But, she'd had a smile on her face when she asked him to take her home. He'd been surprised to tell the truth, having expected her to stay until he moved her along, which he never would have done if he had a say in it. It was as though the tables had turned, and he'd turned into a clingy woman.

She told him that she hoped to see him later, but as of yet, he hadn't heard from her. Nor had he called or stopped by to see her and he was feeling like a complete and total asshole. The funny thing was, he wasn't avoiding her because he didn't want to see her again.

Shit, if he had a choice, Zoey would be in his bed every night, and he'd wake up to her beautiful face each morning. And wasn't that a swift kick in the nuts? He did not do relationships, not since the psycho bitch had all but torn his heart out.

"What's up, Bubba?" Braydon called out as he came banging through the back door, a cluster of energy, just like always. He'd come to call every one of them "Bubba", with the exception of his twin, and he still did so, even at twenty nine years old. Half the time they had no idea whom he was talking to but since Kaleb was the only one in the small office he knew he was the intended target.

"Why are you here?" He asked. "Thought you'd be out at that garage tear down."

"Brendon's got it covered. His job's been pushed out a couple of days. Problems with the permits or something. He didn't want to be stuck in the office, so he offered to head on over there."

Fucking permits. Kaleb hated that part of the job, but thankfully Sawyer had taken over that piece, along with his sales position. Something about being better equipped to flirt with the ladies down at the permit office in order to get what he wanted. *Flirt.* Right. Sawyer was likely bedding them if they were under the age of thirty anyway.

"So, what's up with you and Zoey?" Braydon asked, grabbing an energy drink from the fridge and plopping down in one of the chairs across from Kaleb's desk. As if he needed any more fucking energy.

Kaleb didn't answer the question, just threw a glare in his general direction, one that told him that he wasn't interested in having this conversation.

"Come on, man." Braydon leaned back, sitting his drink on his flat stomach and eyeing him with that look that said he was in it for the long haul. "I always knew you had a thing for her, but seriously? I'm surprised she'd give you the time of day."

Braydon and Brendon graduated with Zoey, and Kaleb knew his twin brothers liked to give him a hard time about her, but it was only because they were close to her. They might not have been as close as she and Kaleb had been as far as friends go, but they looked out for her just the same.

"Shut the hell up." Kaleb grumbled, clicking through the images on his screen. They had a big project coming up, and it didn't have anything to do with demolishing something. If he didn't figure out a way to get his shit together, he might just be single handedly responsible for sending Travis over the edge. The man was hanging there as it was.

"Did you get ol' Stranford to come around on the land?" Braydon asked, apparently giving up on the Zoey conversation, which Kaleb certainly wasn't prepared to have.

"Not yet." That wasn't exactly true because Kaleb had another meeting with Carl Stranford that afternoon, at the other man's request.

To his surprise, Carl had called Monday morning, asking Kaleb to come by so they could work out the deal. It looked like Kaleb's frequent visits got the man to thinking, but now, based on the news Kaleb had learned just that morning, there might be a bigger problem. He only hoped he could figure out what to do about it before Travis got involved.

"I'm meeting with him this afternoon." Kaleb told Braydon when he continued to stare at him.

Surprised when Braydon leaned forward, lowering his voice, Kaleb stared back at his younger brother.

"Seriously," Braydon said, his voice tight, "be good to her, man. That Jason prick she was married to... He was a class act. She might not know all that he did, but the bastard was running around on her for quite some time. Too bad for him, Bren and I found out about it. Let's just say he was inspired to want to see the world."

Fuck.

Kaleb stared back at Braydon, trying to grasp what he'd just told him. His brothers had run Zoey's husband out of town because the slimy bastard was cheating on her. "What the fuck?"

"It wasn't pretty, Kaleb. He'd been through more women than all of us together." Braydon said with that lopsided grin that women flocked to. "That's saying something."

"Does she know?" Of course she didn't know, or Zoey might very well never forgive the twins for interfering in her life.

"Hell no. Let's just say Jason *relocated...* With his pregnant girlfriend. I warned him not to make his presence known when he comes back to visit his folks."

Holy shit.

Kaleb couldn't believe what he was hearing. Granted, he didn't know much about Zoey's split with her ex-husband, but that was because his own life had been in utter chaos at the time and it had been all he could do not to drink himself into a blind fury each and every night.

"She's a friend." Braydon confirmed, sitting up straight once again. "No one wants to see her hurt."

Kaleb was top of that list. The problem... He wasn't so sure he wouldn't be the one to do just that. The woman stoked a fire in his blood, one he feared he wouldn't be able to control. More than that, he worried he'd push her beyond her limits and she'd be disgusted by what she learned about him.

The rumors about the Walker boys weren't just rumors. It was a hard fact – one their parents weren't exactly fond of, but had chosen to turn a blind eye to – that they shared women. Braydon and Brendon were notorious for it, but the others, with the exception of Ethan that they knew of, had had many of women between them. At the same time.

Kaleb would be the first to admit the difficulty in denying the urges. The pleasure that they could bring a woman when there was more than one of them was intoxicating. They didn't flaunt it, but they didn't deny it either. Kaleb knew when it came to Zoey, he'd dreamed about taking her, watching her come apart at the hands of one of his brothers, or hell, his best friend Gage, but he also knew he could restrain the urge if needed.

He hated himself for it, but heaven help him, he didn't want to hold back. And that was what he feared would be the final straw when it came to what might be happening between them.

"You don't have to worry, Bray. I hear you loud and clear." Kaleb mumbled as his brother walked out of the room, but he knew he heard him.

Now if he could just get the situation with Carl Stranford taken care of, he might have half a chance of proving to Zoey that he had her best interest in mind. Not that what he had to do was going to be easy, nor was it going to make any of his brothers happy with him.

Chapter Ten

♂♀

"Mr. Stranford?" Kaleb called from the porch, after rapping his knuckles on the door.

Zoey's truck wasn't in the drive, which meant she was probably working or maybe out with Vanessa. Likely Carl's reason for scheduling this impromptu meeting so late in the day.

Being that it was a little after five, Kaleb wasn't sure when Zoey was going to be home. He only hoped he and Carl could come to a decision before then because he was almost certain she wouldn't be any happier about the situation than his brothers were going to be. Which couldn't be helped.

"In here, boy." Carl's gruff voice called from the interior of the house.

Kaleb let himself in, glanced around just to reassure himself that Zoey wasn't there. Not that he didn't want to see her. Just the opposite. But if he was supposed to have a conversation with Carl, having Zoey close by would likely be too much of a distraction.

"Thanks for coming over here." Carl said from his reclining chair.

Kaleb glanced around the tidy living room; one he remembered being exactly the same for most of his life. Only now it seemed a little dated. That didn't say much for Kaleb's age either. There was a time in his life when the room would have been in style so to speak.

"Have a seat." Carl pointed to the couch, and Kaleb did as he was told. Folding himself down to the couch, he leaned forward, resting his elbows on his knees, giving Carl his attention.

"I've been thinking about this offer. You know," Carl said, swinging his arm as though encompassing everything around him, "the one you boys made."

"Yes, sir." Kaleb replied, knowing exactly which offer he was referring to.

"If you've done any research, I'm sure you found out more than you should have." Carl continued, not looking directly at him.

On the short drive over, and for the better part of the afternoon, Kaleb wondered whether Carl was going to bring it up. He'd been struggling with how he was going to approach the man with his new offer. One that would likely have his brothers going ape shit, but not something Kaleb had given a second thought to.

"I'm aware of your situation, Carl. Which is why I came without Travis. My brothers aren't yet aware, and I didn't want to bring them into it until I spoke with you."

"Son, this house has been in my family for generations. My great, great grandfather built it with his bare hands, and knowing I'm going to lose it after all this time has been almost as heartbreaking as losing my sweet Isabelle."

"Sir, about that..." Kaleb interjected, but Carl quickly cut him off.

"When you boys first started talking about buying the land, I was furious. Completely out of my mind with grief knowing that I was being backed into a corner, and didn't have any way out. It's a good offer," Carl said, looking at Kaleb for the first time. "Not the best," he chuckled, "but a good offer."

For a few minutes, both men sat in silence while Kaleb tried to come up with an easy way to say it. When he finally realized there wasn't an easy way, he blurted out what had been hanging on the tip of his tongue just a few minutes before.

"Mr. Stranford," Kaleb clasped his hands between his knees, looking down, then back up at Carl, "I'd like to buy all of the land." When Carl would have interrupted yet again, Kaleb held his hand up. "Now wait, hear me out."

There was a glassy sheen in the old man's eyes, and Kaleb swallowed hard before he managed to force the words out. "As you may know, Travis, Sawyer and I are looking to build this resort, which is why we approached you in the first place. My younger brothers will take over Walker Demolition completely while the three of us focus on this. We've secured the approvals and have submitted the permits, but without the land, we can't move any further.

"I'd be happy to show you the plans, which consist of the one hundred acres we approached you about originally."

Carl stared back at him, speechless, but giving Kaleb his full attention.

"I talked to the bank this morning, Carl." Kaleb admitted reluctantly. "I'm prepared to offer you the original amount we discussed for the one hundred acres adjacent to the Walker land. That's where we'd like to build the resort."

Carl nodded his head, and Kaleb didn't know if it was an agreement to their offer, or just an acceptance that it was being made. Either way, he continued.

"You're going to lose your house, Mr. Stranford. You're on the brink of foreclosure."

Carl turned away, his eyes glassy yet again.

"From where I sit, you've got three options. First, you take that money, and you refinance to save your house. Or, you let me buy the entire property," Kaleb didn't have a chance to continue because the gasp from behind him told him that Zoey was standing there, obviously listening to the conversation.

"Daddy!" Zoey exclaimed, not looking at Kaleb.

Fuck.

Kaleb turned, saw her standing in the doorway, looking just as radiant in a pair of leggings and an oversized t-shirt with her hair pulled back in a ponytail as she had on Saturday night dressed up in that sexy, frilly dress.

"Zoey." Her name was on his lips, but he couldn't seem to move from where he was. The glare she shot him was filled with confusion and... Anger.

"Honey," Carl said firmly, "this doesn't concern you."

"That's where you're wrong." She insisted. "I've heard about the Walker's plan to buy out the land, and if you want to know the truth, I wondered why you were being so damn stubborn, holding onto it, but Daddy, you can't sell them everything. You just can't."

"Zoey, that's not –" Kaleb tried again, his legs once again working, so he pushed to his full height. When she turned and stormed out of the room without speaking another word, Kaleb turned back to Carl, then back to the empty doorway where she stood only seconds before. "Damn it."

"What the hell are you waiting for?" Carl groaned, looking defeated. "Go after her."

For a second, Kaleb was torn. Did he run after Zoey, try to explain? Or did he stay and try to explain to her father? Both had to be done, but he knew which was more important.

Kaleb turned and walked out, going straight for the kitchen where he heard the screen door slam. By the time he caught up to her, Zoey was walking through the front door of her small guest house, another screen door slamming hard enough to rattle the windows.

Without knocking, Kaleb let himself in, his eyes adjusting to the dim light as he tried to find Zoey. He fully expected her to be waiting for him, ready to lay into him with all of the fury he'd seen radiating from her only moments before. "Zoey!"

She didn't answer, so he wandered into the small kitchen, but when he didn't see her, he headed for the bedroom. The house wasn't unusually large, which meant there was only one other place she could have gone.

"Talk to me, Zoey." Kaleb stated firmly when he found her standing in the middle of her bedroom, hands on her hips, head hanging low.

"About what?"

Really? Kaleb felt his own ire growing steadily. He hadn't even had a chance to tell Carl the third option, which in his opinion was the best of the three. It consisted of Zoey buying out the remaining acreage, either from the bank, or from Kaleb. Either way, he wasn't about to let the Stranford's lose their home.

"Look honey," Kaleb began, but Zoey looked up at him then, and he was pretty sure she was trying to shoot daggers from her eyes.

"Don't call me that."

What? Kaleb was dumbfounded for a moment.

"You haven't called me; you haven't come to see me... I should have known. I should've known you were out to get what you wanted..."

Kaleb cut her off immediately, closing the distance between them in three short steps, pulling her flush against him and lifting her chin forcefully until she had no choice but to look at him. "Don't. Don't fucking do it."

He wasn't sure where the anger was coming from, but he was not going to let her belittle what they had shared because when it came down to it, Kaleb didn't give a fuck about the land, or anything else for that matter. Not at Zoey's expense anyway.

Her eyes were wide as she stared up at him, and Kaleb realized how harsh he'd been with her.

"Why haven't you called?" She asked, and when she pulled away, he let her go.

Why *hadn't* he called? Kaleb wasn't able to answer that question. At least not out loud. He hadn't called for a myriad of reasons. The first being she scared the shit out of him. Both by what he wanted from her and by what he felt for her.

"I've been busy," he lied

"Ah." Turning away from him, Zoey wrapped her arms around herself as though she were cold. That or she was trying to hold herself together.

"Zoey, I'm sorry." For so many things. Taking her like a crazed man being the first on the list.

"I'm sorry, too." She said quietly.

That didn't sound good at all. "For what?"

"For scaring you off. For ruining our friendship. For wanting too much from you." She admitted but didn't look at him.

Kaleb couldn't go another second without touching her. He moved quickly to her side, pulling her into his arms and he was once again flooded by the emotions this one woman evoked in him. So many emotions, he didn't know how to deal with them, and he couldn't name each of them either.

"God, I've missed you." Kaleb whispered in her ear, rubbing his hand down her back, soaking up the feel of her against his palms. Being close to her was exactly where he wanted to be, and touching her caused his frustration and anger to subside, replaced with a much stronger emotion. "So much." It was the first truth he'd said to her since he got there.

And now that he had his hands on her, he would be hard pressed to stop.

Without thinking, he lifted her shirt, pulling it over her head, tossing it to the ground as he backed her against the wall. His emotions - all of them swirling into one - took over.

His brain was at least paying attention because he hesitated long enough to see whether she would push him away. When she didn't, he pressed her firmly against the wall, grinding his erection into her lower belly, his mouth seeking hers and finding exactly what he'd been searching for.

Zoey wasn't holding back, and the anger from moments before exploded into passion, the air thick with it as they went at one another with barely restrained fury. In the blink of an eye, they were both naked, and Kaleb was once again pressing her into the wall, but he wasn't wasting time. Lifting her, he used the wall to his advantage as he let her slide down on him, one hand guiding his cock into the hot, fiery depths of her pussy while the other strained to hold her.

Once he was buried inside of her, he gripped her ass, holding her easily as he slammed into her, their eyes locked, everything they felt, portrayed in their gaze. No words were needed, not a single sound penetrated the air, with the exception of their harsh, choppy breaths and Zoey's sexy moans.

Kaleb had never lost control like this. Never let emotion lead him, but the hunger was there and for the life of him, there wasn't any other way to sate it than to be buried inside her luscious body.

"Kaleb," Zoey moaned his name, her fingernails digging into his shoulders as she pushed against him, keeping her back flat against the wall while he tried to thrust harder, paying no mind to anything but fucking her.

"Come for me." Kaleb breathed. "Fucking come for me."

Zoey's eyes widened briefly before her head went back into the wall, and she was screaming her release, her body clamping around his cock until he couldn't breathe. Letting go, Kaleb stilled, his cock pulsing and exploding inside her while he watched her writhe in his arms.

He wasn't sure what it was about her, and why since that first time he was overcome with the need to take her with crazed lust. Whatever it was, Kaleb knew he couldn't control it. He just prayed Zoey could live with that.

Chapter Eleven

♀♂

The instant her feet were back on solid ground, Zoey felt the urge to flee.

"Where are you going?" Kaleb called from behind her, but Zoey didn't stop. She needed a minute.

Once in the bathroom, she shut the door and locked it, before turning on the shower. What the hell had they just done? One minute her anger was bright and hot, and the next she was filled to overflowing with the sexiest man she'd ever known. It was amazing and shocking all at the same time.

Ignoring Kaleb's insistent pounding on the door, Zoey stepped into the shower, letting the warmth wash the fog from her brain. What they had done was by far the most erotic thing she'd ever done and yet she knew that it wasn't in the same hemisphere as Kaleb's most aggressive sexual adventure. Just the way she felt his power flowing just under his skin had lit her up, made her so wild, she had thought of nothing else but having him buried inside of her. But when he insisted she come for him, Zoey's world had exploded in brilliant fluorescent colors as her orgasm tore through her.

Turning her face into the spray, she let the water pelt over her as she fought to stop her entire body from trembling. It was the aftermath, and she was shaken to her very core in the most exquisite way imaginable. Worse than that, she wanted him again.

So why was she freaking out?

The shower door opened, startling a scream from her chest as she turned to face Kaleb stepping into the shower, looking none too happy with her.

"What the hell?" Kaleb spoke the same words that were on the tip of her tongue. She glanced at the bathroom door only to see the doorknob was missing.

"Don't shut me out, Zoey." The words were laced with a warning, and a shiver ran down her spine. "Do you understand me?"

His aggravation was palpable, but Zoey sensed he wasn't so much upset at her as he was with her reaction to him. What was she supposed to say? *Please, Kaleb, take me harder next time because although you rocked my world, I still want more.* Ummm... Probably wouldn't go over well with him. Not right now anyway.

The water was pouring down over them, and as she stood facing off with the big, brooding man in her shower, she noticed he hadn't so much as touched her since he walked into the small glass enclosure.

"Answer me, Zoey." Kaleb demanded.

"Yes." She huffed, turning back to face the wall. She understood him clear as day. Didn't mean she was happy about it. She just needed a minute to get her head on straight and with him filling her shower, towering over her, there wasn't a chance in hell she could wrap her mind around what was happening between them.

Zoey stood motionless when Kaleb wrapped his arms around her, pressing his warm chest against her back. His touch was like the warm and brilliant light of the sun, infusing her while chasing away all shadows of doubt that had plagued her the second her feet touched the floor.

"I'm sorry." His gruff voice echoed in the small space. "I shouldn't have done that."

"Why?" Now he was confusing her. She wasn't by any means offended by the wild way they'd just come together, she was just a little surprised. Her past experience with sex had been missionary for the most part, definitely lacking fireworks the likes of which the two of them created when they were together. But it damn sure didn't mean she wanted him to stop, she just wasn't exactly sure how to handle it.

Kaleb's hands trailed around to her breasts, cupping them as she intently watched the stark contrast of his sun bronzed hands against her pale skin. She was mesmerized, caught up in the sensation of his callused fingers teasing her pebbled nipples while his palms sensually scraped the tender underside of her breasts.

"You deserve more than that. I should've teased you, got you hot... wet... Before I rammed my cock inside of you."

Her stomach flipped, his words setting off mini flames on the tips of her nerve endings. How did he do that? Was it intentional? Or was there something wrong with her that she liked the lewd words and the raspy sound of his voice?

He continued to pinch and pull one nipple while his other hand trailed down her stomach before sliding between her thighs. She opened her legs wider, giving him better access because she was on fire now, her body prepared to take anything he had to give her.

"I should have teased your clit with my tongue."

God! Could his voice get any sexier? He mimicked the action with the tip of his finger, slowly pressing against her clit until she would've been sweating had it not been for the water.

Leaning back against him, Zoey lifted her leg, placing it on the low ledge in the shower, opening herself, all but begging for him to continue.

"Or buried my finger in your sweet pussy."

Zoey moaned. His finger delved deep inside, not thrusting, but swirling over nerves she hadn't known existed. "Please, Kaleb."

"And I should've had you begging." He kissed her neck, suckled the sensitive skin there as he continued to drive her mad with his finger. "Damn, Zoey. All the things I want to do to you."

"Tell me." She groaned. If he wasn't going to fuck her again, he could at least give her that much.

"I want to watch you come apart. Touch you in ways you've never even dreamed of."

His finger slipped from her pussy while his other continued to pinch her nipple – a sharp burst of erotic pain that had her whimpering.

Her body stopped responding when he moved his hand around behind her, sliding over her bottom, easing down between her cheeks to that forbidden place no one had ever dared to touch. She held her breath, fear and excitement waging a war in her stomach.

"I want to fuck you here, Zoey."

His finger caressed her anus, not breaching it, just teasing. Who would've known it would feel that good?

"Kaleb," she didn't want to respond to his touch, especially one so carnal, but she suddenly wanted more.

"You like that, don't you, baby?" He nipped her ear lobe and Zoey heard his tortured groan as he continued to tease her.

"I want to bury my cock in your ass. Fuck."

Heaven help her, she wanted it to. She wanted Kaleb in ways she shouldn't. She had imagined him doing wicked things to her, but never like that. There'd even been a time when she dreamed about him and Gage...

"Kaleb!" Zoey screamed his name when he thrust two fingers in her pussy, not giving her time to accept what was happening before her body exploded in a rush of heat and flames.

"Bend over." Kaleb instructed, and her brain fought to process his words.

The water was beginning to cool, but it was a welcome relief to the heat swamping her senses. She leaned forward, putting her hands on the tiled wall, bending at the waist. When he pushed her feet apart, she braced for the invasion, and he didn't disappoint. Oh, God, he was going to torture her until her body came apart at the seams.

"Fuck me!" She bit out as she tried to push against him, wanting to take him deeper into her body. It couldn't have been ten minutes before when his cock had been filling her, but her body didn't seem to realize that. She was desperate, aching for the feel of him.

With his chest pressed against her back, Kaleb slid forward, filling her to overflowing before gently moving his hips until she thought he would pull out entirely. One forceful thrust and he was inside of her again.

"Fuck me, damn you!" She was tired of this game, needed more and if he wasn't going to give it to her willingly, Zoey was prepared to take what she wanted.

Thrusting her hips back, she took him inside of her again, and Kaleb groaned, standing again as he gripped her hips.

"Fuck me, Zoey. That's it, baby. Fuck me just like that."

He was standing still as she rocked forward and back, unable to move much in the small shower with the wall so close, but she was doing everything she could to increase the friction, another orgasm just out of reach.

He must have heard her frustrated breath because he began pumping into her, holding her hips still as his movements became harder, faster until he was once again slamming into her, the only sounds were those of their wet bodies slapping against one another, the water as it continued to rain down on them, and the various grunts and groans as they both were lost to it.

Searching, reaching, taking...

White dots filled her vision, and she slammed her eyes closed as her orgasm tore free, radiating from her core before shattering.

It was all she could do just to keep standing.

♂♀

After the shower, Kaleb dried them both, then pulled Zoey into her room and right into her bed with him. Now, he was lying on his back, her small body curled up next to his, her head in the crook of his shoulder. It was the peace he had been searching for over the last few days.

Ever since that one night and morning, Kaleb had been torn about what the hell they were supposed to do now. Did they turn back to their friendship and pretend none of this had ever happened? Or worse, were they going to let whatever this was slip away? Truthfully, he hadn't known the answer until now.

"Zoey," Kaleb whispered her name, wondering whether she had fallen asleep. Although it was still daylight, because technically August was still the middle of summer in Texas and the days were still long.

"Hmmm?" The vibration of her voice rippled over his chest as he pulled her closer.

"About what you heard earlier..." Kaleb needed to make sure Zoey understood exactly what was going on with her father's land, and he wasn't so sure she did, but before he could say another word, the sleepy, cuddling woman disappeared from his grasp, darting up out of bed.

Kaleb had no choice but to get up, find his jeans and pull them on as he watched her walk out of the room, wearing nothing but the t-shirt he had discarded earlier. Damn that was sexy as hell.

"Zoey, damn it!" He called out as he followed her to the kitchen, zipping his jeans and buttoning them as he went.

"You listen to me, Kaleb Walker," Zoey stated adamantly turning on him as she stood in her kitchen.

He nodded, waiting to hear what she had to say.

"First of all, I'm all for this friends with benefits thing," Zoey stated, lifting and lowering her hands, "but there are some rules to this little game."

Little game?

"And what would those be?" He asked, humoring her.

"Rule number one. You can't ignore me."

"Ignore you?" Kaleb stood up straighter. "It works both ways, sweetheart."

"Fine. *We* can't ignore *each other*." Zoey bit out, turning to the refrigerator and pulling out a pitcher of tea. "And two, I expect us to be friends like we were before we started this."

Now Kaleb was all for the not ignoring one another part, but he wasn't so sure the friendship thing was going to work for him anymore. Not after what they had just done. From his eyes, the friendship thing consisted of them hanging out, talking, and then going their separate ways, usually with him having some woman on his arm for the night. That wasn't going to happen ever again. Not while this was going on. Instead of arguing with her, he just nodded his agreement.

"And three, you cannot use me to get to my father."

"Now wait just a fucking minute." Kaleb demanded, seriously getting pissed. "I have never used you, Zoey. You walked into this with your eyes wide open. I didn't try to hide the fact that we were looking to buy your father's land before this started, and since that is still my intention, I'm not hiding it now."

"No? So why are you talking to my dad about buying all of the land, including his house."

Kaleb turned and headed toward the living room, needing a minute to breath.

"That's what you're doing, aren't you?" Zoey asked; her voice much softer, sadder.

"No, honey, that's not what I'm doing." Kaleb refused to lie to her, although he would much rather her hear this from her father.

"Then what are you doing? I heard you tell him you were going to buy the land with the house on it too."

He knew when he'd come over here that she had heard that part of it, but he suspected now that she hadn't heard all of it. "Zoey, have you talked to your father about his finances?"

Now it was her turn to turn away from him. She went back to the kitchen, pulled down two glasses from a cabinet and proceeded to pour tea into them.

"Zoey?" Kaleb knew from her reaction that she was aware of what was going on, but did she know how serious it had just gotten in the last week?

"Yes, I know my father is running out of money. I know he's been having a hard time lately. Since he remortgaged the house a few years back, it has gotten worse." She said, turning to face him once again. "I can't afford the land on my own, Kaleb. I've tried. I went down to the bank and tried to get a loan, but they denied me. My company isn't strong enough to support that kind of loan."

Kaleb knew every gory detail, and it broke his heart to stand here watching Zoey.

"But I can." He said, placing one hand on her shoulder and lifting her chin, so she looked at him once again. "That's the offer I am making your father."

"What do your brothers think about this?" She asked.

Well, that was the hard part. His brothers didn't know the whole story. And Travis would likely go ape shit once he found out, but Kaleb didn't care. If it came down to it, they would buy the one hundred acres for the resort and Kaleb would do the rest on his own.

"We're only looking to buy the acreage that backs up to the Walker ranch." He told her. "And I haven't told them about the foreclosure, Zoey. I didn't think it was any of their business."

When her eyes brightened with unshed tears, Kaleb's heart constricted. He'd had a hard enough time in the past dealing with Zoey when she cried because his heart broke for her every time. Now, after what was happening between them, he didn't think he'd survive her tears.

"I want to do this, baby." Kaleb whispered. "I refuse to let Carl lose his house, so I'm offering to buy the land and let him or you make payments to me."

"What did he say?"

Kaleb fully expected Zoey's pride to interfere because that was who she was. Zoey was a strong, independent woman, and he had never known her to accept help from anyone, let alone him. So he considered this progress.

"Well..." Kaleb grinned. "Since I've spent the last hour here, I never did get a chance to talk to him about it."

Zoey nodded again and turned away.

"It's a good offer, Kaleb." Zoey began, and Kaleb expected to hear the 'but' that would tell him to take his offer and go away. "I think he really needs to do this. I don't want to lose our home. I don't think my dad will survive it if we do."

Kaleb understood that. Theirs was a deep rooted community, many of the families having been there for generations, including the Walker's, so Kaleb knew all too well what she was saying. If he could help her, he was going to do so.

He only hoped his brothers and Carl Stranford would agree.

Chapter Twelve

♀♂

Two weeks later, Zoey found herself knee deep in the
biggest mess she'd ever seen. Literally. What she and Vanessa had
walked into that morning would rival any one of the hoarder's
shows she had watched on television.

"Please tell me you'll do it." Anderson Croft had been
pleading for the last hour as he tried to give Zoey and V a tour of
his mother's home. Thankfully he'd insisted that his mother move
in with him while he tried to figure out what to do with this mess.

"When do you expect to have it cleared out?" Zoey asked,
glancing around at the mountains of stuff piled on every surface
possible. If she had to guess, it would be nothing short of a miracle
to expect anything less than a month, just to make a dent.

"I've found a couple of people who said they would come
and help me go through it, but with only three of us, it might take a
couple of weeks." Anderson stated.

Zoey had known the Croft family for most of her life, having gone to school with Anderson herself. She wouldn't go as far as to say they were friends because honestly, she hadn't talked to him since high school, but standing here now, Zoey felt a deep tug on her heart. This man was beside himself and she could see why.

"So, what do you say? Will you come in and clean it once we have it cleared out?"

"Yes, we'll do it." Zoey committed while Vanessa nearly choked, glaring at her from across the room.

"Oh my goodness." Anderson all but cheered. "Thank you! You don't know how many people we have had come out here and take one look only to turn and run the other way."

Zoey could only imagine. If it were up to V, she knew that's exactly what would have happened today, as well.

"When are you going to start trying to get it cleared out?" Zoey asked, wondering if two weeks were a realistic timeline.

"We're planning to start after work on Friday. If we work through the weekend, we might just make a dent."

A dent? Maybe in one room.

Zoey fished out her iPhone from her pocket and dialed the all too familiar number.

"Hey, baby. I was just thinking about you." Kaleb's sexy voice crooned in her ear, making her smile.

"Well, I was thinking about you, too." Zoey said, turning away and wandering outside where she could breathe a little fresh air. Whatever was in that house was no longer living based on the stench that permeated every room. "I need a favor."

"Hmmm... I like favors. That means if I do something for you, then you do something for me in return, right?"

Zoey laughed. That was definitely how Kaleb's mind worked. "I'll give you whatever you want in return." She said, knowing his naughty mind would likely come up with something that she would be begging for anyway.

"Honey, be careful what you sign up for." Kaleb's voice was deeper, huskier than moments before, and Zoey felt the impact deep in her belly.

"You haven't asked me what *I* want. I promise, once you hear this, you might just rethink your answer." She told him, turning around to see Anderson and V talking by the truck.

"Ok, lay it on me." Kaleb muttered.

"You know Anderson Croft?" She asked, knowing that he did.

"I know of him, sure. Not personally, no."

"Well, he needs some help." Zoey said before explaining in detail exactly what the help would entail. Five minutes later she was hanging up the phone and smiling back at V and Anderson.

"Is everything ok?" Anderson with his coke bottle glasses and little boy cuteness looked skeptical.

"I've called in the big guns." Zoey told him, smiling. "I've recruited the Walker boys to help us get this place cleaned out."

Ten minutes later, Zoey had given Anderson the instructions on what he needed to do in order to prepare for the weekend. If all went as planned, two weeks were just reduced to about two days.

"Are you out of your mind?" V asked as they drove back to Zoey's house.

Probably. "Why do you ask that?"

"Did you not see that house? Oh my God! It's so gross!" V stated excitedly.

"Exactly the reason Anderson needs our help." Theirs was a small town and Vanessa knew as well as Zoey that when it came to helping their neighbors, everyone would pitch in.

Figuring V would only start complaining – good naturedly of course – Zoey chose to change the subject.

"So how're things going with Zane?" She asked, glancing over at her friend when she pulled up to a stop sign.

"Who?" V asked, sounding none too happy.

"Uh oh. What happened?" It wasn't like V not to open up to her, but Zoey could tell that whatever was or wasn't happening with Zane was bothering her friend.

"Oh, don't worry, the sex is still fantastic."

"Fantastic sex." Zoey pondered that for a second. "So why the sour face?"

"Hell, I don't know, Zoey. Shit. I told myself not to get mixed up with one of the Walker's and here I went and did it."

"*Did it*? Care to clarify?"

"No, not really." V laughed, but there wasn't an ounce of humor in it.

When they pulled into Zoey's father's driveway a few short minutes later, V bolted from the truck. Zoey barely managed to climb out before her friend was climbing into her own car.

"If you want, we can have coffee and talk." Zoey offered, knowing full well V was going to turn her down flat, but she had to try.

"Maybe tomorrow." There was a sheen of tears in V's eyes, and Zoey's heart cracked for her friend.

"I'll see you in the morning, right?" They had two houses to clean on Friday, and Zoey knew they'd need to get them done early in order to meet Anderson out at his mother's house in the afternoon to start working.

"Of course." V said and quickly drove off.

♂♀

Kaleb was sitting in the small office of Walker Demolition shooting the breeze with Sawyer, Zane and Ethan when the door opened and in walked Gage.

"Well, I'll be damned." Kaleb greeted his best friend, standing and walking toward him. With a quick sideways hug and a couple of thumps on the back, Kaleb took a step back. "Finally back from your world tour?"

Gage laughed before turning toward the coffee pot sitting on the counter. "World tour, huh? Being a truck driver isn't nearly that glamorous, bro."

It seemed as though Gage had been driving a truck since the minute he graduated from high school and Kaleb had gotten used to his friend being gone for weeks at a time. And each time he came back, it was as though a part of himself had returned.

Since the very first day Kaleb met Gage, back in the fourth grade, they'd been friends. Well, that wasn't entirely true. They'd actually become friends after that first visit to the principal's office when they'd bloodied each other's noses on the playground. They'd both been cocky little boys, both wanting to be king of their own little worlds, and until that year, they had been. It wasn't until fourth grade when they'd had the same teacher that they realized there was someone else wanting to fight for the title. But after that day, when they'd been forced to sit side by side for an hour while they waited for Ms. Thompson to dole out their punishment, he and Gage had formed a friendship the likes of which had survived even their childhoods.

"So, what'd I miss while I was gone?" Gage asked, sipping his coffee and pulling up an empty chair.

"Shit, man. It's like the fucking twilight zone around here." Sawyer said, glancing at Zane, then Kaleb and back to Gage with a shit eating grin on his face.

"Yeah?" Kaleb could see the interest in Gage's eyes, and he knew Sawyer was about to spill every last damn detail. At least the ones he had.

"Zane here has gone off and hooked up with Vanessa Carmichael." Sawyer stated.

Kaleb watched his brother, noting the evil glare Zane shot Sawyer, but he didn't say a word. He knew better because the more one of them denied something, the more the others would pester them about it.

"Then there's Kaleb. That boy's long gone. He went off and fell in love with Zoey Stranford. But, we all knew that one had been coming for a long time."

"Fuck off, man. I did not go and fall in love."

He hadn't.

Gage stared back at Kaleb, and he recognized that heated look in his friend's eyes. It had been a damn long time since the two of them shared a woman, especially one that either of them was remotely serious about, but Kaleb knew exactly what the question in Gage's eyes was. He was not about to have this conversation right now, in front of his brothers. Instead, he nodded his head, acknowledging the question, but he turned to Sawyer.

"And what about you?" Kaleb questioned, and all eyes turned to Sawyer. "I heard something about you."

"I heard it too. Something about you and Kennedy Endsley." Zane offered, grinning.

"Oh shit." Ethan chimed in. "You going after women your own age now?"

That got the room laughing, but just like always, nothing fazed Sawyer. "Ain't nothing going on with me and Kennedy."

Well, if that statement didn't speak volumes, Kaleb didn't know what did. Sawyer never had been one to keep his interludes to himself. That didn't mean that what he did say was all truth, but for the most part, Sawyer was as wild as everyone thought he was. But Kennedy Endsley. That was surprising. The woman was the exact opposite of anyone Kaleb had ever known Sawyer to go after.

Kennedy was sweet and more than a little prim and proper for his taste. She was also the town's veterinarian, and her father was the sheriff, which in Kaleb's opinion meant she was off limits to any one of them. At least if they wanted to live another day.

"So, you and V, huh?" It was Gage's turn to contribute, and he turned his attention on Zane.

They all knew Vanessa Carmichael because she had gone to school with both Kaleb and Gage, but she was a few years older than Zane, which was probably what surprised Gage the most. It had Kaleb. The woman was a dichotomy. On one hand, she was the fun loving friend they'd all hung out with from time to time and on the other, she was an extraordinarily complex, somewhat tortured soul. She'd had a rough life, they all knew that and although she did run in their circles, she tried to keep to herself as much as possible.

"It's not like that." Zane stated, then stood and walked right out the door, leaving them all speechless in his wake.

"What the fuck?" Sawyer asked, staring at the door that Zane just exited through.

"Well, I think that's my cue." Ethan added before standing from his seat. "Glad you're back, Gage."

Kaleb was glad Gage was back too. It'd been a couple of weeks since he'd seen or heard from him, and it was high time the two of them caught up on a couple of things. Not that they would do that with Sawyer in the room, but hopefully later that afternoon they could grab a beer together.

There was something Kaleb needed to talk to him about.

"Throw a brother a bone, would ya? Tell me how exactly you landed Zoey Stranford." Gage grinned, the two of them sitting in Kaleb's living room several hours later.

"Hell if I know." Kaleb admitted. "One minute we're just friends, and the next. Well, fuck. That's all I can say."

"Just all of a sudden, huh?" Gage questioned, looking not at all convinced.

"It's been a long time coming." Kaleb mirrored Sawyer's words from earlier, which was an understatement as far as he was concerned. Twenty years of lusting after her and suddenly he finds himself in Zoey's bed – or her in his. Whatever it was that had gotten them to this point, Kaleb wouldn't change a damn thing.

"No, shit. Remember back in high school," Gage chuckled, "right after we had our first threesome? The next day we talked about what it would be like to have Zoey between us?"

Shit. Kaleb remembered that conversation like it was yesterday. He and Gage had fumbled through what qualified as a threesome because yes, there were three of them. Kaleb, Gage, and Jennifer Sorenson. Damn, that had been an awkward night, to say the least.

A knock on the front door interrupted Kaleb's memory, but he didn't move when Gage propelled himself off the couch and headed to the door.

"Little Zoey Stranford." Gage greeted Zoey and Kaleb's dick suddenly went rock fucking hard. Not that he wasn't happy she was there, but holy fuck, he did not expect her.

"Gage Matthews. Ever the handsome devil." Zoey's voice drifted from the other side of the door, and Kaleb watched as Gage leaned down, probably hugging her if he had to guess.

Seconds later she was walking in the door, carrying a six pack of beer and wearing a pair of short white shorts and a black t-shirt that hugged every luscious curve. Her trim, tan thighs had Kaleb's mouth watering and more blood pounding south.

"Hey," Zoey smiled, sitting the beer on the table between them. "Having a party without me?"

If she wasn't careful, they would be having a party *with* *her* in about two minutes flat. A naked party. Glancing up at Gage, Kaleb noticed the man eyeing Zoey's ass, and he had to bite back a smile. Yep, same ol' Gage. He might give Kaleb a hard time about lusting after Zoey for all these years, but he knew his friend had some pretty intense fantasies about the woman himself.

Their ménage days might be a thing of the past, but Kaleb suddenly had the urge to have one for old time's sake.

"What were you boys talking about?" Zoey asked, grabbing a beer and joining Gage on the couch.

He had to admit, this was a fairly common situation to find himself in – him, Zoey, Gage, all three of them hanging out – but something certainly felt different.

"Threesomes." Gage said, and Kaleb damn near choked on his beer.

"Is that right?" She asked, glancing back and forth between Kaleb and Gage, seemingly unfazed by Gage's admission. "Threesomes?"

"Have you ever had a threesome, Zoey?" Gage asked, suddenly sounding serious.

"Nope." She answered easily, obviously brushing off the question as if it weren't the segway that Kaleb knew it to be.

Kaleb couldn't speak, so he took a long pull on his beer, keeping his eyes glued to Zoey's beautiful face. He was looking for any sign of discomfort, but he saw none.

"I know you two have." She stated, looking at Gage. "More than once."

"That we have." Gage replied, glancing over at Kaleb.

"So, what's the fascination with threesomes anyway?" Zoey asked, and once again, Kaleb fought to keep from choking on his beer. Were they seriously going there?

"It's hot as hell." Gage answered as if he wasn't completely affected by the fact that Zoey was actually showing interest. Kaleb knew he sure as hell was affected by it. The incessant pounding in his dick was the first telltale sign.

"Yeah? How many threesomes have you boys had?" Zoey asked, this time turning to Kaleb. He merely shook his head and smiled. Nope, no way. He was not going there.

"Ok," Zoey laughed, "if you don't want to admit to how many then tell me this," she glanced back to Gage, "when was the first time you had a threesome together."

"That's easy." Gage spoke up glaring at Kaleb. "We were talking about it when you walked in. High school. Eleventh grade. Jennifer Sorenson."

"Holy shit. Jenny? Seriously?" Zoey laughed. "That's surprising. That girl couldn't keep her mouth shut, but never once did she let on about that."

"Well, it was a little weird." Gage leaned forward, grabbing another beer and putting one hand on Zoey's thigh as he did. Kaleb did not miss the movement and a possessive spark ignited in his gut, followed by an intense jolt of lust.

"Weird how?"

Holy shit. If they were really going to talk about this, Kaleb unquestionably needed another beer.

♀♂

Threesomes?

A little surprised that they were actually talking about this, Zoey suddenly couldn't hide her interest. Hadn't she just been thinking about this exact thing that morning in the shower? It had been that damn dream that spurred it on, but still, Zoey's mind had taken her on a wild ride – one starring none other than herself in the middle of an intense sex sandwich with these two magnificent creatures.

Zoey had no idea what compelled her to question Gage and Kaleb about their previous sexual exploits, but she would admit to being curious over the years. The three of them had hung out on multiple occasions, but never had their conversations ventured down this path. Even when they'd been drunk and acting stupid.

Glancing back and forth between the two men, Zoey noticed the look that passed between them and a chill ran down her spine. Based on the way Kaleb reclined in the chair - acting totally unaffected - Zoey knew better. First of all, he was doing his damnedest to hide the hard on he was sporting.

"Come on. Spill it." She encouraged.

"Not a one of us knew what the hell we were doing," Gage began, "so how we managed to get through it, I still don't know."

"So, was it like double penetration? Or did you just share her?" Zoey asked and almost laughed when Kaleb choked on his beer.

"Nope, no DP." Gage stated, laughing. "That didn't happen until years later when we finally figured out what the hell we were doing."

Zoey's mind drifted to an image of her crushed between the two of them, filled to overflowing and screaming in pleasure. Over the years, she'd had the same dream time and again, but never would she admit it. Not even after plied with alcohol.

"So, since you won't tell me how many times, tell me what the wildest one you had is?" This time she pinned Kaleb with a look. She wanted to hear it from him.

"What?" He asked as if he didn't have a clue what she was talking about. "Do you really want to hear about this?"

"I do." Did she ever. She wanted to know details – explicit details.

"It wasn't a threesome." Kaleb stated, rearranging himself in the chair, no longer trying to hide the evidence of his reaction to their intimate conversation.

"No? More?" *How the hell did that work?*

"Yes. There were four of us. Me, Gage, and Sawyer."

Holy fuck.

"Oh, shit." Gage laughed. "I almost forgot about that one. Tina, that girl from the bar, right?"

Kaleb nodded his head and smiled.

"She was a feisty one." Gage stated, still smiling.

"Crazy was more like it." Kaleb offered, not looking at Zoey.

If she didn't know better, she would think Kaleb was a little embarrassed.

"She had taken all three of us at the same time. Sawyer hadn't been easy on her either, fucking her mouth like a crazy man."

Gage's lewd words sent a tingle straight to Zoey's core. She squeezed her thighs tight, and she wasn't surprised that Kaleb noticed; the heat in his eyes evident.

"Have you ever thought about having a threesome?" Kaleb asked, surprising Zoey with his straightforwardness.

Did she tell him? *Could* she tell him? Downing half her beer in one swallow, Zoey leveled her gaze on him once again. "Yes."

This time, Kaleb took it one step farther, using his hand to rub the erection clearly outlined beneath his jeans.

"With who?" Gage asked, his voice sounding strained, no longer laid back and laughing.

Well, fuck.

Admitting to having thought about it was one thing. Telling them the details was entirely different. Her face flamed with embarrassment, but she forced herself to answer. "The two of you."

Zoey's heart rate spiked and her blood pounded in her ears as she waited for someone to say something. The room was so quiet, only the sound of their breathing could be heard as the seconds ticked by slowly.

"Me and Gage?" Kaleb asked, still subtly rubbing his crotch.

"Yes." Oh hell, she might as well go for it. For the last few weeks, Zoey had been thinking more and more about the crazy sexual fantasies she'd had for Kaleb, not to mention the dream from last night had rocked her to the point she almost believed it actually happened anyway. And, yes, there was certainly a time when she would've jumped at the opportunity to explore these two men at the same time. How could she not? Hot is what they were, and if given half a chance to be the object of their lust for even a few minutes, Zoey wouldn't hesitate. Even now.

Maybe it was because she had thought about having a threesome and Gage and Kaleb had been her two closest guy friends. She felt safe with them, and she knew they would never hurt her.

"What about now?" Gage asked, his voice sounding closer than only moments before.

Zoey turned to face him, noticing how he was leaning a little bit closer. "What *about* now?"

"Would you let us fuck you, Zoey? Both of us? Right now?"

Zoey's head jerked to Kaleb, his question startling her and making her pussy clench. They were serious.

But so was she.

She couldn't find her voice, so she nodded her head in agreement.

"Right here. Right now." Gage said, not a question.

Zoey didn't know which of them to look at. She wanted to see Kaleb's reaction because he was the one she wanted above all else. The fact that this was turning him on only pushed her further. If he was all right with it, she certainly was.

"Kiss her, Gage." Kaleb ordered, and Zoey had to force her jaw shut. She met Kaleb's eyes, and the stark naked hunger was evident, but so was something else. He needed her to trust him. Turning her attention to Gage, Zoey felt the butterflies erupt in her tummy, and a slight tremble in her hands.

She kept her eyes trained on the sexy man sitting beside her as he leaned closer, his eyes darting down to her mouth. He didn't rush, he merely leaned closer, and the intoxicating smell of his cologne mixed with the sweet scent of beer on his warm breath had goose bumps breaking out on Zoey's arms.

When he cupped the back of her neck, Zoey leaned closer, anxiously anticipating the feel of his lips on hers. Never would she have thought that kissing another man could've been so hot. Especially after having kissed Kaleb. She could feel Kaleb's eyes on them; heard the way his breathing accelerated. It made her ache for his touch, yearn for his kiss.

When Gage placed his firm lips on hers, Zoey melted into him, giving herself over to the moment.

Chapter Thirteen

♂♀♂

Kaleb watched.

He did little else, including breathe.

Seeing Zoey give in to Gage, watching as she allowed him to kiss her so sensually, so easily, had him gripping the arms of the chair just to remain seated.

It was fucking hot!

Been there. Done that. That was normally what came to mind when Kaleb thought about a threesome with Gage and a woman, but not this time. Not this woman.

With Zoey, it was like they were doing this for the very first time; experiencing the wonder of the pleasure that could be wrought from the three of them together. Only this time, there was no awkwardness, no fumbling to figure it all out. Just anxiety and lust, combining together for a heady mixture of passion and need.

Kaleb knew Gage had always been attracted to Zoey, but he also knew he didn't have to worry about anything more than his friend giving in to the temptation with him present.

That was something he and Gage had. They had a strong friendship, one based on trust and understanding. And through all the years they were friends, neither of them ever attempted to do anything behind the other's back. Kaleb considered Gage a brother, and he knew Gage felt the same. They always had the other's back and always would.

When it came to their ménage's, they were in it for the pleasure. Despite the awkwardness of that first time, they'd been hooked. And yes, there had been a time when they talked about a threesome with Zoey. But shit, they had been teenagers, hyped up on hormones and erotic cravings.

Come to think of it, they were pretty much the same right this very minute.

When Gage groaned, Kaleb fought off the thought, insisting he remain in the moment, watching with a voyeuristic fascination as Zoey slid her small hands up over Gage's chest, then his neck, before linking her fingers in his hair. The position had lifted her arms to the point that Gage was able to ease his hands beneath her body molding t-shirt, lifting it as he went.

Zoey's frilly white bra did little to cover her full breasts, and Gage easily unhooked the front clasp, allowing her breasts to spill free. From Kaleb's vantage point, he could only see them in profile. He needed to get closer.

Without hesitation, he stood, walking around to take a seat on the coffee table, having to move their beer bottles out of the way in order to do so.

Definitely more like it.

From his new perch, he could see Zoey's sweet, pink nipples, hardened and begging for their touch. Figuring it would be in their favor for Kaleb to sit this one out for a few minutes – either that or risk it being over before it got started – he decided to provide some verbal assistance.

"Stand up." He wasn't talking to anyone in particular, so he just sat patiently waiting while they managed to untangle themselves from one another before they both stood.

Zoey was much smaller than Gage, and although Kaleb still had several inches on his friend, Gage definitely wasn't a small man. He worked out religiously and had the toned, thick body to prove it. With Zoey and Gage facing one another, their size difference was significant from where Kaleb was.

"Take her shirt off." This time he was talking to Gage, but it didn't need clarifying. Gage knew how this worked, he'd been privy to a number of them before, but Kaleb knew he wouldn't have to explain how remarkably different this time would be.

Gage easily lifted Zoey's shirt, disposing of it quickly before taking a step back so he could get a better view. Kaleb didn't have any room to move, but there was at least a foot between where he sat and where Zoey stood, so he didn't need to.

"Remove your bra and unbutton your shorts, but don't take them off." Kaleb told Zoey.

He watched as her face flushed and noticed how her hands trembled, but she didn't shy away from them. Her bra slid down her arms and tumbled to the floor seconds before she slipped the button on her short from its mooring.

"Now take Gage's shirt off." Kaleb told her, wanting her to be a participant and not just a bystander.

He didn't have to tell her twice. She moved forward, gripping the hem of Gage's t-shirt before lifting, sliding her hands over his chest as she went.

Kaleb briefly made eye contact with Gage, noticing his friend's hooded eyes and the lustful expression on his face. Nope, he definitely didn't have to explain how different this way. Gage understood clearly. Zoey was their friend – though she had become much more than that to Kaleb in recent weeks, but he wasn't going to tell her that. They had always looked after her. And they always would.

Gage helped Zoey by pulling his shirt over his head and tossing it behind him.

"What do you want her to do to you, Gage?" Kaleb asked.

Gage used his thumb to brush Zoey's lower lip as he stared down at her. "I want to feel your mouth on me. I want your lips wrapped around my cock."

Kaleb's dick throbbed yet again. The idea of watching Zoey with another man's dick in her mouth was enough to have his balls aching for release.

"Sit on the couch." Kaleb told Gage, his gaze holding Zoey's now that she was looking at him. "And you, take off your shorts and panties. I want you naked."

While Gage situated himself on the couch, Zoey eased her shorts and panties off and left them in a puddle on the floor. For a second, he thought he saw hesitation in her eyes, but she masked it quickly.

"On your knees." Kaleb insisted, watching her reaction.

This was the side of himself that he worried Zoey wouldn't be able to deal with; the beast that lurked just beneath the surface, the one that was interested in pleasure for the sake of it and nothing more. There weren't any sweet words, no loving kisses, but they weren't needed either. This was about extracting the most pleasure possible while pushing boundaries. As long as she was willing, which she apparently was, Kaleb wasn't going to hold back. Zoey was a strong, independent woman, and if she didn't want it to go any further, he trusted that she would tell him.

Watching her, Kaleb's eyes traveled down the length of her spine, past her tiny waist, over her curvy bottom as she lowered herself to her knees in front of Gage.

"Tell her what you want her to do." Kaleb told Gage who had toed his shoes off before sliding his jeans off as well, leaving him entirely naked sitting on Kaleb's couch.

"Put your mouth on my dick, baby." Gage told her, his voice thick with arousal. "Suck me. Awww, God! That's it."

Zoey hadn't wasted any time doing as Gage told her. Standing to his full height, Kaleb watched the lascivious scene before him while he too removed his clothes. He wasn't going to play bystander any longer. He needed to touch her. To taste her.

After moving the coffee table out of the way, Kaleb kneeled behind Zoey, pressing his chest against her back as she continued to lave Gage's dick with her sweet mouth. Kaleb couldn't tear his eyes from his friends cock buried deep in Zoey's mouth, and he knew what Gage was feeling. Knew the sweet warmth she bestowed upon him as she teased with her tongue.

"Damn, baby." Gage groaned. "So fucking hot."

Kaleb slid his hands along the curve of Zoey's spine, then over her hips, gliding around to her flat stomach before roaming upward until he cupped her breasts with both hands. Leaning in closer to her ear, he fondled her nipples with his fingers while nipping her earlobe. "Suck him, baby. Suck him hard, just like you do me."

Zoey whimpered, and Kaleb's cock swelled even more, which he wouldn't have thought possible.

"Yes. Just like that, Zoey." Gage encouraged as he gripped the base of his cock. "Lick my balls."

Kaleb continued to grope Zoey, applying more pressure to her nipples as she moaned and whimpered, using her tongue to tease Gage's balls while she stroked his cock with her hand.

"Fuck." Gage groaned. "I'm not going to last much longer." He informed them, lacing his fingers in Zoey's hair before pulling her head toward his cock once again. "I want you to take me all the way in. As far as you can."

Gage was no longer holding back, thrusting his cock deep into Zoey's mouth, his urgent groans filling the room. Kaleb let go of Zoey's breasts, gliding his hands down between her legs, sliding two fingers through her slippery slit before thrusting up inside her, making her moan louder. He could feel the vibrations in his chest, which was still pressed up against her back, so he knew Gage could feel them on his cock.

"Oh, fuck! Zoey! Holy shit!" Gage rambled, "It's so fucking good. Baby! Shit! I'm gonna come!"

Kaleb watched as Gage gripped her hair painfully, holding her still as he thrust once, twice, and then again before he threw his head back and roared his release.

♂♀♂

Zoey wanted more.

Maybe she should've been ashamed, but she was too turned on to care that what she'd just done was the wickedest thing she could imagine. And yes, she had just had Kaleb's best friend's dick in her mouth, but holy hell. It had been hot. Knowing what she was doing to him, listening to his sensual moans and groans had spurred her on. Then to feel Kaleb's hands on her body, she'd been grounded, safe.

Now, with Gage looking at her like he was ready to eat her up and Kaleb continuing to thrust his fingers inside her pussy, Zoey didn't know if she'd survive much longer.

"Kaleb!" She moaned his name, leaning back against him as he continued to impale her with his fingers. Still sitting on the couch, Gage was watching intently. His eyes glued to where Kaleb was finger fucking her with such skill, she couldn't keep herself from trying to ride his fingers.

Just when she was about to give herself over to the orgasm building insistently, Kaleb pulled his fingers out of her, and she wanted to scream. "No, don't stop. Please!"

Ok, now she was begging.

"Come here." Gage told her, taking her hand and helping her to her feet.

He lay on his back on the sofa, still holding her hands and pulling her toward him. "Sit on my face, baby. I want to taste that sweet pussy."

Oh fuck.

She'd been reduced to a jumble of curse words and wanton lust. Unable to say no, and clearly not wanting to, Zoey situated herself above Gage's head, his thick arms coming around her thighs, his fingers separating the swollen lips of her pussy before he began lapping at her with his wicked ass tongue.

"Oh, God!" Zoey wanted to close her eyes, wanted to lose herself in the sensations, but before she could, Kaleb was standing in front of her at the end of the couch, his beautiful cock standing out from his body, beckoning her. She wanted to taste him. Looking up, she met his eyes and the naked lust reflected there almost had her orgasm ripping free.

"Suck me, baby. But don't make me come." Kaleb ordered, and the demand in his tone had her entire body tingling.

She teased the head of his cock with her tongue, sliding over and around the engorged crest, teasing the underside where she knew he was sensitive. He threaded his fingers into her hair, but he didn't pull hard, just held her there as he used his other hand to guide his cock past her lips.

Sucking and licking the way she knew he liked, Zoey tried to focus on him, but Gage's tongue was stroking her clit relentlessly, and she began grinding down on his mouth.

"That's it, Zoey. Ride his mouth." Kaleb said, pulling his cock from her mouth. "Sit up," he told her as he stroked his cock, "I want to watch while he licks your sweet pussy."

Zoey sat up, putting one hand on the back of the couch, the other on her thigh as she too looked down between her legs to see Gage's handsome face and his devious tongue as he thrust inside of her over and over.

Easing one leg off of the couch, Zoey couldn't stand it anymore. She began lifting and lowering herself onto his mouth, increasing the friction, pushing his mouth against her clit. "God yes! Gage!" There was no holding back when her orgasm erupted like a tsunami, a gentle trembling in her core at first before wave upon wave crashed through her, her legs went weak as her clit pulsed and her internal muscles locked.

By the time her molecules had once again met up, Zoey found herself straddling Gage on the couch. When she glanced down, she noticed his cock was once again rock hard and sheathed with a condom. She was resting her forehead against his while he held her against his chest.

"Hey." He grinned. "Welcome back."

Zoey laughed. No, she hadn't passed out, but she wasn't sure how she hadn't. That orgasm had rocked her to the point of near oblivion. Literally. "Hi."

Zoey pulled back and looked deep in Gage's sexy, chocolate brown eyes, wondering why it felt so normal to be here like this with him. Granted, Kaleb was behind her, she could feel his presence and had he not been there, she wouldn't have been comfortable by any means. Or maybe she would, shit, right now, she wasn't sure which way was up anymore.

Gage cupped her neck and pulled her in until their mouths met and she tasted herself on his lips. Then he slid his tongue in her mouth, and she was once again lost in the sensations. Gage's mouth, Kaleb's hands, her body was on fire yet again, and she needed to feel one of them inside of her.

Taking matters into her own hands – literally – Zoey guided Gage's cock right where she needed him, lifting and then lowering herself onto him. She pulled away from the kiss as he eased inside of her, an initial bite of pain before pleasure coursed through her. He was huge. Bigger than Kaleb, and Zoey hadn't thought that possible.

It took a few seconds for her body to acclimate to the intrusion, but once it did, she began moving, lifting and lowering on him, focused on the glorious friction. He was brushing every nerve ending over and over, and it only took a few strokes before her body was once again preparing itself for an earth shattering release.

"Lean into me." Gage told her, and she did as she was told. It didn't take a rocket scientist – or someone who had done this before – to know what they were getting ready to do. Had she not been on the verge of begging them to fuck her into oblivion, she might've been worried.

Kaleb's warm mouth trailed kisses down her spine as she continued to impale herself on Gage's cock. She couldn't quicken her pace because both men were controlling her movements, and she was beginning to get frustrated. Then, just when she was about to tell them to get on with it, something cool slid down the crack of her ass, followed by a warm finger.

Kaleb's big hand pressed down on her back, flattening her against Gage and holding her still. She was filled entirely with Gage's iron hard erection, and Kaleb was teasing her anus with a gel slicked finger.

"Oh!" Damn it felt good. "More." Zoey wondered if she'd ever be able to look at either of them again after this. They'd turned her into a wanton slut in just the last hour, proven by her begging.

When Kaleb's finger slid into her, Zoey tensed momentarily, her body instinctively trying to force out the intrusion.

"Relax for me, baby." Kaleb said, his mouth shockingly close to her ear. "Let me fuck your beautiful ass, Zoey."

She couldn't verbally respond because her breath was locked in her chest, but she nodded, trying to grind down on Gage to increase the friction in her pussy and ignore the discomfort.

As if he read her mind, Gage began to move his hips slowly, trapped between her body and the couch, he couldn't do much, but her nerve endings lit up yet again, the sensitive tissue eagerly clutching his cock as he rocked inside of her. Then Kaleb began to increase his pace, thrusting his finger – first one, then two – into her ass, over and over until she was pushing back against him, anxious for more.

Her orgasm was building, the slight tingle in her womb blossoming into all out pleasure as both men continued to thrust into her.

"Fuck me, Kaleb. Fuck me now!" Zoey couldn't wait. It was too intense, too intimate, too... everything. She suddenly wanted to feel both of them inside of her, fucking her until she couldn't take anymore.

When Kaleb's fingers retreated, Gage slid down on the couch, remaining lodged inside of her, but reclining back a little more. Then he pulled her flat against him yet again, his mouth locking with hers as he kissed her so hard she saw stars. Their tongues battled, her hands cupping his head, holding him to her.

The diversion worked momentarily, but then the pain was back and much more significant than before, but thankfully, Gage didn't let her go. He began thrusting his hips upward, burying his cock to the hilt as Kaleb held her hips in place, his thick cock sliding inch by painful inch into her ass. There was a brief moment when her entire body flashed hot, probably from the pain, but then it was gone and there was movement.

Fast, feverish, amazing.

Kaleb and Gage never lost their rhythm, impaling her repeatedly, sometimes at the same time, filling her until she thought her body would shatter, then alternating. The delicious rasp of their cocks against the delicate tissue and oversensitive nerve endings had her moaning, her nails digging into Gage's shoulders as she tried to hold on.

"Oh, yes!" She screamed. "Harder."

They gave her exactly what she asked for, slamming into her once, twice, three times before Gage stilled, his powerful arms circling around her waist, holding her to him as he pulsed inside of her.

"Kaleb!" She screamed his name as another orgasm blasted through at the same time Kaleb stilled, his fingers digging into her hips as he came hot and fast into her ass.

Moments before she gave in to exhaustion, she wondered where that threesome ranked on their list. On hers, it was undeniably the best yet, but hopefully there'd be more to compare it to later.

Chapter Fourteen

♀♂

"Holy shit!" Anderson exclaimed as he approached Zoey.

She had the same sentiment when she arrived just a few minutes before. Apparently calling in the cavalry had worked. Standing in front of Anderson's mother's house were six of the seven Walker brothers – everyone except Travis – and a handful of their friends.

Zoey had come prepared, but Kaleb had come even more prepared. Standing in a group, aside from Kaleb, Sawyer, Brendon, Braydon, Zane and Ethan, she picked out Gage, Aaron Haines and Beau Bennett – friends of Zane's, Jaxson Briggs – a cousin of the Walker brothers, and last but not least, Trevor Townsend – one of Ethan's friends. On top of that, there was Anderson and two other men that Zoey didn't know.

"Oh my God." V whispered beside Zoey. "If every one of them would take their shirts off, we could make a calendar of hot, hunky men."

Zoey laughed which made Kaleb turn toward her. She smiled, watching as the sexiest of all the hunk's approached. When he bent down and kissed her firmly on the mouth, her breath hitched in her chest. If it hadn't been for the catcalls and whistles, Zoey might've just gotten lost in Kaleb's seductive kiss. Rather than giving everyone more to ridicule them about, she pulled away and smiled up at him.

"I've missed you." Kaleb whispered for her ears only.

Zoey laughed. "Yeah? Ever since you crawled out of my bed this morning?"

Oh, yeah. Last night had been phenomenal. They hadn't seen one another much that week, so when Kaleb had shown up at her house last night, Zoey had immediately invited him in and had her wicked way with him. Now, standing next to him and breathing in the fresh, clean smell of man, she wished they'd never crawled out of bed at all.

"What are you doing after this?" She flirted shamelessly, staring up at him.

"You. I hope."

"Mmmm... I like that idea." Zoey said as she turned her attention on the others, her gaze landing on Gage standing at the back of the group, a seductive smile tipping his lips. She looked up at Kaleb and noticed he was still smiling.

"Yea, Gage had the same plans."

An answering tingle surged through her core at the thought of being with the two of them again. It had been a couple of days and her body had needed the rest, but she was anxious to do it again. Wanton slut she was. At least where these two were concerned.

Although, it might just be Kaleb's fault because she could not get enough of him. From the minute he stepped through her door last night, she'd been on him. She'd easily become addicted to his body as well as the way he verbalized all of the things he intended to do to her.

"Thanks for coming." Anderson called out, catching Zoey's attention and redirecting her errant thoughts.

"I would've never imagined having this kind of help, but I can tell you it's greatly appreciated." Anderson turned his gaze on Zoey, and she decided to take charge. It's what she did, and since she'd spent some time putting together a plan of action, she figured now was the time to deploy it.

"Guys, there's a lot of work to be done today, but I'm hoping if we all get in there, we can knock it out quickly."

"The Dumpster should arrive shortly, so let's go inside, check it out, and Anderson, you can tell us what needs to be done." Kaleb added before turning toward the house.

After a few minutes of trampling through mounds of trash, Anderson laid out what he needed to be salvaged and how they could go about doing so. Not ten minutes later, everyone got to work.

"How's it going?"

Zoey turned to see Kaleb standing a few feet behind her in the front yard. She'd been sorting through some of the items the others had retrieved from the house, trying to ensure they did not throw out anything valuable or possibly sentimental.

Wiping her arm across her forehead, she looked up at Kaleb. "I'd kill for a shower right about now."

"Yeah?" Kaleb's blue gray eyes darkened, and the heat in his eyes rivaled the three digit temps of the scorching August day. "I'm thinking I could help you out with that."

Oh yeah. Zoey liked where this was going. When Kaleb pulled her against him, she let him, although they were both sweaty and nasty from working so hard. Being in his arms had become her favorite part of her day so on the days she was lucky enough, she tried to latch on to it whenever the moment arose.

"I'm thinking about how fucking hot you look with my cock in your mouth." He growled in her ear, sending a shiver down her spine. "And about how sweet your pussy tastes."

Zoey heard the lewd words, and for some unknown reason, they made her body tingle and her insides go a little haywire. She craved this man, plain and simple.

"And I think about how I nearly came watching you suck Gage's cock." He leaned down closer, lowering his voice considerably, "Then I think about how it felt to fuck your ass while Gage took your pussy."

Zoey whimpered involuntarily and tightened her grip on Kaleb because her legs threatened to give out on her. He wasn't the only one who'd been thinking lately. A vivid replay of that encounter ran through her mind at frequent intervals throughout the day.

"Again, Zoey. Tonight." Kaleb whispered, nipping her ear lobe with his teeth.

Zoey pulled back and looked in Kaleb's eyes, now the color of storm clouds at night. When Kaleb's gaze darted across the yard, Zoey followed his eyes until she noticed Gage standing beside his truck, staring back at them. If she wasn't mistaken, there was heat in his eyes, mirroring what she had previously seen in Kaleb's.

"Tonight?" Zoey asked, anxiety flooding her bloodstream. She wanted this probably more than Kaleb. Or Gage. And what did that say about her?

Hussy.

She laughed out loud, grinning like a fool. "Tonight. My house this time."

If this was a path they were going to venture down, she needed all three of them to be open and honest with one another. She was in no way looking for a permanent relationship. Although she might've developed some strong feelings for Kaleb – she was still denying those adamantly – Zoey wasn't about to think toward the future.

Kaleb looked back at her and had they been alone, she would've been naked by the sheer determination in his eyes. At this point, she was ready to strip right there in the front yard from how hot he was making her.

"Now get to work." She ordered before turning away, glancing quickly in Gage's direction, she smiled.

Definitely tonight.

♂♀

Kaleb did allow Zoey to take a step back, but he couldn't take his eyes off of her. Part of him was shocked that she had agreed to another foray with him and Gage, but the other part of him wondered why she hadn't brought it up before now. Since that day, she'd been a little on the wild side.

Which was entirely not what he expected from her.

Over the years, he'd gotten to know the wild child, but Zoey was only wild when it came to partying and hanging out with her friends. She was spunky and fun, usually the life of the party, but she wasn't promiscuous, nor did she flirt with anyone. Ever. So, needless to say, her behavior was a little out of character for sweet little Zoey.

From what he'd gathered in the last few weeks, Zoey Stranford wanted sex. There were times when she all but attacked him the moment he walked through her door, her lips plying him with hungry kisses, her teeth nipping with urgent need. She wanted rough, dirty sex. Then, there were times when she wanted slow and easy; exploring him as if she were a virgin who'd been locked away her entire life, using her tongue and her hands to map out his body in ways he'd never even imagined.

Just the thought of her had his cock throbbing in eager anticipation.

Who would've thought she'd be interested in a ménage.

And now, Kaleb was about to have another one with the object of every single one of his teenage fantasies?

Kaleb watched as Zoey returned to the house, admiring the intensely sexy sway of her hips as she went up the stairs. Those jeans she wore were almost more than he could bear. As he stood ogling her, Gage approached.

"Holy shit." Gage whistled. "I'm impressed, man."

Kaleb shot a look at his friend. "With?"

"How the hell you managed to convince her to go to bed with you is beyond me, much less the two of us." Laughing, Gage slapped him on the back and headed into the house. Kaleb followed.

Once inside, Kaleb noticed they'd made some significant progress over the last few hours. If they were lucky, they'd only have to spend half of Sunday finishing up. If that was the case, he had a big night planned for Zoey.

Sharing Zoey with Gage had proven to be both erotic and unnerving. He'd been like a randy fucking teenager, barely able to control himself. And that had been just from watching her.

Thinking about the amount of pleasure had from that one encounter and how Zoey was a more than willing participant, still made his cock throb. Which didn't surprise him if he honestly thought about it. Over the last couple of weeks, the two of them had shared some hot and heavy make out sessions in damn near every place they could come up with. The sex was off the charts, and her eagerness was downright thrilling. Especially considering he'd initially been worried about how she would respond to the desires that plagued him.

Loud voices coming from the living room interrupted Kaleb's thoughts, and he rushed quickly through the house to see what was going on. What he came upon shocked the shit out of him. It only took a few shoves to get the others to move out of his way.

"I dare you to fucking say it again, mother fucker!" Zane growled, his hand clutching the throat of one of Anderson's friends – Jake was his name, Kaleb thought.

"Whoa." Braydon said as he approached Zane and the other man as Kaleb flanked Zane's other side.

"What's going on?" Kaleb asked, watching as Zane continued to squeeze the man's throat. "Let go of him, Zane."

Jake's eyes were bulging out of his reddened face, but he wasn't making any move to try and fight Zane off. Maybe that was because Zane towered over him and probably had at least a forty pound weight advantage to boot.

Releasing his hold, Zane kept his hand on Jake's throat as he spoke. "If I ever fucking hear another word come out of your mouth about Vanessa, I promise, I'll rip your fucking voice box out."

Kaleb glanced over to see V standing beside Zoey in the doorway, tears streaming down her face. Kaleb had no idea what the hell had happened, but apparently Zane wasn't having any of it. Pulling Zane back, Kaleb and Braydon led him to another room while Anderson approached Jake. They shared a look and Kaleb made sure the other man understood what his options were. Either Jake would leave, or the Walker's would be.

Zane pulled away from Kaleb and Braydon and headed straight for Vanessa, putting his hand on the back of her neck and pulling her against him before leading her through the house and out the front door.

"What the hell happened?" Kaleb asked Zoey when she joined him.

"It was nothing." Zoey whispered, glancing around as the others began to disperse.

"Nothing my ass." Kaleb stated firmly. "My brother doesn't go off like that for no reason." As a matter of fact, Kaleb wasn't sure he'd ever seen Zane react the way he had.

Granted, they'd all probably defended the honor of one woman or another because when jealousy reared her ugly head, there was usually at least one Walker in her path. But this time, something was different about Zane.

Glancing over at Jake, he witnessed the argument between him and Anderson as he was asked to leave.

"Fuck you all." Jake yelled as he headed to the front door. "You let that bastard know this ain't over."

An automatic response had the remaining Walker brothers standing tall and facing Jake as he walked out the door. Kaleb would have to admit, although there were only five of them standing there, it was still an intimidating sight to see them. Jake must've thought so too because he hurried out the front door, not looking back.

When Zoey would have turned away, Kaleb put a hand on her arm. "What really happened, Zoey?"

Looking weary all of a sudden, she glanced around to make sure no one else was listening before turning her attention back to him.

"That guy Jake has been hitting on V all morning," She began. "V wasn't encouraging him, but she was trying to be civil by ignoring him. Apparently he didn't like that because he quickly turned to bad mouthing her. He made it personal." Zoey looked right in his eyes. "He started calling her and her mother whores and then he just turned nasty."

Well, in that case, Kaleb should've let Zane do his worst. Fucker.

"Is she all right?" Kaleb asked as he looked around, trying to find Zane and V.

"She will be. That woman's got thick skin." Zoey forced a smile. "Let's get back to it so we can get out of here." With that, she turned abruptly and went back to working in the kitchen.

Kaleb managed to stay busy for the next two hours and by the time they were at a stopping point, it was well past dark, and there were only a few people still hanging around. Zane had left earlier with V, insisting that he just take her home. Following them, Braydon and Brendon headed out.

"You ready?" Kaleb asked when he found Zoey standing in the kitchen, sans anything other than the cabinets and the sink. "Wow. This looks like a different room."

"It smells like a different room, too." Zoey laughed. "I think that smell has gotten into my pores. I seriously need a shower."

"There you go again with that shower invite. All right, twist my arm already." He laughed, linking his fingers with hers as he led her through the house.

When they stepped out on the front porch, they came face to face with Gage. "We done?"

"For today, we are." Kaleb stated.

"Where're you two headed off to?" His friend asked, glancing back and forth between the two of them.

Kaleb peered down at Zoey, wondering what the answer to that was. He heard what she said earlier, but he wanted to make sure she was still onboard. Especially after such a grueling day and the drama with Zane and Vanessa.

"Why don't you boys go home, take showers, and then come over to my place, say in," Zoey checked her watch, "about an hour? I'll make dinner as my way of saying thank you."

"Can't argue with dinner." Kaleb grinned as he looked at Gage.

"Nope, can't argue. All right, then I'll meet up with the two of you at Zoey's in a bit." Gage said before walking away.

"You ok with that?" Zoey asked when it was just her and Kaleb standing on the porch.

"Well, I can think of other ways for you to say thank you, but yes, I think dinner is a good start." With a quick kiss, Kaleb left Zoey standing on the porch staring after him.

Lord have mercy. The woman was going to be the death of him.

Chapter Fifteen

♀♂

Dinner consisted of country fried steak, mashed potatoes, okra and of course biscuits.

No, Zoey was by far a gourmet cook, but there were a few things she could make and yes, this was one of them. In the past, both Kaleb and Gage had requested her to make the well-known southern meal, so she figured she might as well go for it tonight.

After a quick shower, Zoey spent the last half hour working in the kitchen, trying to get everything ready before either man showed up. Thankfully they must've been taking their time because the steak was almost finished and she had just pulled the okra out of the fryer.

Needing something stronger than beer to calm her frazzled nerves, Zoey was on her second glass of Jack and coke, not that it was helping much. She actually felt just a little out of control and hoped they'd be able to make it through dinner before she went off the deep end.

Five minutes later, just as she was taking the biscuits out of the oven, Kaleb came strolling through her front door with Gage not far behind him.

"Did y'all ride together?" She asked, wondering how they could have timed that any better.

"Yeah, I stopped and picked him up on my way over." Kaleb said right before he pulled her into his arms and crushed his mouth down on hers. It was funny how dinner was now the last thing on her mind.

When they both came up for air, Zoey found she was damn near climbing Kaleb's body in an attempt to get closer. If it hadn't been for Gage clearing his throat and laughing, she might've done just that.

"We figured it would be best if both our trucks weren't parked outside of your house late into the night." Gage offered.

Ahhh. Good point. In a town the size of theirs, rumors spread like wild fire, and with their track record, it wouldn't take long for speculation to run rampant. Not that it would be untrue, but Zoey appreciated the fact that they wanted to be discreet.

"You know," Kaleb said, his hands still gripping her hips, "you didn't have to go all out with dinner. We're a sure thing."

Zoey swatted his chest and laughed, pulling away in the process.

"I know how grumpy the two of you can get when you're hungry." She moved to the table, followed by both men.

They waited for her to take a seat before doing the same.

Southern charm.

It was so damn sexy.

Probably due to such a long day, and the fact they were all starved after working at Anderson's mother's house for the better part of the day, the conversation was minimal while both men inhaled their meals, going back for seconds before Zoey even finished half of hers.

"Where was Travis today?" She asked when they were pushing their plates away a short while later.

"He had a meeting with a couple of potential investors up in Dallas. Sawyer and I offered to go with him, but he said he'd rather go by himself."

"Investors, huh?" Gage asked, spinning his beer bottle in his hands. "For the resort, right?"

"Yeah. Luke and Logan McCoy. They own Club Destiny, some nightclub in downtown Dallas. Travis is still waiting for a final decision on the land we're looking at, but he wanted to meet with the McCoy's just to outline his plan."

Zoey didn't say a word. She wondered whether Gage
knew what land Kaleb was referring to. Since they were good
friends, she figured he did, but no one made a big deal out of it, so
she left it at that.

"So, what's for dessert?" Kaleb asked, turning his
attention to her once again.

Zoey smiled. She knew exactly what she was planning to
have for dessert.

"Oh no. What's the grin for?" Gage asked, trying to sound
leery. Zoey knew better. If she reached over right now, she was
pretty sure his cock would be begging to be released from those
tight jeans.

"First of all, there's this little issue of the dishes that need
to be taken care of first." Zoey grinned. "Since I cooked, you boys
get to clean."

"And what do we get if we do the dishes?" Kaleb asked,
leaning forward in his chair, definitely looking interested in a
possible turn of events.

"Well, that depends..."

"On?" Gage asked, mirroring Kaleb's position, putting his
elbows on the table.

"Whether you can get this task accomplished."

"Oh, honey, I think we've done our fair share of dishes."

"Maybe." Zoey wasn't about to make this easy on them, and quite frankly, it was time to have a little fun. They might've figured she was the passive bystander all this time, letting everyone else take control, but that was no longer the case. "But, you probably haven't done the dishes naked before, have you?"

Kaleb's eyes rounded, and a seductive grin tipped his lips. "Naked."

"Naked." She confirmed, although he hadn't been asking.

Kaleb pushed his chair back, standing abruptly before unbuttoning the first of many buttons on his shirt. He took his time, and Zoey looked her fill. It didn't take long before his shirt was hanging on the back of the chair, and her eyes were grazing the scrumptious planes and angles of his chest, the ripples of his abs, and the tiniest hint of the muscular 'V' that dipped into the waistband of his jeans.

The man was sex personified. Smooth, tan skin and a spattering of dark hair on his chest had her wanting to run her fingertips over every exquisite muscle, followed by her tongue.

Her attention was immediately drawn to Gage as he stood from his seat, using one hand to grip the back of his shirt before easily pulling it over his head. Gage was significantly bigger than Kaleb when it came to muscles, thanks to an apparent commitment to the gym. The hair on his chest was thicker, and her fingers itched to slide into the soft, silky curls.

Oooh la la.

She wasn't quite sure what she'd done to deserve this, but she wasn't about to turn down an opportunity when it presented itself.

Pretending not to be affected was harder than it looked, but Zoey somehow managed. When both men moved to toe off their boots, she let her eyes drift back and forth between the two hard bodies standing before her.

Holy hell, it should be a crime to be that damn sexy.

"Naked, right?" Kaleb grinned, humor evident in his eyes.

"Completely."

A few minutes later, Zoey was forcing her jaw shut as she stared at the finer than fine cowboy butts in front of her. Both men had easily disrobed before carrying the few dishes they had used over to the sink. Lucky for them, Zoey had cleaned up her mess before they arrived, so the task should only take a few minutes.

Not long enough as far as she was concerned. She wanted to sit there and admire the masculine perfection for as long as possible. Both men were trim, toned, and absurdly sexy and watching the play of their back muscles had her thighs clenching.

It was going to be a long damn night.

♂♀♂

Kaleb had never had an issue with being naked. Nor did he have a problem being naked around Gage. They'd been in too many situations in which they found themselves without clothes for it to matter. He'd never thought much about it, but with Zoey's eyes tracking him like a heat seeking missile, he was having a hard time focusing.

Dishes.

Naked.

He hadn't seen that one coming.

As he loaded the last dish into the dishwasher, he turned off the water, grabbed a hand towel from the counter and turned to face her. His cock was rock hard and standing at full attention. When her eyes darted downward, his dick pulsed and jumped as though begging for her attention.

She was enjoying herself, he could tell, and Kaleb was reaching for every last ounce of his patience because he was more than a little tempted to lay her over the kitchen table and fuck her senseless. Instead of acting on that impulse, he leaned back against the counter and cleared his throat.

He had to bite back a grin when her eyes widened as they met his. Yep. Busted.

"Is it time for dessert yet?" Gage prompted, standing a couple of feet to Kaleb's left. Apparently the man didn't have any issues with being naked either.

"I've been trying to think about what I want for dessert." Zoey looked like she was contemplating her choices, but Kaleb knew better.

Zoey had an agenda, and if he had to guess, she'd already come up with the plan for the night. Doing dishes in the nude was only the beginning.

Since he was used to being in control, it was undeniably difficult trying to leave the decision making up to her, but he could sense that's what she truly wanted, so he let her. A bit surprised by her assertiveness, Kaleb had to wonder how long she'd been planning this out.

Standing from her chair, Zoey approached both him and Gage, her eyes lingering on their face before trailing down to the rigid erections they both sported. If she so much as breathed on his dick, he was likely going to come. That was another unfamiliar characteristic she drew out in him. Until her, Kaleb had never known such an intense need to fuck, to bury his cock in her as deep as possible and feel her tight, wet heat as her body pulled him in. He'd always kept himself carefully under control, but she tempted him.

Watching her, Kaleb held his breath as Zoey used both hands to stroke their cocks simultaneously. She didn't apply pressure, just merely slid her soft, smooth hands over the shaft, not lingering.

"If you want dessert, you'll need to have a seat." She told them before turning back to the table and pulling two of the chairs out. She sat them side by side, facing her. "Perfect. Now sit."

Kaleb and Gage glanced at one another before they both headed over to the chairs. The hard wood wasn't his ideal place to sit, especially naked, but if she had something specific in mind, he was all for it.

"Earlier today," Zoey said, turning away from them and going to the refrigerator, "I had a craving for a sundae."

Oh fuck.

"But," she continued, "I realized I didn't have any ice cream."

Kaleb bit his tongue as he watched her pull out a can of whipped cream and a bottle of chocolate syrup. *Holy fucking shit.* He was not going to survive this. There was no fucking way.

His heart rate spiked as he thought about what her intentions might be with those toppings and he was almost certain he knew what she planned to do to them.

"Be right back." Zoey sat the whipped cream and syrup on the table before disappearing from the room.

When she came back, Kaleb damn near choked on his tongue. He hadn't seen her grab his shirt, but she apparently decided she would change. Standing before them, she was wearing his shirt, unbuttoned, and a smile. Nothing else.

That wasn't the worst of it.

In each hand, she had black scarves, which she sat on the table beside the other items she had procured a few minutes before.

Picking up one of the scarves, Zoey moved to Gage first, taking one of his hands and pulling it behind him where she proceeded to tie it to the chair back. Then she did the other.

Kaleb wasn't so sure he was onboard with this.

Staring at his friend now tied to the chair, it was clear that Gage was turned on by this. Kaleb wanted to deny it, but the proof was throbbing between his legs. He held his breath, praying for patience as she took his hands and successfully secured him to the chair, as well.

When she reappeared in front of them, she put her hands on her hips, the shirt covering remarkably little of her sweet, lithe body. Although he would prefer to feast on the glorious exposed skin, Kaleb couldn't help but wonder what she was going to do next.

"So, like I was saying," Zoey picked up the chocolate syrup, "oh, wait. Hold on."

She disappeared from the room yet again, and Kaleb groaned.

"Fuck. She's killing me." Gage exhaled.

"No, shit. If she doesn't get on with it, I'm going to take her over my knee and paddle her sweet little ass for torturing me." Kaleb wasn't kidding either.

Thankfully she was back within seconds carrying a small pillow that she placed on the floor at their feet.

What the fuck?

Picking up the whipped cream, she held one bottle in each hand, staring back at them like they were the ice cream.

Oh hell.

Zoey smiled.

"Like I was saying. I was craving ice cream, but since I'm all out, I figured this would be the next best thing."

When her eyes darted to Kaleb's cock, he sucked in a breath. And when she knelt between his legs, he was tempted to tear his arms from their bonds so he could grip her hair and drive his cock deep in her throat.

"Holy fuck! That's cold." Kaleb groaned as Zoey dripped chocolate syrup over the length of his cock.

She didn't say anything, just smiled before her little pink tongue darted out and licked the throbbing head repeatedly, lapping up the chocolate before she drizzled another small amount.

"Mmmm..."

The vibrations shot up through his cock while the heat from her mouth counteracted the cold chocolate, and Kaleb knew he was up against the greatest test of his patience and willpower.

But then she was gone. Switching, Zoey moved over to Gage and took the whipped cream and applied a small amount to the head of his cock. Kaleb watched in utter fascination as she licked him clean.

Zoey repeated this action two more times on each of them, using the chocolate on one, the whipped cream on the other and getting more aggressive with her sucking each time. Kaleb tried to thrust into her mouth, but with his hands tied, he couldn't pull her forward each time she pulled back.

What she did next had Kaleb damn near screaming in pleasure.

Using the chocolate syrup, Zoey dripped some into her palm, then swiped her index finger through the chocolate, coating it and then tracing his balls with her cool finger before she licked every last drop off of him.

"Oh, God, baby." Kaleb groaned. "Don't fucking stop." It was a demand, but he knew she wouldn't heed it worth a damn. No, she was in control, but he had to try. "Suck my balls into your mouth. All the way. Oh, fuck. That's it."

He fisted his hands at his back and sucked in a breath while Zoey rolled his balls in her mouth, her mischievous tongue tormenting him.

Zoey left him, his balls literally aching while she teased and tortured Gage. His friend's groans filled the air, proving Zoey was getting to him as much as she was Kaleb. This was one of those times when Kaleb questioned the idea of a threesome.

"I think I'm finished with dessert." Zoey grinned as she stood up, making a point to flash them both. Kaleb bit his tongue.

"Untie me." Kaleb demanded, instinct causing him to pull at the bonds. "It's my turn for dessert."

That seductive little grin of hers damn near had him bolting up from the chair. Although he could've easily gotten out of the flimsy knot she used on the scarf tying him down, Kaleb was trying to give her her moment.

Only because it was about to come to an end.

♂♀♂

Zoey walked around behind them ever so slowly, then untied the scarves holding their hands to the chair. The second they were free, she giggled and ran, and Kaleb, in all of his naked glory, took off after her. She hadn't made it far before her feet left the ground, Kaleb's arms coming around her, pulling her against him. She was out of breath from laughing, but the instant his body touched hers, a flame ignited in her core.

Yes, she had teased them.

Yes, she had enjoyed it. Immensely.

And yes, maybe secretly she hoped there would be a little retribution on their part.

As Kaleb buried his face in the crook of her neck, his teeth nipping that sensitive spot that had a direct link to her clit, Zoey moaned. She loved when he did that.

But then Gage was there, and as Kaleb held her suspended above the ground, his warm mouth latched onto one of her nipples and she gripped his head, holding him to her as though he would disappear before she could experience the thrilling sensations his mouth inflicted.

Zoey was startled back from the overwhelming intensity when Kaleb began carrying her through the living room to her bedroom. Once there, he deposited her on the bed, tossing her mind you, making her laugh once again. Now sprawled across the bed sideways, Gage moved around to the side where her head was while Kaleb spread her legs and eased between them.

She wasn't sure when she'd come to crave this, but there was certainly something to be said about two men dousing her with attention. Especially this kind of attention.

Standing above her, Gage took her hands and pulled them above her head, securing them with his knees against the side of the mattress.

"Tell me if I'm hurting you." He whispered as he leaned over, once again sucking one painfully hard nipple into his mouth. He wasn't gentle with her either, but that was entirely ok because she didn't want gentle. She wanted fast and dirty, forceful and fulfilling, anything to help ease the ache between her thighs.

With Gage's body over hers, she couldn't see what Kaleb was doing, but the instant his tongue lashed through her slit, she knew his intentions, and she instinctively thrust her hips up toward his mouth. His large, warm hands came to rest on her thighs, holding her down on the mattress as he began tormenting her the same way she had him.

So sweet. So good. She wasn't sure she would be able to hold her orgasm back as two mouths tickled her flesh, sucking and nipping and pushing her closer and closer to that razor sharp edge.

She opened her eyes, spotting Gage's iron hard erection directly above her and found that if she tilted her head, she could graze the engorged crest with her tongue. His moan was instantaneous, and she felt the vibration through her nipple and straight to where Kaleb was currently flicking his tongue.

She moaned again, tipping her head a little more before sucking Gage fully into her mouth. His cock was satiny smooth, and granite hard, and the smell of musky man filled her senses, increasing the hunger that had never been sated by food.

When his hips began thrusting, his cock tunneling through her mouth, Zoey had to focus on not gagging, especially at this angle. But his beautiful cock was long and thick, filling her mouth. Then his knees released her hands as he knelt on the bed, straddling her head, but he easily trapped her arms between his legs and her head, hanging over the edge of the bed. She couldn't adjust the angle, and he apparently knew that when he began fucking her mouth insistently, pulling out altogether before sliding back between her lips, groaning out his pleasure as he did.

As she continued to focus on sucking his steely shaft, there was movement between her legs and suddenly she was filled to overflowing. One cock filling her mouth while another filled her pussy, both men ramming into her until her body was a jumble of tingles and overstimulated nerve endings.

Kaleb lifted her legs, holding them out to the side as he pummeled her pussy over and over, faster and harder until she was unable to stop the tremors that had started only moments before. Fighting to keep from biting down because she was trapped beneath Gage, Zoey tilted her head, allowing Gage to thrust as far as he could until groans erupted in the room.

Theirs and hers.

Her pussy spasmed around the huge intrusion, gripping Kaleb's cock as his fingers dug into her calves where he held her legs, and her orgasm erupted at the same time they both let go.

Gage filled her mouth, slowing his movements while lifting his upper body to keep from crushing her as he held the base of his cock.

Before she tumbled back to earth, she was being pulled and turned; Kaleb's sexy, familiar scent once again comforting her as his arms came around her, holding her close.

Heaven.

The man had somehow figured out how to rock her world in every way imaginable, all the while, Zoey knew she was falling way too fast for this man.

Way too fast.

Chapter Sixteen

♀♂

"Zoey!"

Zoey set the clean plate down on the counter, turned off the water and headed to the living room where her father was. She cocked her eyebrows at him, seeing him sitting in the chair, a smile tipping his lips.

"What's up, Dad?"

"Sit with me."

Ok.

It wasn't very often that her father asked her to join him, but when he did, she knew it wasn't so they could watch television together. He knew how very little interest she had in the Old West reruns he enjoyed so much.

Curious as to what it was he wanted to talk about, Zoey set the dish towel she used to dry her hands on the arm of the couch and sat down close to his chair.

"I've been thinking about the offer from the Walker boys."

Well, that was a good thing, Zoey thought to herself. She'd been thinking about it too. Although she and Kaleb hadn't talked about it after that one day when she walked in on the conversation, Zoey had wanted to ask both her father and Kaleb whether they had come to a decision.

For Zoey, it was a no-brainer and yes, that made her feel both selfish and as though she might be disregarding what her family had worked so hard to build. The Stranford land had been in the family for generations, however, the hard times that had fallen on her father in recent months were slowly taking their toll on him. And her.

She didn't know what the offer was exactly, and she hadn't bothered to ask her father, although she felt she deserved some more information. It was still his decision to make, and she decided she would support him either way. If he wanted to hold on to the land, Zoey would make sure they worked on getting it back to its former glory and making money again. Or, if he chose to sell it, she would ensure the money was used to take care of her father as it should.

"Have you made a decision, Dad?" She asked when he didn't say more.

"I have." He turned his navy blue eyes on her; the same eyes she saw every day when she looked in the mirror.

"And what did you decide?"

"Honey, I don't want you to be mad at me, and I don't want you to think you don't have a say in this because you do."

"Dad –" Zoey tried to tell him that it wasn't her decision to make, but he silenced her with a wave of his hand.

"This land has been in my family for an awful long time, and those before me fell on hard times too, but somehow they managed to get through it.

"Now, I might not have told you this, but it has always been my plan to give you the land and let you choose what to do with it."

Zoey didn't speak, she let her father talk, but her brain began pondering what he was trying to tell her. She didn't want to make this decision. She absolutely didn't.

This would be something that could come between her and Kaleb, and despite the relationship, for lack of a better word, that had developed between them, Zoey knew their friendship alone might not survive this type of complication.

"I've met with my lawyer." Carl said, looking both sad and relieved. "And as of yesterday, this land no longer belongs to me."

Zoey held her breath, waiting to hear that her father had actually accepted Kaleb's offer and the Walker's now owned the one hundred acres they had been pursuing.

"I didn't accept Kaleb's offer, honey."

Her heart dropped, and her stomach churned.

"All of the land including both houses now belongs to you. I didn't do this to make it hard on you, but I felt as though, in my current situation, you would be the one to make the best decision."

Zoey wasn't so sure about that.

She knew what her father was referring to. Over the course of the last few months, his memory had been failing him significantly. And she knew her father was only trying to protect them both by transferring everything over to her, but that meant she was now responsible for his financial hardship. Not that she hadn't been before, but it was quite different now.

"Dad, I don't –" This time Zoey stopped herself. She didn't want to burden her father, especially not in his current condition. If this was a decision she had to make, then she would.

"Do you have any concerns?" She asked.

"It's not going to be easy either way. They have caught us between a rock and a hard place, and I hate that I had to put all of this on you, but Zoey, this is your birth right. And if you want a monstrosity of a resort in your backyard, then that's your decision. I support whatever you choose to do."

Oh Lord. When he put it that way...

Two hours later, Zoey was pulling down the long dirt drive toward the office building of Walker Demolition. She had called Kaleb and asked that he and his brother's meet with her to talk about the land. She didn't bother telling him that her father had signed it all over to her because quite frankly, she didn't want to deal with that right now.

What she did want was to know what their plans were. How it would affect her home, her father's home and the rest of the town. Until today, she found herself supporting Travis' idea, but selfishly that had been because she didn't want to lose her home. If she sold the land to the Walker's she would be able to pay off the house and there wouldn't be any chance that her father would lose his home.

What that meant for her community was another story. This resort, as they referred to it, was going to draw in all sorts of people. And she felt she deserved to know more.

Parking her truck, she shut off the engine at the same time Kaleb descended the stairs from the back door of the office. Her eyes were glued to him as he approached. Just like always, even before they started up this little rendezvous of theirs, her heart did a little happy dance the moment she laid eyes on him. He was beautiful. With his white button down shirt, those tight Wranglers accentuating his thick legs and his delicious butt, Zoey found her hormones coming to life yet again.

She couldn't afford to be led by her hormones anymore. Especially not today.

"Hey." He greeted as he opened her door. "You all right?"

No. No, she wasn't.

"Are Travis and Sawyer here?" She asked as she slid down from the driver's seat and stood before Kaleb. He was standing so close she could smell that musky, mouthwatering scent of his cologne, the same kind she bought him for Christmas one year.

"They are." He stated, sounding unsure of himself. "What's going on?"

Zoey met his gaze and saw the concern in his eyes, and she knew he'd see the same in hers.

"Let's go inside, please." She couldn't do this here. Not with Kaleb. She had a better chance of standing up against all three of them than she did Kaleb alone. Her heart wanted to give this man anything he wanted, even if it wasn't in her best interest. And that was something she couldn't chance with the biggest decision of her life thus far.

Taking her hand, Kaleb walked alongside her, glancing down a time or two, but Zoey kept her eyes trained on the building. This was hard enough as it was, and looking at him only made it that much harder.

"Hey, Zoey." Sawyer greeted as soon as she stepped through the door. The man was up and out of his chair, immediately pulling her against him. Zoey steeled herself, hugging him back and soaking in his warmth. That was what she got for befriending the Walker's. They were a very sweet bunch, not to mention, devilishly handsome.

"Hey." She replied when he pulled back. She noticed Travis sitting in a chair, a cup of coffee in his hand, staring back at her.

"Travis."

"Hey, Zoe." He said, using the shortened version of her name as he always did. Travis was the only one of the Walker's that felt like a brother to her. He was considerably older, and she hadn't gone to school with him, which meant she didn't know him nearly as well either.

"Afternoon." She said when she found her voice. "Thanks for agreeing to meet with me."

He nodded his head, sipping from his coffee mug but never taking his eyes off of her. "What can we do you for?"

She released Kaleb's hand, trying to find the nerve she lost somewhere between her house and their office. She knew she had to do this, but she suddenly wished she wouldn't have jumped to do it so quickly. Although time obviously wasn't on her side because she spoke with the bank just before coming over, and her days to come up with a solution were definitely numbered.

"I'd like to see the plans for the resort." She told them, glancing between Sawyer and Travis, but avoiding Kaleb's gaze. She could feel him looking at her from where he stood near the coffeemaker.

"Yeah?" Travis asked, not sounding nearly as friendly as moments before. "What for?"

"Just show her the fucking plans." Kaleb groaned, handing Zoey a fresh cup of coffee, which she took. "You can sit there." He pointed to an empty seat near his desk.

The room was small and in it were three relatively large desks, one for each of the three oldest Walker brothers. She knew Braydon and Brendon preferred not to be in the office, so they didn't need desks and Ethan and Zane had an office near the other shop where the vehicle maintenance was handled.

"Thanks." She said to Kaleb, sitting in the chair and placing her cup on the desk. "I want to talk about the offer you made my father, and in order to do that, I need to see what the plans are for this resort."

Travis didn't look all that happy, but he opened his desk drawer and pulled out a cardboard tube which he placed in front of him. After popping off the end, he pulled out a set of rolled up papers before flattening them on his desk and setting a couple of items on each corner to hold them open.

"Well, come here." Travis stated gruffly as he shot a look at her.

Zoey stood, then hesitantly approached the desk as if Travis were a coiled snake ready to strike. There in front of her was a jumble of lines on a grid. If she looked closer, she could see the architectural layout of what they obviously envisioned for the resort.

The thing was undoubtedly a monstrosity as her father had said.

"How big is it?" She asked the obvious question.

"The plan is for four hundred thousand square feet in total, including five hundred guest rooms, shopping, dining, two clubs, and meeting rooms."

Holy crap. "How many acres does it sit on?"

"Roughly one hundred acres." Travis said.

"So why do you need so much land?" Zoey asked. She heard they purchased two hundred acres of adjoining land from two other ranchers in the area, so she wasn't quite sure why they needed more.

Watching as Travis moved the page before showing her another. This one was more her style, and it nearly took her breath away. It looked like a computer design of what they envisioned the resort to look like from the outside. It encompassed their small Texas town by keeping to the rustic, natural theme. Not quite a log cabin, but it resembled one on the exterior, yet it seemed remarkably quaint, which Zoey thought was odd.

When Travis removed that image, replacing it with several others, she saw the design for the suites as well as some of the shopping and dining areas. Then, as she looked on, he revealed the obvious draw for the entire resort. Two massive, state of the art clubs. Not just any club either.

"Holy shit." She whispered, her mind overwhelmed with images of the types of people this kind of place would draw to their innocent, unknowing little town.

"Before you freak out," Sawyer said, his tone much sharper than moments before, "have a seat, and we'll give you some of the details. It isn't what you think it is."

"I have eyes, Sawyer," Zoey retorted, "I know what that is."

"But you don't know all of the details yet." Kaleb chimed in, his posture no longer reflecting the laid back cowboy she was familiar with. He was leaning forward, his forearms resting on his desk and his eyes locked with hers.

With a deep breath, Zoey plopped down in her chair.

"We've acquired two hundred acres already, but I'm looking to have the entrance on the south side, for two main purposes." Travis began, his eyes lighting up for the first time. "The south side will allow us to remain farther away from town, and it also offers a measure of privacy we wouldn't have otherwise."

"Privacy?" Zoey didn't understand. "This is a resort. Wouldn't you want to blast its existence to everyone so they can bring in the money?"

"That's where this resort differs." Sawyer spoke up.

"We have secured the investors needed to get this place off the ground, and along with their financial backing, they will be assisting us in understanding how to run an exclusive, invitation only resort." Travis added. "We won't be open to the public, Zoey. At least not to the general public."

Baffled, Zoey waited for him to continue.

"The purpose of the resort is for entertainment purposes, of course. But our resort will be discreet as well as secured." Sawyer tacked on.

Zoey glanced back and forth between the three men. She didn't know what to think about this, but the images of the clubs told her everything she needed to know about why they wanted to be discreet about it. "Those are sex clubs." She stated the obvious.

No one spoke, all three men just looked at her.

"Do you even have approval to build that here?"

"We do." Kaleb assured her. "Everything is contingent upon securing your father's land."

"My land."

"What?" Kaleb asked, looking confused.

"It's my land, Kaleb. My father signed it over to me. It's no longer his decision. It's mine."

Chapter Seventeen

♂♀

Kaleb didn't know what to say. He didn't know what to think. And worst of all, he didn't know what Zoey was thinking. She wasn't animated like she normally was. In fact, she looked distraught. Ever since she had seen the images of the club their resort would include, she'd been different.

And now she was telling him that they had been talking to Carl Stranford for the better part of six months only to find out the man wasn't going to make a decision at all. Now it was up to Zoey?

"What are you saying, Zoey?" Travis asked, and it didn't escape Kaleb that he didn't use the shortened version of her name that he had given her when she was younger.

"I'm saying my father no longer has a say in this matter." She said smartly, sitting the coffee cup on the desk.

"Does that mean you've made a decision?" Travis was quickly losing his patience, Kaleb noticed.

"No, it doesn't mean I've made a decision." She said, standing. "But I will. I'm going to request a little more information from you and you can expect my answer in one week."

"A fucking week?" Travis stood, shoving his chair into the wall behind him. "I've been waiting six fucking months for an answer, and now you're putting me off the same way your father did?"

Zoey stunned Kaleb as she went toe to toe with Travis. Although the man was significantly taller, she didn't seem intimidated, even when Travis came closer. She placed her hands on her hips and cocked her head back to look up at him.

"That's what I said. One week. You provide me with the information I request, and we'll meet again. One week from now."

With that, Zoey walked out the door, and she didn't look back. It took a second for Kaleb to realize she'd just walked out on him too. He stood abruptly and all but chased her down in the parking lot.

"Zoey!" He called after her, but she seemed determined to ignore him. "Don't fucking do it." He warned her. This was the second time she'd walked away from him without looking back, and it pissed him the fuck off.

By the time he reached her truck, she was backing out, purposely avoiding his gaze.

Bullshit.

Kaleb fished his truck keys from his pocket and walked to his truck. He was down the driveway and on the main road before her truck was out of his sight. Two minutes later he was parking in front of her house beside her, but she once again hurried out and ran inside.

Ran.

Kaleb couldn't believe it. He took off and managed to stick his booted foot in the door seconds before it would've been slammed in his face.

He used force to push against the door, opening it until Zoey was backing into the room; her eyes wide as saucers as she stared back at him. He slammed the door, then locked it.

"What the hell are you doing?" Zoey screamed at him.

"What am *I* doing?" Kaleb stalked her. "*Me?* What the hell are *you* doing? You storm out of my office and ignore me when I try to talk to you."

"I didn't have anything to say to you." She insisted, backing up until she met the ungiving wall behind her. Kaleb didn't stop moving toward her.

"No?"

"No. I told you I'd get back to you in a week."

"I don't give a fuck about that." Kaleb couldn't believe what she was saying. Did she think that the only reason he was there was for her father's – no, change that... *her* – land?

He stared down at her, invading her personal space when he put his palms flat against the wall on each side of her head. He bent at the waist in order to bring their faces level. "I consider myself a pretty tolerant man, Zoey," he began, "but there are some things I don't do."

She didn't question him with words, but her eyebrow cocked with interest.

"First of all, I don't mix business with pleasure." It would never end well if he did, and he knew it. "And two, I don't tolerate being ignored."

"I didn't ignore you."

"You walked away when I called your name. I know you heard me."

Zoey broke eye contact, looking down, but then back up at him. With an exasperated sigh, she melted against the wall. "I don't have the energy for this, Kaleb."

What the fuck?

"So, this is how it is?" He knew he should shut his mouth because he was beyond pissed, but he couldn't. "Yesterday I had my cock buried in your pussy while my best friend was fucking your mouth until we all three came. And today, you're treating me like the only interaction we have is related to business? That's bullshit, Zoey, and you know it."

"What do you want from me, Kaleb?" Zoey lifted her arms, her hands slapping down on her thighs. "There is nothing I can do about this. Whatever this is that you and I have, it can't last. I know that. Especially not after my father gave me the land. I know what you're after, and I don't have the energy to pretend with you that it's anything else."

Kaleb stood up straight, plunged his hands into his hair, but he didn't move. And Zoey didn't either. He closed his eyes, took a deep breath, then opened them again. This time when he met her eyes, he made sure she saw everything he was feeling.

"Honey, if you think I'm only after the land, you've got another thing coming." And he would damn well prove it to her. Taking her hand, he reined in his temper and pulled her along behind him. She was reluctant, but she wasn't trying to pull away.

"Where are we going?" Zoey asked, sounding just as pissed as he felt.

How they had gotten to this point, he had no clue. But, Kaleb was going to show her exactly what happened when she made assumptions about what it was that he wanted.

♀♂

Zoey followed Kaleb into her bedroom because she didn't know what else to do. He was livid, she could feel his anger radiating off of him. Well, that was good and fine. She was pissed too. She hadn't been until it dawned on her that she was now the key to what the Walker's wanted, which meant what she and Kaleb had would never be real. Not again at least.

He had an end goal, and now she would be his means of getting what he wanted. She refused to do it.

Once inside her room, Kaleb abruptly stopped, turning to face her. She nearly ran in to him, but she managed to stop herself just in time.

"Take off your clothes." Kaleb insisted, and there was a demand in his tone she hadn't heard before. As angry as she was, she couldn't deny the way her pussy flared to life, clenching in need at his tone.

"What?" No, she wasn't giving in that easily. No way.

"You heard me." Kaleb said, sliding his hand into her hair and pulling her head back. Hard.

There was a bite of pain that rippled through her scalp and like lightning, it flashed downward, making direct contact with her clit.

"Take off your clothes, Zoey. Or I'll do it for you." There wasn't an ounce of humor in his eyes, and his stern command made her pussy wet. Wetter than she thought possible. What the hell was wrong with her? She was supposed to be pissed at him, but she couldn't seem to remember why.

"No." Maybe that was a mistake, but Zoey was going to push him the same way he felt he could push her.

"No?"

Zoey recognized the question in his eyes. She knew Kaleb. Knew him to his very core. When a woman said no, it meant no. And he was questioning her meaning. She decided to clarify, "I'm not taking off my clothes. If you think they need to come off, you do it yourself."

Her mind whirled with the events that happened next. Kaleb gripped the hem of her t-shirt and without anything resembling gentle, he proceeded to strip her totally naked. She was breathing hard, and her nipples were pebbled by the time he was through. Other than getting her clothes off of her, he didn't touch her in any other way, but heaven help her, she wanted him to.

"Turn around." He ordered, his tone clipped, his eyes hard.

Zoey turned away from him, unsure of what he was going to do next. Kaleb took her hands hanging down at her sides and lifted them while pressing his chest against her back. Although his chest wasn't the only thing pressing into her. His erection nudged her bottom and Zoey squeezed her thighs together. This was too much, and she had no idea what was going on to even know what to expect.

First she walked out. Then he was pissed. Then she was pissed. Then she was wet and so damn horny she was shaking with it. Something was off in the chain of events, at least in her opinion.

"Put your hands flat against the wall and don't move."

Zoey started to take a step closer, because from where she stood, if she had to touch the wall she would be bending over.

"Uh uh. Don't move your feet. Just put your hands on the wall."

She did as Kaleb told her, feeling incredibly foolish as she bent over at the waist, her butt sticking out. It was an odd position, but if he were naked, it could be a position that might just get her what she very much needed.

Still leaning over, she got a glimpse of Kaleb's t-shirt as he pulled it off, tossing it to the floor behind him. From between her legs, behind her, she could see him taking off his jeans. Biting her lip, she kept her hands on the wall feeling a sudden rush of embarrassment. What happened to her rage? How did she end up standing naked before him with her hands on the wall like she was being punished?

Her eyes widened as realization dawned. She went to stand, but Kaleb's firm hand landed on her back, holding her in place.

"Kaleb, wait." She whispered, not understanding the strange desire that had set forth in her belly.

"No waiting." He replied. "And don't you dare move."

She whimpered because her body instinctively knew that whatever was to come would result in a mind blowing orgasm. If he would just line up behind her, she could spread her legs farther apart, and he could thrust into her hard and fast, exactly like she... *Oh God!!*

Her ass burned, and she nearly face planted into the wall when she went to move her hands to her now stinging ass. "What the fuck was that for?" She screamed as she stood, covering her bottom where she figured there was an imprint of his hand.

"Turn around. Put your hands on the wall, Zoey." Kaleb growled the instruction. "Now."

She turned, not saying another word because honestly, her ass might've been burning, but her pussy was throbbing and she figured she could endure whatever it was he wanted to do to her as long as he would fuck her.

This time when she faced the wall, Kaleb's hands braced her hips and she felt the head of his cock sliding down the crack of her ass. Then the warmth of his body disappeared, and another stinging slap came down on her bottom, the opposite side as the last one.

"How many, Zoey?" He asked, and she had no idea what he was talking about.

"What?"

"How many spankings do you get?" He chuckled, his warm hand caressing the sting he'd just left. "How many until you understand how much I cannot tolerate you walking away from me?"

How many? Shit, two was plenty. She had no idea how many he expected her to say. "I don't know."

"I do." Kaleb said, pressing one hand on her back, pushing her down farther until she couldn't keep her hands on the wall any longer. "Put your hands on her ankles."

This was humiliating. Zoey was now bent over at the waist, her hands clasping her ankles and the backs of her thighs screaming from the burning stretch. She wasn't all that flexible, but she couldn't seem to argue with him.

Another slap landed, and she nearly tumbled over, but Kaleb put his hand on her back, holding her still.

"Count them." He instructed.

Did that mean the three that he'd already given her? She didn't know, but decided to start with four.

Several additional slaps landed, and Zoey tried to keep up with the count, but the tears were running down her face, the burning sensation almost too much. However, she was so turned on, she couldn't move, praying that, after the next slap, Kaleb would bury his cock in her pussy and put her out of her misery.

But he didn't.

Another two slaps landed before Kaleb's warm, moist tongue was on her ass, licking the heated flesh before dipping into the crack of her ass. She spread her legs apart, keeping her hands on her ankles and although the blood was rushing to her brain, she didn't want him to stop.

When he started reaming her anus with his tongue, she knew what he was preparing for, and Zoey wasn't above begging. Then he stood again, two more slaps landed on her ass before he thrust one finger inside her ass, slowly, gently pushing in and pulling out repeatedly until she was moaning and pushing her bottom against his hand.

This went on for several long minutes, two or three slaps on her behind alternated with his fingers thrusting into her ass. She was on the brink of an explosive orgasm when he stopped altogether and told her to stand up.

"Move over to the bed and bend over."

Oh, she certainly liked that idea. Her ass and the backs of her thighs were on fire from where he had spanked her – she still didn't understand why she liked it so much – and her back was tight from bending over. At least laying on the bed would allow her to relax a little.

"Please, Kaleb." She begged when her upper body was laying on the bed, her ass still sticking out, begging for his touch.

"Please what?" He asked, and Zoey heard the rusty, gravelly sound of his arousal. Their little spanking session had apparently affected him as much as it had her.

"Fuck me."

"How? Where do you want my cock, Zoey?"

"In me." Kaleb chuckled again, but he didn't give her what she wanted and she groaned. "Please, Kaleb."

"Tell me. Where do you want my cock? In your pussy? Or in your ass?"

God, why was he leaving it up to her? She was so fucking turned on, she didn't give a damn where he fucked her as long as he did it soon. But she knew what he wanted, and quite frankly, what he wanted was what she wanted. "In my ass. Fuck my ass, Kaleb."

"I'm going to fuck you hard. I can't hold back." His words sounded like a warning, but Zoey wouldn't tell him that they were more of a promise to her ears.

"Please." She begged again slipping her hand beneath her body, finding her clit with her fingers.

"That's it, baby." His sexy voice boomed through the room as he moved around behind her. "Play with your clit. Then I want you to bury two fingers in your pussy when I fuck your ass."

Oh yes!

Zoey worked her fingers furiously over her clit as Kaleb moved behind her. She expected him to separate her ass cheeks and press inside of her, but once again, another slap landed on her ass, and she screamed, her fingers stilled.

"Now, Zoey." Kaleb exclaimed, pushing his cock into her faster than she expected, stealing her breath, but the pain disappeared as fast as it had come on.

"Fuck your pussy with your fingers, baby."

She tried, she honestly did, but the only thing Zoey wanted was for him to move faster. She needed to come, and it didn't matter how he made that happen, her body was pulled tighter than a bow, begging, pleading for release.

Kaleb gripped her hips and began ramming into her ass, harder, faster, over and over until she was moaning and having a hard time focusing on what her hands were supposed to be doing.

"Come for me, Zoey. Come for me, baby." Kaleb's voice sounded strained, as though he were fighting to hang on.

Zoey cried out, "Please, Kaleb. Make me come."

She didn't know what was stopping her, didn't know why she couldn't reach that pinnacle that would rocket her into ecstasy, but she couldn't. It was then that Kaleb's fingers replaced hers, burying deep in her pussy, curving until he hit that perfect spot that had fireworks detonating behind her eyes and her body tightening painfully.

"Come for me!" Kaleb's sexy voice boomed louder than before, a command, not a request and Zoey's orgasm tore through her as Kaleb roared his release.

♂♀

Kaleb couldn't close his eyes, although Zoey didn't seem to be having any problem with it. What had just happened between the two of them had been the most intense situation Kaleb had ever found himself in. Did he go around spanking his partners? Ummm... That would be a no. Until Zoey, Kaleb had never spanked another soul. Ever.

Yet when she had walked away from him for the second time, trying to shut him out, he'd been so pissed off; his only thought was of making sure she remembered not to do it again. He didn't want her to shut him out. He didn't want her to walk away from him. What did that mean? Hell he didn't know, but he knew he couldn't take it if she turned away from him now.

Holding her in his arms, her soft, warm body lying across his, cuddled into him like she was meant just for him, Kaleb knew he wasn't walking away from this unscathed.

Not this time.

For twenty years, he'd been her friend. He had stood beside her, both of them listening when the other needed someone to, hanging out so they wouldn't be alone, and just having a good time in between. But, this. This was more.

And Kaleb wanted more. Hell, he wanted everything with Zoey.

That should've been easy to convey, but with her stunning news from earlier that afternoon, there was no way he could just drop that little bomb on her. She'd think it was a setup, and he wouldn't be able to blame her. But what he wanted from Zoey wouldn't change, even if she decided not to sell her father's land. Travis might be pissed at first, but they were resilient, and they'd figure out another way. In truth, they didn't need the land, but it would make it simpler.

The woman got under his skin all those years ago when he first met her and he'd been enthralled with her ever since. And now... Now he was just flat out in love with her, and there wasn't a single thing he wouldn't do to make her happy. He just didn't know how to tell her now, so he'd bide his time, and pray that the right moment would present itself.

Chapter Eighteen

♂♀

Kaleb was sitting in the office when Zane walked through the door, making as much noise as possible it seemed.

"What the hell is wrong with you?" Kaleb asked, not looking up from his computer.

"Fuck off."

Well, that was one hell of a greeting. Kaleb stopped typing the email he'd been working on, and looked up at his youngest brother. "Seriously, what's up?"

Zane took his coffee mug and sat in the chair across from Kaleb's desk, not looking at him. When he didn't speak, Kaleb broke the silence. "How's Vanessa?"

That got Zane's attention and his eyes darted upward, meeting Kaleb's. What he saw on his brother's face could only be described as torment. *Oh, shit.*

"Hell if I know."

"Are you still seeing her?" He asked, not knowing whether Zane wanted to talk or not, but figuring while he was there, he might as well ask.

"You mean fucking her?"

Ouch.

"No, that's not what I meant, actually." Kaleb remembered what had happened that first day at the cleanup at Anderson's. The way Zane acted hadn't been that of a man just interested in fucking a woman.

"She said I went all caveman on her." Zane admitted, sounding defeated.

Well, hell.

Before he could say anything more, in walked Braydon and Brendon right in time to save the day.

"What's up, Bubba?" Both Zane and Kaleb glanced at Braydon, unsure which of them that he was talking to. Probably both.

"When the two of you are together, it can only mean trouble." Kaleb said, leaning back in his chair now. There was no way he was going to get any work done. Not that he knew what he was supposed to be working on anyway. His mind was so cluttered with thoughts of Zoey, he had a difficult time focusing on any one thing.

"Have y'all closed on that land deal yet?" Brendon asked, grabbing an energy drink from the refrigerator before joining them in the small office area.

"No. Zoey's going to get back with us at the end of the week."

"How is she anyway?" Zane asked, sounding interested for once.

"Good. Why?"

"No reason."

Ok, this conversation was going precisely nowhere.

"Why are you here, Zane?" Kaleb decided to be blunt. "What the hell is going on?"

"Shit if I know. Vanessa won't talk to me, and I don't know what the fuck I did wrong."

"Well, that's easy." Brendon offered. "You went all caveman on her ass. Going after that jackass Jake and all."

"He fucking deserved it. He deserved to get the shit kicked out of him." Zane said, looking none too happy with Brendon's two cents.

"Maybe, but did you have to do it in front of everyone?" Braydon asked. "You called attention to it, and after you left, everyone was talking about it."

"Shit." Zane leaned forward, elbows on his knees, holding his head in his hands.

"She'll get over it." Kaleb said because that's what the moment called for. He had no idea whether Vanessa would get over it or not. He still didn't know what the hell had happened, other than the little bit Zoey had told him.

"Bullshit, man." Brendon laughed. "Vanessa Carmichael does not get over anything. The woman holds a grudge forever."

Braydon laughed. "She sure does. Remember that time we colored the ends of her hair with chalk in Mrs. Rose's class?"

Brendon smiled. "Oh shit. I remember that. She didn't talk to us for the rest of the year."

"Y'all are lucky any girl talks to you anymore. The ones you haven't fucked, you've tormented in some way."

"They keep coming back for more." Brendon laughed. "They come *begging* for more."

Kaleb knew the twins were popular with the women, always had been. He also knew they were as promiscuous as they came. And yes, the women flocked to them, even knowing they would only sleep with them if the two of them were there at the same time.

"How's Zoey?" Braydon asked, looking serious all of a sudden.

What the hell? Didn't they just go through this? Kaleb cocked his head, trying to figure out what his brother might be referring to. "She's fine."

"Yeah?" Brendon asked, glancing over at Braydon and then back to Kaleb.

"What the hell are you not telling me?" Kaleb asked, suddenly getting irritated.

"Nothing, bro."

"Bullshit. What the fuck is going on?"

"I just happen to know that Jason Tribbons is back in town." Braydon informed him, and the hair on the back of Kaleb's neck stood up. He didn't know Jason Tribbons, nor did he care to know the man. If what Braydon said was true, Kaleb wanted to beat the living shit out of him just for the hell of it.

"Does she know?" Kaleb asked, glancing between the twins. It was uncanny how fucking similar they looked. Most people couldn't tell them apart, which they happened to find amusing.

"Not sure."

"What do you mean you're not sure? Does she or doesn't she?"

"What the hell does it matter, Bubba?" Braydon asked. "Are you worried? Jealous, maybe?"

"Hell no." He wasn't jealous. He just didn't want the bastard anywhere near Zoey. "But you two should be worried. If Zoey ever finds out the two of you ran her husband out of town, forcing him to divorce her, she'll have your hide."

The telltale gasp had every single one of them stilling.

Fuck.

As though they were all being pulled by a single string, the four of them turned toward the back door to see Zoey standing there, complete and total shock on her beautiful face.

"You did what?" They barely heard her devastated whisper, but they all knew she had spoken.

"Hey, Zoey." Leave it to Braydon to pretend nothing had happened. He sauntered over to Zoey, throwing his arm around her like the woman wasn't shooting daggers out of her eyeballs. At six feet five inches, Braydon was significantly taller than Zoey, but the look in his eyes as he glared back at Kaleb said he was terrified of the woman.

He should be.

"What do you mean they ran my ex out of town?" Zoey asked again, her voice much stronger.

Brendon looked at the floor, and Zane looked at the wall. He probably didn't know any of what was going on, but he was smart enough not to chime in.

Braydon pulled his arm from around her shoulders and took a step back, instinctively covering his junk. The woman could be vicious when she wanted to and they'd all seen it a time or two. Sweet and innocent, Zoey definitely was. But what Kaleb had learned about her in recent weeks made that sweetness seem like a thing of the past.

"Why?" Zoey asked, turning to face Braydon.

Kaleb held his breath, unsure what to say, if anything, and waiting anxiously for Braydon to speak.

"You heard me." There was more conviction in Braydon's tone. "We ran the bastard out of town, Zoey."

"You forced him to divorce me?"

"Well, if you mean did we hold a gun to his head, no, we did not. We were doing you a favor."

"*A favor?*" The incredulity in her tone was evident. "You think forcing my husband to divorce me was doing me a favor?"

"I do, actually." Braydon stated even more firmly, moving closer to Zoey.

Kaleb's natural protective instinct kicked in, and he stood from his seat. Normally the instinct kicked in when his brother's needed backup, but this time, it was all about Zoey.

"And how could you ruining my life possibly be a favor to me?"

"Me?" Shocked, Braydon laughed. "Honey, that bastard had a baby on the way, and you want to tell me that I'm the one who ruined your life?"

"A..." Zoey staggered, and both Braydon and Kaleb reached out to catch her. Thankfully Kaleb reached her first. Pulling her against him, he tried to turn her in his arms, but she pushed him away. Hard.

"Get away from me." Zoey stormed out of the office, leaving Braydon, Brendon, Kaleb and Zane staring at one another.

"What the fuck?" Zane asked, looking more than a little surprised. "He got some chick pregnant while he was married to Zoey?"

"Yeah." Brendon said sounding defeated.

"Let me at the bastard." Zane pushed to his feet while the others just stood there, mirroring their brother's sentiment.

♀♂

A baby?

Jason got some girl pregnant while they were married? How the hell did she not know about it?

Zoey tried to focus on the road, but she had a hard time with tears streaming down her face. Oh, they weren't sad tears because she'd gotten over the bastard years ago. No, these were tears of rage, and once she got her hands on him, he was going to be crying too.

Figuring there was no way she could go home and be alone at the moment, she headed into town. In desperate need of a drink, she set her sights on Moonshiner's.

How in the world had Brendon and Braydon known about this pregnancy and she hadn't? And why the hell didn't Jason just tell her?

Well, that question was probably a little easier to answer.

Zoey had never been good with her temper when pushed. The man probably figured it was in his best interest. Or his balls best interest. Either way.

Forcing back the tears, Zoey scrubbed her face with her hands before heading inside. She couldn't help but wonder how many people knew about this and kept it from her. Hell, she'd heard it straight from Kaleb's mouth, so obviously he knew. And he'd sat back all these years and let her look like a complete idiot.

The damn tears threatened to spill once more, and Zoey ground her teeth together, hoping the pain would ease some of her frustration. Without looking around, Zoey went straight to the bar and ordered a vodka and 7-Up, telling the bartender to go light on the 7-Up.

She had just settled onto her barstool, drink in hand when she heard an all too familiar laugh from somewhere behind her.

No, no, no. This could not be happening.

Turning around slowly, Zoey's eyes grazed the room, sliding over each face until the object of all of her current anger appeared before her. Sitting not twenty feet away, Jason was talking with a woman, one Zoey didn't recognize from this angle, as well as a couple of guys she didn't know, but recognized from town. Not only was Jason apparently having a good time, he didn't even seem to realize that his ex-wife – wait, make that *oblivious ex-wife* – was sitting behind him.

How was it possible that he got some woman pregnant and was run out of town without her knowing about it? Oblivious was an understatement. More importantly, how could he have done that to her?

Granted, she wasn't as blind as she allowed people to think back then. Of course she was aware Jason was stepping out on her, but to what extent, she didn't know. He'd been fond of the bars back then, and when she refused to go out all the time, he wound up going alone. Or so she thought.

Without thinking, Zoey launched up from her seat and stomped across the room, hell bent on... hell, she didn't know, but she was geared up for a confrontation at the very least.

"Damn it, Gage." Zoey exclaimed when Gage stepped directly into her path, successfully stopping her

"Hey." He greeted, tipping her chin up at him when she didn't bother to look. "Where're you headed?"

"Don't tell me you know, too."

"Know what?" Gage asked, looking sincerely confused.

"Never mind." Figuring there was no reason to shout it to the world, Zoey took a deep breath but didn't move. She'd much prefer Gage to get out of the way so she could continue with what she was doing. Surely by the time she reached Jason, she'd come up with a plan.

"Have a drink with me?" Gage asked, easily turning her – physically – and ushering her back toward the bar.

Definitely not the plan.

Once she was reluctantly seated on her barstool yet again, Zoey quickly downed half of her drink, doing her best to ignore both Gage and the bastard still laughing from across the room.

"Where's Kaleb?" Gage asked.

"Who cares." She didn't care to see Kaleb – not right then, and maybe not ever. How could he have kept this a secret from her? Glancing around the room, she suddenly wondered whether there were other people who knew what happened. How many more people had kept this from her and were whispering behind her back?

"Care to talk about it?"

Jerking her attention back to Gage, Zoey let her eyes linger on his face for a brief moment before glancing down at the nearly empty glass in front of her. With a quick flick of her wrist, she made it definitely empty and then shook her head to answer Gage.

No, she didn't want to talk about it. What was she going to say? Her current romantic fling – also known as her former best friend – had known about her ex-husband cheating on her and getting some girl pregnant. To top it off, he'd never told her.

God, she must look like an idiot.

Turning to look behind her again, Zoey noticed the blond woman beside Jason turning... Tiffany Folsom, seriously? Was Tiffany the woman Jason got pregnant and ran away with? Or was she just another of his conquests?

"Ok, then don't talk." Gage grinned, glancing down at his phone.

"Who're you texting?"

"No one." He was obviously lying because his fingers were still flying over the keyboard on the phone.

"Bullshit. You're texting Kaleb. Well, you can tell him to go take a flying leap for all I care."

Another booming laugh sounded from behind Zoey, and she wanted to scream. Right after she punched something. Realizing her glass was still empty Zoey motioned for the bartender who acknowledged her with a subtle head nod.

"So, does your attitude have anything to do with the jackass sitting across the room?"

"How'd you guess?" Zoey bit out.

"I'm lucky like that." Gage laughed. "So, what'd Kaleb do to piss you off? Seems to me like you have more than enough to be mad at right here in the room."

"Did you know that the twins ran him out of town?" Zoey asked, figuring she might as well ask.

"Who? Kaleb?"

"No." With her frustration levels reaching critical mass, she took a deep breath and exhaled slowly. "Not Kaleb. Jason."

"Out of town? What do you mean?"

Shit. The question in Gage's pretty brown eyes told her that he had no idea what she was talking about.

"Speak of the devil." Gage grinned, looking toward the door.

What the hell? All seven of the Walker brothers filed in, turning damn near every head in the room, including Zoey's. She had to admit, watching Kaleb, Braydon, Brendon, Zane, Ethan and Sawyer walking in, all big, strapping and so damn good looking... it nearly hurt to look at them. Pulling up the rear, none other than the eldest of them all, looking like a total badass with his black Stetson pulled low over those gleaming blue eyes.

Good Lord.

When the bartender set the drink in front of Zoey, Gage handed over money to cover it, and she quickly downed it, not tasting a thing but feeling the burn as her sinuses caught fire. *Damn it.*

She wasn't about to give any of them the satisfaction of letting them know what they had the power to do to any female within a fifteen mile radius, so she pretended she hadn't seen them by turning to face the bar, her hands clasped tightly around her now empty glass.

She was both surprised and a little irritated when Kaleb came to stand directly behind her, successfully boxing her in so that she didn't have an escape route, even if she wanted one. That insanely delicious scent of him overwhelmed her senses and nearly made her eyes cross. When the warmth of his breath teased her ear, a body wracking shiver ran down her spine. When the hell was her body going to get onboard? She was mad at him, dammit, so now was not the time to get all hot and bothered by his nearness.

"I had no idea, I swear. Not until a couple of weeks ago." Kaleb whispered before planting a kiss on her cheek. "If I had known, I would've told you, Zoey. You know that."

Ok, so maybe she did know that. But it was easier to be mad at him. It was easier to be mad at all men at the moment. Especially the cheating bastard laughing it up like a fucking hyena across the room.

When Kaleb went motionless, his hands tightening on her shoulders, Zoey realized he just figured out that Jason was there.

"Well, I'll be damned." Braydon's deep baritone reverberated through the bar, causing the gentle rumble of voices to go eerily silent. When Zoey turned in her chair, she realized all of the Walker brothers, as well as Gage, were standing directly behind her, but they weren't looking at her. Instead, their attention was focused on the two people directly responsible for Zoey's now pissed off mood.

The only consolation – Jason wasn't smiling anymore.

"If it isn't the lying, cheating bastard in the flesh."
Brendon added, apparently looking to start shit as he took a
menacing step forward, his big, powerful body prepared to pounce.

Aside from the one step Brendon took, no one else was
moving closer to Jason, although the fear that flashed across his
too handsome face said otherwise.

"Oh, and if it isn't Tiffany Folsom." Braydon tacked on,
smiling, but looking none too happy. "I have to say, I'm surprised
he kept you around this long."

And that's what started it all.

Chapter Nineteen

"It's Tiffany Tribbons, thank you very much." Her nasally, whiny voice penetrated the air and made Brendon and Braydon chuckle, though Kaleb wasn't sure what the hell was funny. "And we're still together because he only kicks the trash to the curb."

Zoey flew out of her chair, although Kaleb easily pulled her back, holding her firmly in place. Kaleb knew that all hell was about to break loose and should Jason Tribbons get any bright ideas about throwing insults, he wasn't so sure any of them would be able to hold back. That was the one thing about the brothers – they were a protective bunch, and every one of them had grown protective of Zoey over the years.

"Well, that's funny." Brendon said, taking a step closer to their table, Sawyer right by his side, probably to hold him back if necessary. "From what I remember, Jason tucked his tail between his legs and ran out of town *with* the trash. Ain't that right, Jason?"

When Jason didn't say anything, not even attempting to defend the woman who had declared herself to be his wife, clearly the mother of his child, it was obvious where this was going to lead.

"Oh, and look." Tiffany said in a fake sweet voice, "little Zoey Stranford is hooking up with a Walker. Or are you hooking up with *all* of them these days?"

"If you've got the cream of the crop," Zoey offered, not moving from her position in front of Kaleb, "what does it matter who I'm with?"

"Oh, honey, Jason was smart enough to leave your ass long ago. He told me what a bore you were in bed."

Zoey smiled, and Kaleb knew there was a storm brewing. With a nod of his head, Kaleb acknowledged Jason before speaking. "You might want to take her home."

"Fuck you, Kaleb Walker." Tiffany screamed. "I can go anywhere and do anything I want."

Zoey glanced up at Kaleb and grinned. "It's true. She can. She's particularly fond of doing married men."

Apparently Tiffany took offense to that statement because she came around the table, walking right up to Zoey. Kaleb didn't budge and neither did Zoey. Had he not been leaning against her back, he wouldn't have known she was gearing up for a fight. But he knew her well. She wasn't about to throw the first punch, but she damn sure wasn't going to take any shit off of anyone.

"Why don't you take your sweet self back home, lie down like a comatose woman and let them have their wicked way with you? I hear you're good at that."

"Yeah? That's what I'm good at, huh?" Zoey laughed without mirth. "Ever think that maybe I just didn't know he was there and that's why I didn't move?"

That statement garnered a round of laughter from the other patrons in the bar, but still, Jason didn't move. Tiffany, on the other hand, looked pissed. At least one of them was going to stand up for the other. Obviously Jason wasn't interested in defending his wife because he was still seated, nursing a beer and trying to pretend the whole thing wasn't happening.

"Honey, he's the best I've ever had." Tiffany glared at Zoey.

Once again Zoey glanced up at Kaleb then back at Tiffany. "Well, that's saying something. Considering you've had half the town."

Another round of laughter.

The instant Tiffany reached for Zoey, Kaleb intervened, stepping in front of her and successfully blocking the hand that would have bitch slapped her. Thankfully Gage was right there, holding Zoey back because the woman had just come unhinged.

"Tribbons." This time Travis spoke up, and when he did the entire bar got quiet. They all knew Travis generally didn't intervene, and he wasn't much on talking either, so when he did, people tended to listen. "Take her home. And don't bring her back here tonight."

Kaleb watched as Jason stood, glancing around as though one of them were going to jump him at any minute. It wasn't until he was at the door, the rest of them watching them walk away that it happened.

Out of nowhere, Jake – Anderson Croft's friend that Zane had had words with previously – pounced on Zane's back, effectively tackling him to the floor. Unfortunately for Jake, he wasn't fast enough because Zane went down, but not entirely. Before anyone knew what happened, Zane was on him, and Sawyer and Travis were trying to pull him off. Then three more joined the melee and a free for all broke loose.

Grabbing Zoey by the hand, Kaleb dragged her through the short, narrow hallway that led to the back door. Six of his brother's together was more than enough to handle the brawl and Kaleb wouldn't put it past Tiffany to do a sneak attack while they were all preoccupied, so getting Zoey out of the fray seemed the most logical option.

He didn't let her pull away when she would have tried; instead, he led her to his truck, ignoring her verbal and physical protests. "Just get in."

Obviously irritated, Zoey glared up at him, but she stopped arguing. With a dramatic huff, she finally did as he instructed, climbing in through the driver's door and crawling across the seat.

"Middle." He told her when she would have moved over to the passenger side of the truck. Call him crazy, but Kaleb wanted to keep her close.

Another deep exhale, then Zoey finally settled into the seat, making a gigantic deal out of buckling her seat belt. Kaleb smiled to himself before starting the truck.

"Where are we going?" She asked as he pulled out of the parking lot.

"For a drive." Instead of going back toward his house, he took off on one of the back roads. Zoey needed some time to cool off, and Kaleb wasn't interested in fighting with her anymore tonight. And he had just the thing to take her mind off of what just happened.

♀♂

"Just take me home." Zoey was still angry, but she was calming down some. She truly didn't want to go home, not particularly interested in spending time alone, but she wasn't prepared to give in to Kaleb's high handedness.

Yet she had a difficult time putting any effort in to arguing with him. Maybe it was the distinct scent of Kaleb that overwhelmed her senses, or the fact that she didn't have to look at Jason's face anymore. Or his wife.

Ugghh. The thought still pissed her off. She was so worked up after that little bitch Tiffany mouthed off, she couldn't even speak.

"Why are you fidgeting?" Kaleb asked as they drove down the back road. Zoey recognized where they were going because it was one of the secluded spots they had frequented as teenagers. Just outside of their small town, the abandoned barn had definitely seen better days, but even after all of the partying they'd done there over the years, it was still standing.

"I'm not fidgeting." She lied, stilling her hands as she said the words.

"Baby, if you need something to do with your hands, I've got a suggestion."

Zoey's entire body stilled with that comment as a burst of adrenaline laced passion shot through her bloodstream, making her pussy clench and a chill run across her skin. She squeezed her hands together, ignoring the urge to reach over and touch him. It was tempting, so very tempting.

"Touch me, Zoey." Kaleb insisted, his eyes never leaving the road. When she didn't move, he reached over and took her hand, placing it along the hard ridge of his erection. "Feel what you do to me."

Zoey's mouth hung open at his audacity, but she didn't move her hand. Testing him, she began brushing her hand back and forth along the steely length of him.

"Take my cock out, baby. I want you to stroke me." Kaleb glanced over at her, the intention in those penetrating blue eyes evident. "Now, Zoey."

Zoey gave in sooner than she expected, turning slightly so she could use both hands to free him from the denim confines before using her left hand to stroke him slowly. She wasn't in a hurry and sitting at this angle, she could watch the muscles in his jaw as they tensed.

"Awww, fuck, baby." Kaleb growled, and the vibrations were like a lightning bolt straight to her clit.

Maybe it was because of Tiffany's insults, or the thought that Jason had actually shared some of their most intimate moments in such a nasty way, but Zoey needed Kaleb's encouragement. Even if she didn't believe the cruel words Tiffany said, Zoey's ego had taken a direct hit nonetheless.

"That's it." Kaleb whispered harshly, using one hand to guide her along the velvet covered the length of him. "Your hand feels so good on me."

His groan filled the truck and had her squirming in her seat. Was she actually stroking his cock while they were driving down the road? Kaleb was still paying attention to the road, but his sporadic groans confirmed that she was doing something right.

"Slow." He demanded. "Don't rush it, Zoey. I'm not ready to come yet."

Zoey slowed her movements, paying attention to the soft, smooth shaft beneath her fingers, and the way Kaleb squeezed her hand tightly, still stroking, but now painfully slow. Zoey had the sudden urge to make him lose control.

A few minutes passed before Kaleb steered the truck down the bumpy, dirt path that led to the old, abandoned barn. When he pulled the truck behind it, he turned the headlights off. The interior of the truck was lit by the blue lights in the dash, enough that Zoey could see what they were doing.

"Take off your jeans." Kaleb unhooked both of their seatbelts and then maneuvered to the middle seat, forcing Zoey to move over to the passenger side. The sudden need to be filled by him, to hold him close and feel him buried deep inside was so overwhelming, she was frantically working to remove one boot and her jeans.

"Come here." Kaleb's words were terse, urgent with his own need as he pushed his own jeans down past his hips.

As soon as she had her jeans down, she threw her leg over his, straddling his hips.

"Lift your leg."

Kaleb helped lift her right leg as he guided his cock between them, sliding the wide head through her slick folds. There was no foreplay, no teasing, just a quick, hard thrust of his hips that resulted in him being buried to the hilt inside of her.

"Don't move." He warned, but Zoey was on the edge already, her body working to accommodate his cock as he pushed deeper.

"Kaleb." Zoey needed more of him.

When he pulled her body against his, crushing his mouth to hers, the events of the last few minutes disappeared, and the only thing left was the intensity of her feelings for this man.

"Damn, baby, you're so fucking tight." Kaleb groaned, his mouth still pressed to hers. "I could stay just like this forever."

Forever. Zoey liked the idea of that, but right now, her body had other ideas. She began to move, riding him slowly, taking him as deep as possible before reversing.

"I'm not going to last, baby. I'm warning you now."

Zoey liked the confident way he spoke and the way he lifted her hips, holding her still as he began to thrust upward, controlling her movements.

"Fuck." A brief pause, followed by a tortured groan before Kaleb spoke again, "I'm going to fuck you hard and fast."

"Fuck me, Kaleb." Zoey locked her eyes with his, her hands lacing into his hair as he began to move inside of her. The tight space didn't allow for much movement by either of them, but Kaleb began pushing up as Zoey began pressing down, their bodies rocking, thrusting.

"Oh, God!" Zoey threw her head back, her orgasm surprising her with its intensity, blasting through her with a devastating rush.

"That's it, Zoey. Come for me."

As she came, Kaleb did too, their bodies molded together, their mouths fusing as one, neither of them letting go.

A few minutes passed before either of them moved. With her head resting on his shoulder, Kaleb ran his fingers through her hair and Zoey soaked up the feel of him. The sweet scent of sex permeated the cab of the truck, but she was too content to move, too relaxed to let go of him. If only they could stay just like that forever.

There was that word again.

♂♀

Kaleb sensed the moment Zoey started thinking too much. His cock was still deep inside of her, and yes, he was getting hard again. Just the feel of her tight, warm body wrapped around him was enough to get him geared up for round two. Unfortunately, one round in the truck was enough for him. Now he wanted to get her back to his place where he could take it slower next time.

It wasn't that he didn't want to take her as many ways as possible right there in his truck, it was that he wanted more from her than just a quick fuck – although they'd already done just that. For the life of him, Kaleb couldn't understand it, but he wanted even more from her. He wanted her ultimate pleasure and the cab of his truck wasn't the best place for that.

What had spurred him to take her like this, he had no idea, but he'd been so worked up, he couldn't resist. Seeing that she had been onboard, he hadn't been able to resist.

It didn't take them long to get dressed and resituate themselves, nor did it take long to drive back to his house. For some reason, Kaleb was in a hurry. He could feel Zoey pulling away from him, and he didn't know if it was what they had just done – though the doubted it – or whether she was still upset over what happened earlier.

Instead of asking, he simply linked his fingers with hers as he drove back to his house, giving her a few minutes of silence.

As he pulled down the drive to his house, he glanced over to see Zoey leaning her head back with her eyes closed. Damn the woman was beautiful. Her long blond hair was disheveled from the impromptu quickie, but she looked a little calmer than she had before.

On the inside, he figured that wasn't the case. Having known her for so long, Kaleb still couldn't believe this Zoey. The one who welcomed whatever he suggested, even coming up with some crazy, spontaneous ideas of her own. It only went to prove that he'd assumed she was sweet and innocent when it came to sex games because she wasn't the promiscuous type.

That's where he'd gone wrong. First of all, he never should have assumed anything, and secondly, Zoey had obviously never had the outlet that she needed. Or at least that's what he gathered. Considering the trash talk coming from Tiffany's mouth, Jason hadn't been happy with Zoey, but that was most likely because she'd never been satisfied.

He couldn't have pulled up to his house, but for a second before Zoey was itching to get out, quickly launching herself out through the passenger side door.

Once inside the house, Kaleb locked the front door, not wanting any uninvited guests tonight. Staring at Zoey, he noticed the sudden exhaustion that creased her pretty features.

"Hot tub." Kaleb said before even thinking about it.

"What?" Zoey asked, looking shocked for a second.

"Let's get in the hot tub."

"But..."

Kaleb didn't let her finish before he took her hand and led her through the house to the back door. Once out on the back deck, he lifted the cover from the tub and then removed it altogether. Messing with the controls for a minute, Kaleb got the lights and the bubbles going and notched up the heat a couple of degrees.

Then while Zoey stood there, apparently waiting for instructions, Kaleb returned to the house and flipped off the outside lights. Not that anyone could see them since the house was surrounded by thick trees on all sides, but he'd rather not take his chances.

Returning to Zoey's side, Kaleb turned her to face him before leaning down and brushing his mouth against hers. He let himself get lost in her kiss, pulling her closer when she kissed him back, their tongues dueling while their hands began to wander. His body immediately reached a fever pitch, as though he hadn't just had her a short time ago.

"I want you naked." He groaned into the kiss, lifting her t-shirt until he easily pulled it over her head. He didn't pull away from her for long, only breaking the kiss long enough to remove his shirt, as well.

They continued to grope one another as they took turns removing the other's clothes until they were both fully naked, neither of them speaking with words, but their eyes told a story all on their own. Unwilling to take his lips from hers, Kaleb lifted her up and over the side before lowering her in the water and climbing in after her.

"Come here." Kaleb insisted as he got situated in one of the lounge chairs, leaning back, his body fully submerged in the water. He pulled Zoey onto his lap so that she was straddling him and then once again latched his mouth to hers.

Feeling her breasts against his chest, her stomach against his, and the sweet juncture between her legs resting above his dick, Kaleb allowed himself to relax.

Running his fingers through her hair, he pulled her head back and stared down in her eyes. He wanted to tell her exactly what she made him feel, but he knew he couldn't. Not yet. Although the timing couldn't have been better, Kaleb knew he had to hold out.

Even after everything that had taken place that day, he had to ensure Zoey trusted him implicitly. Considering he gave her another reason not to, letting on that he knew something about her ex that she didn't, Kaleb felt as though he needed to prove it to her.

"I want to make love to you, Zoey." He whispered, still gazing into the warm, blue depths of her eyes. "I want to feel you."

He didn't have to do anything more because Zoey positioned herself, using one hand to guide his cock before lowering her hips and seating him fully inside of her.

He groaned.

She groaned.

And then there was friction as he began lifting her hips, grinding his cock in her wet heat as they once again melded their mouths together. He didn't let her go, holding her head so she wouldn't get away because having her this close had become an obsession with him.

He might get pleasure from the threesomes, and he knew Zoey did too, but they paled in comparison to this. Two bodies, two souls, two hearts, coming together as one. And that's how Kaleb felt when he was with Zoey.

For him, there was no better place to be.

♀♂

Zoey was holding onto Kaleb for dear life.

Swiping her tongue over his, she got lost in the taste of him, the warmth of his body pressed against hers and the incredible feeling of him filling her. This was different from before. They were coming together as one, in more ways than just their bodies. It wasn't much different from in the truck, yet more intimate in so many ways.

Part of her was scared to give in to him, but the other part knew she already had. Zoey had fallen for this man. Her best friend. Her lover. She'd gone and given her heart to Kaleb Walker, and he didn't even know it.

And she couldn't tell him because she didn't want their feelings to influence the outcome of what they both had to do. She still had to make a decision on the land, and she needed to know that whatever she chose to do, Kaleb would support her.

But right now, here in the darkness, Kaleb making love to her was what she needed, and she wanted to hold on to that for a little while. Hold on to him.

"You feel so good." Kaleb whispered softly in her ear.

Zoey couldn't remember ever having felt the way Kaleb made her feel. Never once in the five years of her marriage had Jason ever made her feel like she was the only one that mattered. Yet Kaleb did.

"Kaleb, please." She wasn't sure what she was pleading for, but she needed more. More of him, more of this. Anything to secure this feeling in her memory so she could always hold on to it.

"Anything, Zoey." He responded, holding her hips and thrusting into her. "Anything at all."

The water dispersed around them with every forceful movement, but Zoey didn't care. "I need you, Kaleb."

"I'm right here, baby. Always here."

Zoey felt her release building, the sharp sudden tingling in her womb, her muscles fighting for control, needing to hold on so she didn't shatter into a million pieces.

"Come for me, Zoey." Kaleb told her, and Zoey laced her fingers in his hair, crushed her mouth to his and clamped her internal muscles on his steel hard erection buried deep inside of her.

And then she let herself go.

Chapter Twenty

♀♂

"Morning." Zoey greeted Vanessa two days later. It was bright and early, and they had to meet up at the Wilson's once again, so Zoey was surprised to see V at her house.

"I'm so happy you didn't preface that with a *good*." V replied, barely smiling.

Zoey knew something was wrong with V, she'd known for a while, ever since that afternoon at Anderson's cleanup. After what happened between Jake and Zane, V hadn't been the same. Whether it was the nasty comments Jake made, or whether it was Zane's reaction, Zoey wasn't so sure. She had a feeling it was a little of both.

V wasn't used to someone standing up for her. That's not what her childhood had been about, and although they had a large group of friends, including the Walker brothers, V had never actually allowed anyone to get close. With the exception of Zoey. In recent days, V had been pulling away, keeping herself at a distance from everyone.

"Still pissy, I see." Zoey retorted as she poured a mug of coffee for V.

"Maybe."

There was no maybe about it. Zoey knew V, and she knew something was going on. She just hadn't been able to get her friend to open up to her, until now.

"Here." Zoey thrust the mug toward her friend as she grabbed her truck keys off the counter. "Let's go get this over with."

On the drive over to the Wilson's, V didn't say a word and the silence was beginning to wear on Zoey's last nerve. She had her own issues to deal with. Namely deciding what to do with the land and she really wanted her friend's input.

"Tell me what's going on." Zoey insisted, glancing over at V then back at the road. "Is this about Zane?"

Regardless what V said, Zoey knew it was. The two of them must have gotten pretty hot and heavy, pretty damn quickly which never did work out in anyone's favor.

"Hell no." V said. "Ok, yes. Why the hell did he have to go and defend me like that? I'm sure as soon as I left, everyone was talking about poor, little Vanessa, her mother's such a whore."

"Actually, that's not what anyone was saying." Zoey said, feeling a little defensive. "Nor was it what they were thinking." Pulling into the Wilson's driveway, Zoey didn't move to get out; instead, she turned toward her friend. "Zane obviously cares about you. Wait, let me finish." Zoey held out a hand, stopping V's rebuttal. "Regardless of what's going on between the two of you, Zane is still your friend. We all are. And we care about you, V."

Vanessa didn't look at her.

"You can find whatever faults you want to in Zane, but he wasn't wrong in this." Zoey lowered her voice.

"I heard about what happened at Moonshiner's." V changed the subject, and effectively had Zoey exiting the truck. She didn't want to relive that night.

"I can't believe Jason got Tiffany pregnant and the twins ran them out of town."

Zoey turned to look at V. Could her friend actually not have known? The same as Kaleb? She found it hard to believe neither of her best friends knew what Jason had done. "Are you telling me you didn't know about this?"

"None, whatsoever." V said, sounding a little angry. "Do you actually believe if I had known that I wouldn't have told you? God, Zoey!" V grabbed her bucket from the back of the truck. "Way to show how much you trust me."

Zoey grabbed her bucket and took off after V. It was harder to keep up because V had much longer legs and walked fast. Especially when she was mad.

"Wait. V. Stop." Zoey called out to her, feeling like a total ass yet again. "I do trust you. I just find it hard to believe that the whole town didn't know."

"Well, we didn't. Apparently Braydon and Brendon care about you more than you think. From what I heard, they were all over Jason, forcing him to take his lying, cheating ass out of town as fast as his scrawny legs could carry him."

Zoey laughed. Jason was a little scrawny, now that she thought about it. But, that was probably because she was comparing him to Kaleb. Something she found herself doing to every man she knew. No one compared to him.

"I'm sorry, V. I didn't mean it like that." Zoey knew deep in her heart that V and Kaleb would've been the first to tell her had they known.

V looked back at Zoey, a wicked grin on her face. "I forgive you, but that means you have to clean all of the toilets."

Two hours later, Zoey and V were finally returning to the truck, both of them exhausted.

"I swear I'm never having kids." V exhaled on a sigh as she climbed into the truck. "If there is any chance my house will look like that every week, you can forget about it."

Zoey laughed. She agreed whole heartedly; however, she wasn't so sure about the not having kids part. Admittedly, she'd considered the possibility with Kaleb. In recent days, she'd considered a million possibilities with Kaleb, none of which she thought would actually come true, but she could still dream.

"Hey, V," Zoey began as they were backing out of the driveway, "what do you think about the resort the Walker's want to build?"

"I don't know much about it, except what Zane told me, but I think it sounds kinda cool."

"Do you realize it's not a normal resort?" That was probably the one thing Zoey was having a hard time wrapping her mind around. It was a sex club, plain and simple, yet no one had come out and said so.

"Normal? Define normal?"

"Don't get me wrong." Zoey stated. "I've seen the plans, and the place is going to be amazing. They'll have shopping, restaurants, and even a spa. Hell, you could practically live there and never need to go anywhere else."

"A spa?" Leave it to V to pick up on that one thing.

"And two clubs."

"Two? As in dance clubs?"

"Not exactly." Not that Zoey knew the specifics. From what she had seen on the design, there would certainly be dancing, but the dancers would be on poles. And naked.

"Ok, spill it, woman. What kind of clubs are we talking about here?" V asked, turning in her seat to face Zoey. "*Oh!*"

"Oh is right." It never did take V long to catch on.

"Sex clubs? Like BDSM and shit?" V sounded even more curious now.

"Well, I don't know about all that. I don't think any of the Walker boys are into BDSM, but maybe.

"Travis told me that it'll be by invitation only, and they're looking to keep their guest list secure to protect their privacy. They've hired some security firm out of Dallas, and there are a couple of investors who have already agreed to back them."

"Holy shit."

Zoey glanced over and noticed the seductive smile tipping V's full lips. "What? What are you thinking?"

"I'm wondering if I can be an exclusive member, of course."

"Seriously?" Zoey had never thought of it that way.

"Hell yeah. If I had the money, I'd invest."

Hmmm... That got Zoey to thinking. Invest? Really? Now that could be a logical answer to her problems. Maybe she didn't have to sell the land to the Walker's. Maybe she could just lease it to them. It was definitely a thought.

"Two clubs? Exclusive members? Sex? I like it, Zoey."

V's last comment swirled through Zoey's mind. Maybe she had been going about this the wrong way.

Chapter Twenty One

♂♀

Kaleb couldn't stop pacing the office floor, and he knew he was getting on Travis' last nerve, but he didn't give a shit. Today was the day. Zoey had asked them to meet her at her house at four o'clock, and it was only two. He didn't know if he was going to survive the wait much longer.

It wasn't that he was anxiously awaiting her final decision, although he was, but more importantly, he knew that as soon as this was over – no matter the outcome – he'd have the opportunity to talk to Zoey alone.

Since Gage was leaving town first thing in the morning, Zoey and Kaleb agreed the night before to meet up with him later tonight. It had been Zoey's idea and quite frankly, Kaleb was beginning to wonder about his sweet, innocent little lover. She was out of control. *Way* out of control.

He loved it.

But that was because he loved her.

Yes, he'd finally come to terms about how he felt about her, and now the only thing left to do was to tell her. Show her. Granted, he'd have to wait until later, especially if Gage was going to be at the house, but it was only a matter of time now.

"Would you sit your ass down?" Travis barked, shaking Kaleb from his thoughts.

Kaleb didn't apologize, but he did make his way to his desk, pulling up his email. As he sorted through the junk mail, he tried to get his mind off of Zoey and back on work. Where it should've been.

"The McCoy's want to meet with us." Travis said, finally giving Kaleb something else to think about.

"When?" Kaleb hadn't met Luke and Logan McCoy, although he had had several conversations with Alex McDermott, the owner of CISS – Corporate Investigative Security Services – as well as his partner Dylan Thomas and one of their employees, Cole Ackerley.

Since Travis had sought out CISS for their security, wanting the best for the resort, they'd all become acquainted over the last few months. And he'd heard about Luke and Logan, mainly from Travis, but he had yet to meet them.

"Tomorrow night." Travis confirmed. "I told them we'd have an answer for them today, and we'd meet for dinner to discuss the next steps."

Kaleb knew that regardless of Zoey's decision, there would be next steps. Travis, Sawyer, and Kaleb were all invested in this resort, and if they had to change the layout because of the land, then so be it.

"Dinner?"

"Yeah. We'll meet at the steakhouse in Austin. Their treat, they said. And they're bringing their significant others."

Kaleb glanced at Travis, wondering why he didn't say wives.

"It's an interesting situation, let's put it that way." Travis smirked.

"Interesting how?"

"Logan is married, but Luke is in a three way relationship."

"Three way? Like as in two women?" Kaleb tried to picture it in his mind.

"No. He's in a relationship with a man and a woman. Cole Ackerley is Luke's lover."

"Ahhh. Well, that makes sense." It didn't actually, but to each his own and all that. Kaleb didn't care whom they were with, just as long as they could help to get this resort off the ground. Knowing the plans Travis had come up with, the type of clientele they would be after would likely make a three way relationship look tame.

"So, dinner tomorrow night. Bring Zoey if you want." Travis said, and Kaleb made a mental note to talk to her about it.

Two hours later, Kaleb was pulling up to Zoey's house, both Sawyer and Travis following behind him in their own vehicles. Since Kaleb wasn't planning to run out as soon as the meeting was over, they'd all decided to drive separately.

He had to admit he was a little nervous about this meeting. Since he had left her house that morning, Kaleb hadn't spoken to Zoey, except for a couple of texts during the day. She said she'd been busy getting ready and Kaleb couldn't imagine what the woman was up to. With Zoey, he wouldn't put anything past her.

The thought made him smile.

When he approached the door, he rapped his knuckles on the wooden screen before opening it and walking in. There before him was the sexiest thing he'd seen in his life.

Zoey was wearing a tight blue jean skirt, short enough to make his eyes wander and his dick to rise to the occasion. She had on an oversized cream colored sweater – nearly see thru, mind you – and a brown tank top beneath. She was also sporting her damn cowgirl boots, and he was half tempted to take her straight to her bedroom just to show her what he thought about the outfit.

"Damn, baby." He whistled as he approached. "I thought you wanted to have a meeting."

Grinning from ear to ear, Zoey met him in the living room, reached up and kissed him lightly on the lips before turning back to the kitchen. "Are Sawyer and Travis with you?"

"They're behind me. We took separate vehicles."

A knowing smile tipped her lips and made her blue eyes shine. God he loved that smile.

"Well, as soon as they get here, we'll get started. I've set everything up in the kitchen."

Set everything up? Kaleb glanced in the kitchen and noticed there were some papers on the table. What was she up to?

♀♂

Zoey was nervous as hell, and she'd had more than one pep talk with herself since that morning. Thankfully, she'd busied herself by running down to Austin so she could get a couple of things for the meeting. And now, the time had come for her presentation.

Never in her life had she given a presentation before, but after her conversation with Vanessa, she finally figured out a way to make this work for everyone. She only hoped the Walker's were receptive to her proposal.

"Hey, Zoe." Travis greeted when he walked through the door, followed closely by Sawyer.

"Hey. Thanks for coming." Ok, so now her nerves were making her a jumbled mess. This plan had seemed so easy in her mind, but with her tiny house filled with three of the Walker brothers, she was beginning to doubt herself.

"Let's go in the kitchen." Kaleb told his brother's, obviously picking up on her sudden dry mouth. She smiled at him in thanks.

She noticed the look Travis shot at Sawyer, but they didn't say anything as they made their way through the living room.

Once the three men were seated at the table, she swallowed hard, trying to scrounge up the courage to go through with this proposal. She'd run it by her father earlier that morning and had been pleasantly surprised by his support.

"Have you made a decision?" Travis asked, always the one to get right down to business.

"That depends." Zoey grinned. "I've actually come up with a proposal for you. One I think will benefit us all in the long run."

"A proposal?" Travis sounded skeptical, and the look he threw at Kaleb said so. When Kaleb just shrugged his shoulders and turned his attention back to her, Zoey continued.

"After giving this some serious thought, I'd be interested in letting you use my land."

"Use it? As in letting us purchase it?" Sawyer asked.

"Not exactly."

"What the fuck?" Travis exclaimed pushing up from his chair and startling Zoey with his outrage.

"Sit the fuck down and listen to her." Kaleb demanded.

Zoey jumped, jolted by Kaleb's adamant tone. She'd never seen Kaleb react like that. He was always the level headed one, never showing his anger in public.

Apparently Travis hadn't seen that side of his brother either because he lowered himself back to his chair, looking none too happy about her initial comment.

For the next half hour, Zoey went through her spiel, showing them – on paper – exactly what her proposal looked like. She informed them that she liked the idea of the resort, was more interested once she found out that it wouldn't be open to the general public which would help to keep their quaint little town off the map.

"So, you are willing to lease us the land for thirty years?" Sawyer asked, glancing between her and Travis.

"Yes. That's my proposal."

"Since we didn't actually plan to build on the land," Travis thought out loud, "it's not a bad idea."

"Why the lease?" Kaleb asked. "Why not sell it to us?"

"Honestly, if you're going to make money on this deal, I'd like to make money, too. As you probably know by now, I'm in debt with the land, and if I don't do something by the end of the week, the land will go into foreclosure, which will ultimately tie it up for who knows how long. That won't benefit either one of us at this point."

That was an understatement, but something she hoped would persuade Travis to consider her offer. If she didn't come up with the money by the end of the week, Zoey and her father were going to lose their home. At least this way, she would have the money necessary to get the loan current, and any residual income would ensure they didn't end up in this predicament in the future.

"I'll do you one better." Travis spoke up after a few painfully long minutes.

All three of them turned their attention on the eldest Walker.

"You sell us the land, and I'll pay off the rest of it, including your father's house."

Wow. She hadn't seen that one coming. It was a good offer, but it didn't secure her future. She wouldn't have to worry about losing the house, but she would ultimately be signing away her heritage for money.

"I've got a better idea." This from Kaleb. "Can I have a minute to talk to my brother's?"

Zoey didn't know what to make of Kaleb's request, but she decided to give them a moment to discuss whatever his plan was. "Five minutes. Then I'll be back, and we need to come to a decision." She had to remain firm, or these men would walk all over her, she feared.

Zoey walked outside and paced the gravel driveway, kicking rocks with the toes of her boots as she clenched and unclenched her hands. She had to admit, Travis' offer was more than she expected, and it meant she wouldn't have to have Kaleb's financial help as he had offered before. Not wanting to be in debt to any of them, she wondered if maybe this was the way to go.

Except her proposal was a good one. They would lease the land from her, and even Sawyer said it made sense. They weren't building on the one hundred acres, simply using it as the entrance, which after the lease expired if they decided to do something different, they could. And Zoey wouldn't be out her land.

Zoey glanced down at her watch and headed back in at the five minute mark. She needed to get this out of the way. There were things she and Kaleb needed to talk about. Since the proposal she intended to offer *him* was much more lucrative for her, she was anxious to get on with it.

Her heart tipped and rolled at the thought.

Chapter Twenty Two

♂♀

Kaleb smiled. Travis might not have liked the idea at first, but his brother had come around to it in the last couple of minutes. Hearing the screen door shut, Kaleb knew it was time to face the music.

"Did I give you enough time?" Zoey asked, looking directly at him.

He nodded his head and then glanced at Travis.

When Travis smiled, a genuine smile that none of them had seen in quite some time, Kaleb exhaled the breath he hadn't known he'd been holding.

"Just remember, my last offer is still on the table." Travis began. "But, I think Kaleb does have a better offer, and after listening, I think it would work for all of us."

"And that is?" Zoey looked impatient, and Kaleb knew the feeling. He wanted this conversation over with. For the last seven days, he'd contemplated the outcome of this meeting, but more so, he'd contemplated the outcome of the conversation they would have later that night.

"You sell us the land," Travis stated, holding up his hand to stop Zoey when she looked like she wanted to argue. "You sell the land to Walker, Inc., and in return, we make you a partner."

"A partner?" Zoey's eyes widened, and Kaleb bit his lip. He couldn't tell by her expression whether she knew what they were actually offering her or not.

"Yes. A full partner. Keep in mind, there are seven of us, but that would make you the eighth partner in Walker, Inc." Travis' smile disappeared. "Now, don't go getting ahead of yourself just yet. Being a partner requires a lot more on your part than simply selling us the land. In turn, we'd expect you to invest just as much into this company as we do. The resort won't run itself, and I have always intended for us to be right there on the front lines."

"A partner." Zoey whispered this time and Kaleb wanted to reach over and touch her, but he didn't. "What would I have to do?" She asked, looking only at Travis.

"You'd have to work." Travis laughed. "But don't worry; we won't have you cleaning the rooms, although I think that would be one of your responsibilities. You and V. Managing the housekeeping."

"Me and V?" Zoey appeared dumbfounded.

"She works for you now, doesn't she?" Sawyer asked. "It wouldn't be like you'd have any time to handle your cleaning service if you're busy trying to co-manage a resort."

Kaleb watched as realization dawned. Zoey knew what they were offering her and considering they'd never made an offer like this, it was monumental. A partner. A full partner in their *family owned* business.

"A partner?" Zoey asked again, her eyes lighting up. "You'll buy the land for the agreed upon price that you made my father originally, which means I can pay off the house."

"That's the deal." Kaleb confirmed, smiling.

"Holy crap!"

Zoey's excitement caused them all to laugh, but they were still waiting for her final answer.

"Will you take the offer, Zoey?" Kaleb asked her when she flopped down into the chair.

"Yes. Absolutely yes. I'll take it."

"Thank God." Travis replied, pushing to his feet. "I'll meet with our lawyer as soon as I leave here, and we'll get the papers drawn up. Tomorrow, before dinner, we'll meet up to get everything signed. That work for you?"

"Yes." Zoey said, standing once again and accepting Travis outstretched hand.

Kaleb watched as the two of them shook on it.

A few minutes later, after Sawyer and Travis left, Kaleb found himself leaning casually against the wall, waiting for Zoey to say something. She hadn't stopped smiling for the last five minutes, and he was beginning to wonder if she ever would.

"You ok?" He finally asked when she stood staring at the front door.

"Huh?" Zoey turned to face him. "Oh, sorry."

Kaleb had remarkably little warning before Zoey came running at him, launching herself into his arms. He laughed as he pulled her against him, lifting her off of the ground before turning so her back was against the wall.

Taking advantage of the opportunity, he crushed his mouth to hers, seeking the sweet, exotic taste that was all Zoey. Damn. He'd never get enough of her. Kissing her, tasting her, holding her. All of it combined was so much more than he ever thought it would be, and he'd become addicted to the little vixen in recent months.

Hell. He'd been addicted to her for years. But not like this.

"I take it you're happy?" He asked as he nibbled down her neck, inhaling her scent into his lungs and holding it there so he could savor it. The woman was intoxicating.

"You did this!" She whispered.

"No, baby." Kaleb smiled as he pulled back and looked into her eyes. "You did this. All you."

"I still can't believe it." Zoey unwrapped her legs from around his waist, and he immediately missed her warmth. "I have to tell V!"

Kaleb watched as she danced around the living room, his eyes roaming her body. Still wearing that tease of a skirt and that wispy little sweater, he wanted nothing more than to strip her naked, save for the boots. Fuck. His dick was harder than granite, and his jeans had just become painfully tight.

"So what are we supposed to do now?" She asked when she stopped moving, still smiling.

"I'm thinking dinner is in order. Either you let me take you out to celebrate, or you let me cook for you. Your choice."

"You can cook?" Zoey looked quite concerned, and Kaleb laughed.

"You know damn well I can cook." He told her as he stalked her across the room. "But let's take this little party back to my place."

Zoey lunged at him again, crushing her mouth to his for one of those soul stealing kisses before pulling away quickly. "I think I'll take you up on that offer."

♂♀♂

Sitting at the small table in Kaleb's kitchen, Zoey watched as he worked. She'd only been teasing him when she asked if he could cook. Years of knowing the man, she'd been on the receiving end of one of his gourmet meals on more than one occasion and she wasn't about to pass up another.

"Have you ever cooked naked?" She asked, joking.

"Not when I'm cooking with grease." He told her, not turning around. "Why?"

"I was just wondering. That would be a sight to see." She loved seeing him naked. All of that glorious toned skin and rippling muscle. Her mouth watered at the thought, wanting to run her tongue over his entire body, exploring every delicious inch.

"I was thinking it might be more thrilling to see *you* naked while I cook." This time he did turn around, and the way his eyes smoldered made her skin tingle.

"Get naked for me, Zoey." Kaleb said more firmly, and she realized he was serious. "It's only fair," he continued, "I did the dishes naked at your house."

True. Him and Gage both. That night was burned into her memory.

Apparently he was a little impatient because when she didn't move to do as he told her, he approached. After taking her hand, he pulled her up from the chair and proceeded to remove her clothes, one piece at a time while he made no attempt to pretend he wasn't ogling her with his eyes.

"There." He whispered a few minutes later when she stood before him perfectly nude except for her boots. "That's what I've wanted to see all afternoon."

Turning back to the stove like it was nothing for him to have a naked woman in his kitchen, Kaleb proceeded to finish cooking. At first it was thrilling to see the subtle glances he stole of her as she sat at the table, but when they were actually eating, she had an overwhelming desire to cover herself.

"Nope." Kaleb said, focusing on his food, but looking up at her when she attempted to cover her naked breasts. "Naked is naked, and I want to see every luscious inch of you."

He was killing her. Modesty had never been her thing, but then again, she didn't make a point of being naked in front of anyone. It was enough for Kaleb to see her when they were going at it, but this was too casual. Her face flamed with the embarrassment she'd been battling with.

Finally pushing her plate away, she realized she was definitely finished with dinner and anxious for him to get naked with her.

"I would ask you to do the dishes naked, but I think I'd rather see you busy doing something else."

Her breath hitched in her chest at the statement, and she suddenly worried what he was referring to. When he stood from his chair, taking both of their plates over to the sink before returning, Zoey kept her eyes glued to him.

Then he took the chair he vacated moments before and pulled it closer to her.

"Turn your chair this way." He said as he stood before her.

Not knowing what it was he was after, Zoey did what he asked, hoping like hell he was going to touch her soon. Before she exploded.

"Now put your foot on this chair."

Wait, what?

Holy crap. If she put her foot in the chair, it would expose her completely. More so than she already was, if that was even possible. Unable to move, Zoey didn't put her foot in the chair until Kaleb assisted, lifting her foot and spreading her legs wide.

"Damn that's pretty."

Her entire body flushed at his statement.

"Now, I want to see you touch yourself."

"Oh, my God! Kaleb!" She couldn't believe what he was asking her to do, and she wasn't sure she could do it even if she wanted to.

"What, baby?" He asked, kneeling down between her spread legs.

When he used one finger to slide through her sensitive folds, Zoey gasped.

"You're wet."

Well, yes. What did he expect?

"So fucking wet." His voice was deeper, huskier, and Zoey knew he was just as affected as she was. "Now touch yourself. Show me how you pleasure yourself because I know you do."

Well, yes. She did. But that was between her and her vibrator, thank you very much.

When Kaleb took her hand, placing her fingers against her clit, Zoey's eyes crossed. Was she actually going to do this?

"That's it, baby. Play with your clit. Tease your sweet pussy while I watch."

Kaleb stood and moved back to the sink, quickly rinsing the dishes as he turned his attention back on her frequently. Her hand had a mind of its own, circling lightly over her clit, making her wetter than she had been and eager for Kaleb to join her. When a moan escaped, it surprised her more so than it did him, and she closed her eyes briefly.

That's when the door opened, and she damn near died of embarrassment.

"Holy fucking shit." Gage growled. "That's the hottest thing I've ever seen."

"Isn't it?" Kaleb asked as if this was a casual conversation between two friends. "I love to watch her touch herself."

Gage and Kaleb didn't make a move to come closer; instead, they leaned against the kitchen cabinets, their gazes locked between her legs where she continued to tease her clit. She couldn't believe she was doing this, but the hunger she saw in their eyes spurred her on. And quite frankly, it felt good.

"Can I play with her?" Gage asked Kaleb as if Zoey didn't have a say in the matter. That turned her on too.

Wow, she had officially turned into a wanton hussy, controlled by her inner slut.

Zoey choked on a laugh. *Inner slut.* The idea amused her, considering, until Kaleb and the little rendezvous' with Gage, Zoey had been with two men in her life. And the kinkiest thing she had ever done had been oral sex. Now look at her. She was touching herself in front of two men, both of whom she'd been with at the same time. It was a side of herself that she hadn't known existed, a side she was quickly realizing was a dominant part of her personality.

Kaleb moved closer at the same time Gage did, but neither of them touched her like she hoped.

"I want to watch you fuck yourself, Zoey. Slide your finger inside your pussy." Gage encouraged her, his deep voice seducing her. She locked her eyes on his as he watched how she played with herself, slowly pushing one finger into her pussy, then two.

Her orgasm was lingering, but she was unable to push herself over the edge. She needed more than her own hands, but she knew if she asked they would deny her. This was her payback for tying them up in her kitchen - that was clear.

When Kaleb took off his shirt, Zoey let her gaze linger on his impressive body, wishing he'd do more than stand there. At least now she had an incentive because looking at him was enough to have her flicking her clit more firmly.

Then when he removed the rest of his clothing, Zoey did come, her finger furiously rubbing her clit as she moaned out her pleasure, unable to take her eyes off of Kaleb as he began stroking his cock.

"Damn that was hot." Gage said as he too began quickly disrobing, tossing his clothes about the kitchen.

Kaleb easily lifted her when she wouldn't have been able to stand on her own and carried her into the living room. Sitting her on the couch, he stood before her, as naked as she was, and still gripping his iron hard erection.

When Gage appeared beside him, Zoey looked at them both, doing a mental comparison of their differences. Kaleb, with his dark hair and stormy eyes was a woman's darkest fantasy come to life and Gage, well, the man was a masterpiece. Not quite as tall as Kaleb, Gage was probably right at six feet, but it wasn't his height that captured women's attention. It was his body. He was long and lean, yet thick and bulky through his chest and shoulders. She would've never thought that a long haul truck driver had enough time to work out the way he apparently did.

Mouthwateringly yummy, that's what they were. And as it turned out, Zoey was eager to explore.

As far as threesomes went, until that very first time with Kaleb and Gage, Zoey didn't have any personal experience, but she certainly had read books and even heard some firsthand accounts from a few people she knew. Like the Walker twins. Braydon and Brendon were notorious for their ménages, and they were proud to boot. And if she actually thought about it, it very well could've been the twins that had gotten her intrigued about the prospect of having two men solely focused on her with some of their more graphic tales.

Not that she had ever expected to find herself in this situation. But her fantasies had been vivid; her mind had undoubtedly conjured up images of Kaleb and another man, and yes, Gage had been in them a time or two. So yes, her mind was dirty and her thoughts bordered on carnal. But hell, she was a healthy twenty nine year old woman and if she wanted to explore her sexuality, then that was her prerogative, right?

Right.

And over the course of the last couple of months, she'd more than explored, coming to find out she wasn't the plain vanilla type. Nor was she what Jason obviously described her as. But with him, it hadn't been like this. She didn't burn from the inside out like she did with Kaleb.

And she was quite certain she wouldn't have been nearly as comfortable doing this if it weren't for Gage. He was a friend, and she trusted him implicitly. Since she didn't have the same feelings for him that she did Kaleb, she understood the complexity of the situation. He was there for the pleasure. And they all knew it.

Gage graced her with that lopsided grin, his chocolate brown eyes sparkling with something she'd never seen before. There was a fury of passion reflected in his gaze, and she wondered if it had always been there and she'd just missed it.

"It's my turn to watch." Gage told her as he moved toward her. "Turn around."

Zoey did, allowing Gage to sit down before he pulled her onto the couch in front of him. She could feel the evidence of his desire pressed against her lower back when he pulled her toward him. In this position, with her bottom on the edge of the couch, her back against Gage's chest, they both had a direct view of Kaleb as he knelt between her legs.

Gage pulled her arms up over her head, making her wrap them behind his neck, which thrust her breasts forward.

"Keep your hands there. Don't move them." He instructed, and she did. Clasping her hands behind his neck, her elbows pointed toward the ceiling, Zoey felt entirely too exposed to Kaleb's wandering gaze.

"So fucking pretty." Kaleb's voice sounded strained as he grasped her ankles and spread her legs farther apart. He was taking his time, and she was dying more and more with every passing second. Bringing herself to orgasm in front of them had done nothing to sate the ache that had built to overwhelming proportions in the last hour or so. She needed him to touch her.

"You're so fucking beautiful." Kaleb whispered, and it almost seemed as though they were the only two in the room. Had it not been for Gage's rough hands caressing her breasts, Zoey could've gotten lost in Kaleb's sexy, hooded gaze.

She was grateful that she didn't have to direct this little play of bodies because her brain was overloaded from the onslaught of sensations.

Ok so not a single one of her fantasies had ever come close to what this felt like.

Two men.

Two intensely hard bodies.

Four hands.

Her brain was doing a quick arithmetic lesson about how many orgasms she might have when the pleasure was doubled. Her initial calculation told her that she might just not survive it. She knew from the past exactly how hot they could make her, but for some reason, each time was like the first time.

"I want to watch Kaleb make you come apart." Gage whispered in her ear as he pinched her nipples, sending sparks of fire shooting straight to her clit.

Zoey figured that wouldn't take long, and since she couldn't find her voice, she stared into Kaleb's eyes, the hunger, the passion, all of it right there on display.

He didn't waste another second as he lowered his head between her thighs, his tongue darting out between her slick folds, teasing her with the slightest of touches.

Gage was able to see over Zoey's shoulder as they both watched Kaleb on his knees before her, using his fingers to separate her folds and delicately stroking her clit with his tongue. A shudder vibrated through her on impact. Watching him was hot and the lewd, carnal words Gage whispered in her ear only made the fire that had ignited in her womb burn hotter.

"Spread your legs wider." Gage instructed, and Zoey moved them apart, allowing Kaleb better access as he began to feast on her oversensitive pussy, thrusting his tongue in deep, then retreating only to torture her clit. Repeatedly he brought her to the brink only to hold her back.

"God, Zoey," Gage continued, "it's so fucking hot. Is this what Kaleb does to you when y'all are alone? Does he eat your pussy until you scream his name? Have you ever paid attention to how intense it is to watch him as he devours you?"

Fuck yes. Kaleb had insisted that she watch him, ordered her to lie there while he tormented her with pleasure, but not even then had it been this good.

"Ride his mouth, Zoey." Gage demanded, holding her tighter against him, using his teeth to nip at her ear. "That's it, baby."

Zoey's orgasm was taking hold as Kaleb began fiercely licking her clit, suckling it, flicking ruthlessly with his tongue as she pushed against his mouth, increasing the friction.

"Oh, God!" Even being held by Gage, with Kaleb's arms wrapped around her legs, she felt as though she were going to come apart, the millions of pieces to be scattered in disarray. As her orgasm ripped through her, her arms and legs tingled, and her mind went blank.

♂♀♂

Kaleb watched Zoey as she screamed his name, her body tensing as her release tore through her. It was the sexiest damn thing he'd ever seen. Looking up from his perch between her soft thighs, he could see Gage's arms around her, caressing her flat stomach, grazing her breasts.

He needed to be inside of her, wanted to feel her wrapped around his dick, milking him as only she could do. But this was about Zoey. About her pleasure.

Pulling himself to standing once again, Kaleb nodded at Gage who unwrapped Zoey's arms from his neck before maneuvering out from underneath her and switching places with Kaleb. Once on the couch, Kaleb pulled her onto his lap, his cock nudging against her bottom.

He was tempted to slide his rock hard cock into the warm, recesses of her pussy and forget about everything else because just holding her against him was enough to have him ready to explode.

Instead of losing himself in the heaven of her body, he latched onto her neck, suckling the sweet skin, trying to hold back so that he didn't mark her, yet not caring at the moment whether he did or not.

When Gage approached, kneeling on the floor in front of them, Kaleb's eyes were glued to Zoey's beautiful breasts on full display. Gage had apparently zeroed in on them as well because he gently latched onto one nipple, circling his tongue slowly.

Zoey's arms came up, and she wrapped them around his neck, just like she had Gage, pulling him closer against her back as he continued to lick the soft spot behind her ear. With her new position, her breasts had been thrust out to Gage, and the man was smart enough not to let the moment pass him by.

"Watch, baby." Kaleb instructed. Hell, he was watching, knowing that Gage was getting a taste of the sweetest woman Kaleb had ever known, and the man should consider himself lucky to have had the chance. If it weren't for the fact that sharing Zoey with him only satisfied her that much more, Gage Matthews would be shit out of luck.

And, just as he suspected, Zoey was enjoying herself if her dick teasing moans were anything to go by.

"Please." She begged, and Kaleb moved his hands around to cup her breasts, lifting them to Gage's eager mouth as she watched.

"Please, what?" Kaleb wanted to know what she needed.

"I need more."

Kaleb knew the feeling and watching Gage as he sucked one hardened point into his mouth had Kaleb needing more too.

He needed to feel Zoey's mouth on his cock.

"Turn around, baby." Kaleb told her as he released her arms from his neck. Maybe he was being selfish, but he couldn't stand not feeling her soft fingers or her hot mouth on him any longer.

When she slid off of the couch onto her hands and knees, Kaleb was able to see in her eyes and the hunger he glimpsed there had his dick pulsing. "Put your mouth on me." He demanded, watching as a spark of interest lit her navy blue eyes.

He could sense her eagerness, but she managed to hold back as she gently cupped his balls before grazing her little pink tongue over the engorged head. She teased him for long minutes, likely paying him back for what he had done to her earlier. Only he knew that she wasn't going to be able to focus for much longer because Gage was moving behind her, his head disappearing between her legs.

The moment she sucked him fully into her wicked hot mouth, Gage must've made his move because the vibration of her moans lit him up from inside, his cock throbbing and threatening to explode.

With a firm grip on the base of his cock, Kaleb held himself tightly, trying to force back the release that threatened just from watching her writhe against Gage's mouth and continue to suck furiously on his cock.

Latching one hand in her hair, Kaleb positioned himself so he could thrust into her mouth, holding her still and watching as the wide crest disappeared inside the warmth of her mouth while her tongue thrashed along the sensitive underside.

There'd been a number of women that Gage and Kaleb had shared over the years, but never had one of them been like this. Yes, this was all about the woman's pleasure, but there had always been a driving need, an end point that both of them were working toward. With Zoey, no matter how badly he wanted to come, Kaleb knew he had to wait. He was bound and determined to be inside of her when he did.

Suddenly Zoey pulled away from him, a torturous moan ripping through the room and looking down the length of her back, Kaleb could see the top of Gage's head.

"Oh!" Zoey moaned, her eyes closed. "Yes. Oh, God, yes. Don't stop!"

Kaleb knew exactly what Gage was doing – he was preparing Zoey for what would come next. Leaning forward, Kaleb swept his tongue over her lips; her head thrown back as she pushed back against Gage's invading tongue, Kaleb barely managed to focus.

"Come here." He said as he pulled her forward, lacking any of the gentleness he knew he should've been showing her. Pulling her onto his lap, she straddled his hips as he easily slid his cock into her pussy. With a sharp intake of breath, Kaleb allowed her body to acclimate to him while Gage prepared himself.

Kaleb had to situate himself farther into the couch so she could lay flat against him, allowing Gage access to her ass.

"We're going to fuck you, baby. At the same time." This wasn't the first time, but Kaleb wanted to warn her, even though he didn't think she needed it.

"Yes. Kaleb. Fuck me." Zoey moaned, beginning to move on his cock and making his dick throb, his balls tighten.

"Fuck her, Gage. Now." Kaleb groaned, beginning to thrust slowly into her, trying to keep her from moving, but barely able to restrain the need to pound into her pussy and come with a ferocity he had become accustomed to where Zoey was concerned.

"Fuck me!" Zoey screamed when Gage pressed into her, obviously unable to be gentle either. For a second, Kaleb was scared they would hurt her, but then Zoey bit his chest, grinding against them both and he realized she needed this as much as they did.

With the pain from her sharp little teeth echoing through him, Kaleb held her hips, thrusting as much as he could with both of them almost on top of him while Gage began ramming into her ass, fucking her furiously. His rhythm allowed Kaleb to remain almost motionless as Zoey moved on his cock, her muscles tightening while the feel of Gage's cock tunneling in her ass had him gritting his teeth.

"Come for me, baby." Kaleb demanded, pulling Zoey's head back by latching onto her hair. He stared deep into her eyes. "Now."

When she screamed her release, Kaleb captured the sound with his mouth, holding her to him as his dick pulsed inside of her, his release tearing through him, leaving him breathless and overwhelmed with all that he was feeling for this one tiny woman.

Chapter Twenty Three

♀♂

"Dinner?" Zoey asked Kaleb when she answered the phone the following morning.

After last night's sexcapade, Zoey had escaped to her house after saying goodbye to Gage. He was leaving town – off on the road as usual – but this time he would be gone for about three months. She hated to see him go, but she fully understood. She hadn't even had a chance to talk to Kaleb like she planned because she was too exhausted after all the fun they'd had.

This morning, she'd barely managed to climb out of bed when V was banging on her door. It wasn't very often that V made it to her house before Zoey managed to crawl out of bed, so she knew she'd overslept. Kaleb tended to do that to her. The thought made her smile.

"Yes, dinner." Kaleb confirmed in her ear. She was standing on the front porch of Anderson's mother's house – now thoroughly cleaned out and almost cleaned up.

"Tonight?"

"Yes, honey. What part do you not understand?" Kaleb laughed.

The part where she was supposed to go to dinner with the investors of the resort, that's the part she didn't understand. It would've been nice if Kaleb hadn't sprung it on her at the last minute.

"What time?" Knowing she was going to cave, Zoey checked her watch as Kaleb gave her the time. Shit. She didn't have much time.

"Ok. Should I just meet you there?"

"No. I'll pick you up at seven. Be ready."

She would try, but she wasn't making any promises. It was already five o'clock, and she and V had been immersed in getting the house cleaned completely so they wouldn't have to come back. Another ten minutes and they would be done, but she wasn't so sure that would leave her enough time to get ready.

"V!" Zoey screamed when she walked in the door.

To her surprise, Vanessa came running out of the kitchen, wielding a scrub brush like a mad woman.

"What the hell's the matter?" V asked, her eyes darting back and forth through the room.

Zoey glanced around before looking at Vanessa again. "Sorry. Nothing's wrong. Except I have to hurry up."

"Oh yeah? Hot date tonight?" V teased before turning back to the kitchen, Zoey following close behind.

"Sort of, although I'd really like to sit this one out."

"Is this 'partner' related?"

Ever since Zoey informed V of the deal she made with the Walker's, which they had officially signed on at lunch, her friend had been ecstatic. In fact, she began celebrating by dancing around the living room singing "No more toilets for me!" making Zoey laugh.

Nope, no more toilets. Well, maybe until the resort was built, but that was only because Zoey refused to leave her clients without a backup plan. She fully intended to let them all know next week that she would no longer be in business after the first of next year. That at least gave them a little time to find another cleaning service.

"Yes, its partner related. We're meeting the investors from Dallas for dinner at some upscale steakhouse in downtown Austin."

"Wow. Fancy." V sang. "What're you going to wear?"

Hell if she knew. What was she supposed to wear? Figuring since this was an upscale restaurant, she might have to dig through her closet for a little while before she knew exactly.

"Are you about done?" Zoey asked, ignoring V's last question and grabbing the last of her supplies and tossing them in her bucket.

"I am now!" V exclaimed, dropping her scrub brush in the sink and turning off the water. "Come on. Let's go find you something to wear."

Fifteen minutes later, Zoey was scrambling in the shower, washing her hair, scrubbing her body, shaving her legs, all of the important things, and nothing more. As soon as she was finished, she pulled her hair up in a towel, grabbed another and secured it around her chest and then went to find V. Thankfully her friend was doing the hard part, digging through her closet.

"I found the exact outfit."

Ok. Not bad, Zoey thought as she looked over the outfit lying on the bed. A short gray and black mini skirt, black lightweight sweater and knee high black boots. Why was it that V always picked black for her to wear? Whatever reason, it looked good, and it solved her biggest dilemma.

Now off to do her makeup and hair.

Zoey was pretty sure she never would've made it without V's help, but standing in front of the full length mirror, admiring their handy work, Zoey was pretty impressed. V had blown out her hair and straightened it, which made it look longer than normal, hanging halfway down her back.

Minimal makeup was all she could muster because Zoey wasn't big on makeup. But after a little eyeliner and mascara, a touch of blush and a shiny clear gloss on her lips, she actually looked good, if she did say so herself. Now if only Kaleb would hurry up before her stomach twisted in more knots, she might just make it through the evening.

As if on cue, there was a loud knock on her front door, and Zoey made her way back to the living room to see Kaleb standing before her. Honest to God, she had to put one hand on the wall, the other over her heart because the man standing before her actually stole her breath.

He was magnificent.

Gone were the sexy blue jeans, replaced with a pair of expensive black slacks, black shoes and a crisp white shirt. No tie, but he didn't need one. The man looked like he had just stepped out of GQ magazine.

"What?" He asked, sounding a little insecure.

"I've never seen you dressed up. Well, except for prom, but that didn't count." She admitted, still staring at him in awe.

"Good or bad?"

"The only thing better is when you're naked." Zoey grinned and then moved closer. "And you smell fantastic."

Too good actually. Zoey wasn't sure she'd be able to keep her hands to herself.

♂♀

Kaleb was having a hard time keeping his hands off of Zoey. The woman was beautiful when she didn't dress up, but when she did, she was spectacular. It was rare to see her in anything except blue jeans and a t-shirt, sometimes shorts. On occasion, she would wear a dress, but nothing like the outfit she had on now. Those fuck me boots had his dick stirring in his slacks.

It was a damn good thing they couldn't back out of this dinner because standing in front of her now if given the chance, Kaleb would be undressing her.

With his teeth.

"You're beautiful." He finally whispered as they stood staring at one another. She'd damn near given him a heart attack when she stopped short just inside the room as soon as she saw him. Dressing up was not his forte, and though he might own the clothes, he opted not to wear them if he didn't have to. Not knowing what her reaction was going to be, he admittedly had been a little insecure.

"Let's do this." Zoey told him. "So that way we can hurry back and get naked."

Kaleb growled and then pulled her against him. He couldn't resist kissing her and inhaling the soft, subtle hint of perfume. Something spicy that made him even harder than before. "You're going to be the death of me, woman." He said as he stepped back from her.

After she grabbed a small clutch, she was once again beside him as they headed for his car.

"Ummm... Kaleb." Zoey stopped. "Where's your truck?"

He laughed, looking out at the car sitting in the driveway. "Don't worry, it's at the house. I borrowed this from Sawyer." It was one of Sawyer's many play toys, and the sleek, black Cadillac CTS-V had always been one of Kaleb's favorites.

Kaleb helped Zoey into the car before going around to the driver's side. He resituated himself as he got in, hoping he could just get through this evening without sneaking Zoey off to the bathroom and taking her nine ways to Sunday.

A half hour later they were pulling up at the restaurant, the valet rushing over to open Zoey's door while another came around to Kaleb's. Without a second glance, he tossed the keys to the man closest to him and took his ticket before hurrying over to Zoey. When she slid her arm into his, he held her close as they made their way inside.

Just inside the door, Travis and Sawyer were talking, but stopped the second they approached. Sawyer whistled, and Kaleb glared at him.

"Don't worry, I'm not whistling at you." Sawyer laughed. "I'm wondering how in the world you ended up with this beautiful woman on your arm."

That made two of them. Kaleb had wondered the same thing on more than one occasion, but he wasn't going to admit it.

"Do we have a table yet?"

"Yeah. The McCoy's are here, but we're still waiting on a couple of people." Travis said as he turned and led them through the restaurant to a room in the back.

The table looked like it held about twenty people and there were already several people seated, including two men who looked identical to one another.

"Luke, Logan, I'd like you to meet my brothers." Travis introduced as the two men stood. "This is Sawyer, and this is Kaleb. The beautiful woman on his arm is Zoey Stranford, our partner."

Kaleb felt Zoey tense, her hand clutching his arm more firmly, but she smiled and shook the outstretched hands.

It hadn't been until Luke and Logan stood up that Kaleb realized they were actually identical twins. So much so, he was pretty sure he wouldn't be able to tell them apart.

"Nice to meet you." Logan said before turning to the woman beside him. "This is my wife, Samantha."

"Please, call me Sam. It's so nice to meet you, I've heard so much about you." Sam said, shaking hands with all of them.

Then it was Luke's turn to introduce the two people beside him. "You've met Cole, and this is our wife, Sierra."

Our?

"Oh, hush. Don't freak them out." Sierra laughed. "It's illegal for me to be married to two men, but if it were possible, I'd definitely have done it by now."

After the brief introductions, everyone took a seat; Kaleb and Zoey sitting across from Sam, Sierra and Luke while the others were gathered toward the ends of the table.

"Who else are we waiting for?" Travis asked as the waiter stopped by, pouring wine and placing baskets of bread in front of them.

"Alex and Ashleigh should be here momentarily." Luke offered.

"And Tag Murphy, our attorney and a friend will also be joining us."

Kaleb glanced at Travis, but his brother merely brushed him off with a look. Attorney?

♀♂

Zoey couldn't believe how relaxed the atmosphere was. As soon as she sat down, Sierra leaned toward her and commented on her boots, followed by Sam laughing at Sierra.

"The woman has a thing for boots." Sam said, "So, I'm warning you. If you like them, hide them."

From that point on, the three women laughed and talked and as soon as Ashleigh joined them, they'd barely even noticed the men were there. When Zoey found out exactly who Ashleigh was, she'd damn near choked on her wine. Ashton Leigh. The erotic romance writer. And she was sitting next to her, acting as though they'd been best friends since day one.

She wasn't sure what she expected at this dinner, but this certainly hadn't been it. By the time the meal was served, the table had erupted in separate conversations and the wine flowed freely – well, for everyone except Sierra, Zoey noticed. And she was definitely grateful for the liquid courage, especially when the conversation between the women took the immediate turn that it did.

"So, I take it you don't need any more firsthand knowledge of what it's like to be in a threesome, Ashleigh?"

Ashleigh laughed, and then glanced over at Zoey. "They like to give me shit all the time. You see, I'm the only one of them not in a ménage relationship, nor have I ever been."

Zoey gathered that Cole, Luke and Sierra were in a three way relationship, but she hadn't realized Sam was until the intensely sexy Tag had shown up and planted a scorching hot kiss on her mouth like her husband wasn't sitting right next to her. When Logan glanced over at them, it wasn't anger Zoey saw in his eyes. She saw the same heat and longing she'd seen in Kaleb's, and it was clear he approved.

"What about you, Zoey?" Sam asked, and Zoey blushed crimson.

"Ignore her." Ashleigh chuckled. "She's like that. Sam thinks it's normal for every woman to be with two men at the same time."

"I don't think it's normal." Sam said defensively, her beautiful green eyes dancing with humor. "I just think it's a shame if they haven't."

When Zoey finally found her voice, she realized she might've had one too many glasses of wine if what came out of her mouth was any indication. "Well, I'd have to agree. I'm definitely a different woman now."

"Oh my God!" Sierra squealed, causing the rest of the table to quiet and stare down at them, making Zoey's face heat again. "Sorry, ignore us. Go on about your business." Sierra shooed them off with one dainty hand.

Instead of ignoring them, Luke leaned over, putting his arm around Sierra and gently rubbing her flat stomach.

"Oh, my God!" Ashleigh squealed, followed by Sam.

Sierra simply smiled, and the beautiful woman actually glowed.

"How far along are you?" Sam questioned; her attention, as well as the rest of the table, entirely focused on Sierra and Luke.

"Eleven weeks." Sierra beamed.

Zoey glanced over at Cole noticing how extremely proud the man looked, and the question that immediately came to mind was the same one that came spewing from Sam's mouth.

"Who is the father?"

Surprisingly, not one of the three looked embarrassed, nor did they respond the way Zoey expected.

"They are." Sierra put her hand on Luke's thigh and brushed her cheek against Cole's hand when he reached around Luke to touch her. It was the sweetest thing she'd ever seen, and despite the fact that they both couldn't be the birth father, Zoey felt her heart swell at the way they all three treated it as though they were. "But enough about me," Sierra continued, her eyes zeroing in on Zoey once more, "details, honey."

Thankfully the men at the table went about their own business, resuming the conversations they'd been having earlier.

"I'm the odd woman out again?" Ashleigh asked, pretending to be offended, but looking totally at ease.

"Looks like it." Sam offered.

Dessert came and went and Zoey found herself opening up more and more to these women who were just as laid back and down to earth as those she was most familiar with, like the Walker brothers. It was refreshing after what she had built up in her mind.

When the topic turned to the resort, Ashleigh listened in, but Sierra and Sam were front and center, offering their input at every turn, and the men were taking their every word into consideration. As it turned out, Sam was in charge of managing the project from a time and budget perspective because that was obviously her expertise. And Sierra was in charge of design.

By the end of the night, everyone understood their roles, including Zoey. She also realized that when it came to the enormity of what this resort promised to be, she was way out of her league.

Chapter Twenty Four

Kaleb noticed that Zoey had been quiet since they left the restaurant and she also wasn't paying any attention to him on the drive home. She'd answered his questions with the minimum required answer, but she never contributed any more than that.

When they pulled up to her house, and she moved to get out, he pulled her arm gently, keeping her in place. "Stay there."

Honestly, he was surprised that she listened, so when he came around and opened her door, offering a hand to help her out, he didn't know what to say. Something was off, and he didn't know what.

He'd heard part of the women's conversation, but when they ventured to the topic of sex – namely ménages – he'd figured it in his best interest not to listen. After all, he wasn't a saint, and he could only be tempted so much before he lost control.

But now, with Zoey acting as though she'd just lost her best friend, he knew something else was bothering her. When he walked her to the door, he wondered whether she would even invite him in.

She didn't.

He came in anyway.

When she disappeared to her bedroom, he decided to follow her. That's when he saw her angrily pulling off her clothes and throwing them around the room, replacing them with her worn blue jean shorts and a skin tight t-shirt.

"Talk to me, Zoey." He felt like he'd been here before. Only this time, he was clueless about what might be bothering her. Throughout dinner, she'd been talkative, both with him and the women around them. It wasn't until the end that she got quiet, but he hadn't thought anything of it at the time.

"There's nothing to talk about." She said in a rush before trying to push past him.

Ok. Enough's enough. He didn't let her get by him. With ease, he pulled on her arm, turning her until her back was against the wall and she had nowhere to go. When she didn't look at him, he lifted her chin until their eyes met. The sadness he saw had his heart squeezing in his chest.

"Did you not have a good time?"

"I did. The girls were wonderful." Zoey admitted unconvincingly, closing her eyes.

"Look at me." Gripping her chin more firmly, Kaleb realized he was getting angry. He hated when she did this. When she ran away, hiding herself emotionally from him and everyone else. And he realized why he hated it so much. That wasn't the Zoey he knew. The woman he knew would confront anyone head on, telling them exactly what she thought and why, yet this woman, the one he saw before him didn't look like the confident, intriguing woman he'd grown to love.

"What?" Zoey exclaimed, looking at him. "What the hell do you want me to say, Kaleb? Dinner was fabulous! The people are great! I'm so happy this is going to work out for all of you."

"All of *us*? You're part of this, remember?" Kaleb didn't understand.

"Am I?"

Taking a step back, Kaleb took his hands off of her. "What the hell are you talking about?" Was she going back on their deal? Could she? She already signed the legal documents, and the money for the land was being funded to the bank on Monday morning.

"What exactly am I going to contribute, Kaleb? Other than the land? Huh? I can't compete with those people!"

"Compete?" Kaleb barked, trying to wrap his mind around what the hell she was saying. "Who the hell said anything about competing?"

"You met those people tonight." Zoey nearly screamed, her arms flailing at her sides. "I pale in comparison to those women. I'm not some highly educated project manager, and I'm not some big shot designer. I don't have anything to contribute, and you know it as well as I do."

Reality slapped him in the face, and Kaleb found himself flush against Zoey, pressing her into the wall and tipping her chin until she had to look at him. She tried to move away, but he secured her much smaller body with his until she stopped moving. But when her tears started to fall, his heart cracked wide open.

"Zoey," Kaleb lowered his voice, trying to get her to listen to him, "no one is asking you to be any of those things. And just for your information, Sierra isn't a big shot designer. She owns her own design company, but she's just getting started. In fact, she could probably learn a lot about business from you."

It was true. He had listened to Luke and Sierra talk about her company and some of the things she was hoping to do in the future. At this point, she had a couple of clients, but in no way was she a big shot. As for Sam, well, the woman was an anomaly, Kaleb had to admit. She was successful in ways most people would envy, but in talking to her briefly, she didn't pretend to be any different from the rest of them.

"Baby, those women, and even those men pale in comparison to you."

Zoey's eyes popped open, and she rolled them, making him smile.

"They do. You've got the biggest heart of anyone I know. And I've never known you not to accomplish what you set your mind on doing. They're lucky to have you. *I'm* lucky to have you." Staring into those ocean blue eyes, still shining with unshed tears, Kaleb's heart shot to his throat. "I love you, Zoey."

When she didn't speak immediately, Kaleb froze, wondering if she was going to turn him away. She had alluded to friends with benefits over the last few months, and they'd obviously managed to set the sheets on fire, but they never admitted to having feelings for one another. But he loved her. He had always loved her.

"You love me?" The question was riddled with disbelief, but Kaleb leaned his forehead against hers, sliding his hand into the hair at the nape of her neck.

"I've always loved you, baby. Since the first day I laid eyes on you, I knew I had to have you. And every single day since, I've loved you that much more. I settled on friends because I would've done just about anything to keep you in my life. But, Zoey, I do love you. And I want more from you than just friendship."

"Friends with benefits?" She asked, but he saw a sparkle in her eyes.

"Yes." He stated, and her eyes widened. "I want that and more. I want you to be my best friend, my lover... My wife."

♀♂

Zoey couldn't believe her ears. She was beginning to wonder if maybe she did have too much to drink. A minute ago she'd been wallowing in self-pity, which was so unlike her and now she was standing here, listening to Kaleb confess the exact things she'd been feeling for the last few weeks.

Wife.

Did he really just say wife?

"Zoey?"

She saw the question in his eyes, and that little bit of insecurity made her heart burst. She loved this man. She loved his strength, his nobility, his kindness, and that little hint of insecurity. He was human. And he was a man. And she loved him.

"I love you." She whispered, needing to say the words out loud. "I love you so much."

Those stormy steel blue eyes brightened, and for a moment, she thought she saw a sheen of tears, but then they were gone, and he was smiling.

"Marry me, Zoey. Be my wife." Kaleb gently kissed her lips as he continued to speak. "I want to wake up next to you every morning and go to sleep with you in my arms every night. I want to have babies with you. Grow old with you."

She wanted those things too. She had always wanted those things and maybe that was her problem. Maybe she had always known what was right in front of her, but she was just too blind to see it.

"Yes." She said, kissing him back and pulling him closer.

"Yes, what?"

That dominance she found so damn appealing was back, and she could see Kaleb's need to hear the words.

"Yes. I'll marry you, Kaleb Walker. I'll marry you and grow old with you and have babies with you and go to sleep in your arms and wake up every morning with you. Yes!"

"You make me the happiest man alive, you know that?"

"Well, you'd make me the happiest woman if I could get you out of these clothes." Zoey laughed as she started in on the buttons on his shirt.

Kaleb growled, making her laugh. "You're going to kill me, woman!"

Chapter Twenty Five

♂♀

Two weeks later...

"Hey." Kaleb smiled as soon as Zoey walked through his front door. *Their front door.* She looked good for a woman who had just put in eight hours cleaning without any help. Kaleb offered to go with her that morning, but she refused him, insisting that he had plenty of things to worry about.

Ever since the night when he proposed, and she said yes, their lives had been a whirlwind of activity. As soon as the ink was dry on the final paperwork and the money was transferred, both Zoey and Travis had been out of control. Travis immediately kicked everything into high gear, insisting they'd been sitting around on their asses long enough.

Then, of course, there was Zoey. The woman was a force to be reckoned with, and she didn't waste a single second in getting things moving along. Including the renovations on her father's house. Well, their house – or soon to be anyway.

As soon as Zoey told her father the good news - although he already knew because Kaleb would've never proposed without getting her father's permission to do so – Carl insisted on some changes. First, he was moving to the guest house.

Apparently Carl wasn't happy roaming around the giant house all by himself any longer, and he wanted to move to the smaller guest house where he wouldn't have to deal with the stairs. Or at least that's what he said. In turn, he wanted Zoey to take the house, but he insisted that she fix it up to suit her needs. By needs, Carl told her that he expected grandchildren in the very near future.

Zoey argued, as had Kaleb, but Carl didn't listen to a word either of them said. Instead, he insisted he was going to move his recliner out to the guest house by himself if he had to. In turn, Zoey agreed after seriously trying to convince her father otherwise but to no avail. And thankfully, the renovations were going to take a few months, and since Carl was hell bent on moving into the guesthouse immediately, Zoey agreed to live with Kaleb in the meantime.

Worry, maybe. Do, yes. The most important thing at the moment was greeting his future wife appropriately. He met her halfway, then pulled her against him, crushing his mouth down on hers. A little sigh escaped before Zoey did what she did best, she kissed him back and then attempted to climb his body.

"I missed you." He groaned, licking and kissing her lips, before pulling back to look at her. Holding her in his arms, her legs wrapped around his waist, he didn't hesitate before carrying her toward the bathroom.

"Where are we going?" She asked, chuckling.

"Shower. Now." He knew that was the first thing she did every day, and after the events of the last couple of weeks, he normally left her alone while she did, but today, he wasn't able to keep his hands off of her.

"You're going to join me?" Zoey asked sweetly, running her hands through his hair.

"I'm going to be inside of you is more like it." He warned her as he set her back on her feet in the bathroom. He let go of her long enough to turn on the water so it could heat, but when he turned back to face her, he smiled. She was half naked already and trying to get her jeans off as he stared back at her.

"You're wearing too many clothes, Kaleb Walker." Zoey said when she stood up, gloriously naked.

"Yeah? Well, why don't you help me take them off?"

"Hmmm... I thought you'd never ask." Her sweet smile made his entire body roar to life.

It didn't take long for Zoey's nimble fingers to remove his jeans and boxers, the only clothing he had on when she came in, and by the time she was finished, he was hard as stone and eyeing her sexy mouth.

"Zoey." He warned her, it was the only thing he could do because suddenly, all of the pent up frustration and emotion that had been bottled up for the last two weeks was coming to the forefront and the only outlet he could possibly imagine was her.

When her soft hand gripped his shaft, slowly stroking him as those enormous blue eyes stared up at him, he almost lost touch with reality.

"Tell me, Kaleb." She whispered, slowly moving toward the shower. He followed closely, not wanting her to let go of his cock because the sweet caress was too good.

"I need you." He growled.

"Need me to do what?" She asked again, her voice but a whisper, barely heard over the sound of the water from the shower.

Once inside the slate lined walls of the shower, the warm water pelting down on them, Kaleb was breathing harder because Zoey was stroking him faster. She tore her gaze from his and was watching as she did so, his eyes locked on her pale fingers wrapped around his cock.

"Put your mouth on me, Zoey."

She didn't question him as she lowered herself to her knees before him, the water cascading over them both as she gently sucked him deep into her mouth, no teasing kisses, and no torturous swipes of her tongue. No, this was blessed wet heat, her mouth wrapping around him, pulling him in as she began moving down his shaft.

He slid his fingers into her hair, holding her firmly. "Damn, baby. That's it." He groaned, pushing past her lips, feeling her tongue as it curled around the underside of his cock, her teeth grazing the sensitive nerve endings. "Suck me, Zoey. Harder." He was going to lose it, and she knew it as well as he did.

Not wasting any more time, Kaleb held her head still, his eyes meeting hers as he buried his cock farther into her mouth. He watched her cheeks hollow as she sucked, the head of his dick meeting the back of her throat. A lustful groan emerged from his chest, ricocheting off of the tiled walls as he began fucking her mouth faster. "Fuck, Zoey. It's too fucking good, baby. I'm going to come. Swallow me."

When she swallowed, the head of his dick pressed as far in as he was willing to go, he damn near lost his footing before pulling out and shoving back into her mouth. "Fuck yes!" He groaned, coming fast and hard, filling her mouth and watching as she swallowed again.

When she stood, Kaleb closed in, backing her up against the wall, and pressing his much larger body against hers. Then she was teasing him again, stroking his semi-erect cock slowly. "You want me to fuck you?" He asked, knowing her answer before she said anything.

"More than I need air." Zoey moaned. "I want to feel you inside me, Kaleb."

God, he loved it when she talked like that. Not that Zoey was much for talking dirty, but when she told him what she wanted, or voiced her pleasure while he was buried to the hilt in her pussy, it took everything in him not to come too soon. And just like now, he was hard again because that's what she did to him. He'd come to terms with the fact that he would never get enough of her. Ever.

"Turn around." He told her, taking a step back to give her room. "Put your hands on the wall."

She did, thrusting her ass out toward him. He bent his knees and gripped his cock before guiding it into the sweet, warm depths of her pussy.

"So fucking tight." He groaned as he slid in slowly.

"Not slow, Kaleb. Hard. Fast. Fuck me." Zoey moaned as she rocked her hips back against him.

Never one to disappoint, Kaleb gripped her hips and slammed home. Ramming his cock deep, retreating and then going even deeper, Kaleb fucked her with blind fury, aware of only the feel of her pussy wrapped around his cock, her sensual moans as she begged for more. How he managed, Kaleb had no idea, but the second her orgasm detonated, he followed her right over into the abyss, coming with a rush once again.

♀♂

Zoey was putting the finishing touches on dinner when Kaleb joined her in the kitchen. They had lingered in the shower for a little while longer, but when her stomach growled, he laughed at her and insisted they get out so they could eat.

Zoey didn't bother to tell him that she needed him more than she needed food, although it was true. Instead, she toweled off, slipped into one of Kaleb's shirts – her new favorite outfit – and hurried to the kitchen, wanting to get there before he did. If she let him, he would've cooked for her, but with all that was going on – namely all of the work they were putting in on the resort – Zoey was trying to do all she could for him. It wasn't because she felt she had to, it was because she loved him and right now, that was the only thing she knew to do as they prepared for the rest of their lives.

"How's the resort coming along?" She asked when Kaleb brushed up against her back, pulling her wet hair back and nuzzling her neck.

"Almost ready for the ground breaking ceremony."

Zoey had been on pins and needles ever since they made her a partner, and even more so after she had finally gotten over her serious moment of self-doubt. Thanks to Kaleb, Zoey felt as though she could do anything she set her mind to and decided, rather than feel inferior, which was so unlike her anyway, she was going to give it all she had. This was a new chapter in her life, one she planned to embrace with open arms and an open mind. In the past few months, Zoey had opened up in ways she never could've imagined, and honestly, she liked the woman she had become. She especially liked the woman Kaleb brought out in her.

Did she consider herself lucky? Incredibly. To have found the love of her life, the one who completed her in ways she never even considered, was a gift to be cherished. And to top it all off, he was her best friend.

Was she the same person she was before? Yes. In many ways, she was still that wild, carefree woman, but thanks to Kaleb and the love he blessed her with, she was a better woman. A stronger woman. And that was one of the many reasons she loved him. Their lives were just beginning together, and she had Kaleb to lean on when she needed him and vice versa. She could easily take a page from the Walker's book because when it came to those they cared about, they always stuck together, and above all else, they would always be there for each other.

Always.

Epilogue

♂♀

Kaleb held Zoey's hand, glancing out at all of the familiar faces looking back at them. His brothers were standing beside him, every one of them proud of all they had accomplished.

Together.

Today, well, this was about their dream; the groundbreaking of the new resort, which had thankfully consumed most of his time, taking his mind off of what the future held and the anticipation of the day he would make Zoey his wife. He couldn't help but think that, in just a couple of months they would be doing this yet again, only at that time Zoey would be making him the happiest man on the planet.

But, right now, this was where he wanted to be. He was too busy living each day, sharing each minute with the woman he loved and working on building a life of their own. She was his rock. His anchor. She grounded him when the chaos that was now their world could've very well consumed him too. Building Walker Demolition had been a cake walk compared to the time and effort it required to build a resort the likes of which none of them had ever known.

"I love you." He whispered, brushing his mouth against her ear.

"I love you, too."

And that was what he lived for.

Glancing around him, Kaleb noticed his brothers were lined up, grinning like fools. Sawyer appeared to be on top of the world, in his element as the spokesman for Walker, Inc. And the self-appointed MC of today's groundbreaking ceremony. The rest of them would easily take a step back from the limelight.

Braydon and Brendon, well, they were their usual, rambunctious selves. At the moment, they were mindlessly flirting with a group of women who had arrived for the ceremony. Not uncommon.

Ethan was apart from them all, talking to their father in an animated fashion. The two men had so much in common, probably more so than the rest of them. It was eerie to see how much Ethan resembled their father, in both his looks and his mannerisms. He was definitely the most mature of the bunch and the voice of reason on many occasions.

As for Travis, well, that was to be seen because the man had set himself apart from the rest of them long ago. Whatever happened to him, no one knew, but whatever it was seemed to be eating away at him more and more each day.

Still staring at Travis, Kaleb stopped. There was one missing, and he wasn't sure how they hadn't noticed from the beginning. He didn't see Zane anywhere, and he wasn't sure exactly how they had missed him. Likely it was from all of the hoopla going on, but regardless, his brother should've been there.

"Where's Zane?" Kaleb said out loud, not sure who was listening, but suddenly frantic because his youngest brother wasn't there.

"I don't know." Zoey answered him, taking his hand as she scanned the crowd of at least one hundred for Zane, as well. "I haven't seen V either."

Kaleb turned to Travis. "Where's Zane?"

As though the others sensed something was wrong, everyone stopped what they were doing and made their way over, including their parents.

"Where the fuck is Zane?" Travis asked, irritation, but more so concern lining his face.

"I haven't seen him today." Ethan admitted, looking around as the others were doing the same.

As if on cue, Zoey's phone chirped. She let go of Kaleb's hand and retrieved it from her pocket. Kaleb glanced down at the screen at the same time. By now, Luke and Logan McCoy had joined them, as well as Alex McDermott, Cole Ackerley and Dylan Thomas. They were all staring at Zoey as if whatever information she just received was earth shattering news.

"Oh, my God." The look on her face and fear in her eyes had Kaleb grabbing her phone. It didn't go unnoticed that her hands were shaking, but she let the phone go.

Looking up at his brothers, his parents, and their new business partners, Kaleb couldn't get the words out.

"What the fuck is it?" Travis asked, stepping forward. "Where the fuck is Zane?"

"That was V." Zoey whispered, glancing over at Kaleb's parents. "He's in the hospital."

Kaleb managed to look up into Travis' face, realization dawning. He wasn't going to voice what else was on the text from V, but Travis didn't need any further explanation, neither did the others.

What they thought to be an idle threat just turned into their worst nightmare.

♂♀

♂♀ ■□ ♂ ■□ ♂ ■□ ♂ ■□ ♂ ■□ ♂ ■□ ♂

Check out more from Nicole Edwards:

www.nicedwardsauthor.com

The Club Destiny Series:

Conviction

Temptation

Addicted

Seduction

And coming in 2013 –

Infatuation

Captivated

The Alluring Indulgence Series:

Kaleb

And coming in 2013 –

Zane

Travis

Continue reading for an excerpt from

TEMPTATION

The second book in the Club Destiny Series:

Sierra Sellers has never had a problem finding a date, but when her mother's meddling ways result in her being set up with the intensely sexy Luke McCoy, owner of Club Destiny, Sierra learns she can't fight temptation. When he unleashes her deepest, darkest fantasies, she finds herself in a position she doesn't want to get out of.

Luke McCoy has run fast and hard from the demons that chase him. The hot, fierce need that pushed him beyond the boundaries he hadn't realized he'd erected resulted in a two month hiatus from the world he'd built for himself. A world concreted in lust and forbidden fantasies. So when his twin brother Logan introduces him to Sierra, Luke finds himself up against another temptation that he can't resist.

Cole Ackerley never backs down from a challenge, but that was before he'd been intimately introduced to Luke McCoy. Throw in the black haired vixen with the glowing blue eyes, and Cole finds himself engulfed in a ménage hot enough to rival the sun. When his feelings for both of them ignite, Cole learns the true meaning of self-restraint.

The deep, soul scorching hunger that ignites between the three of them turns into a firestorm of sensuality and lust that only burns brighter and hotter with every encounter. But when Luke continues to push them away, can Cole and Sierra find a way to show him there are no boundaries when it comes to love?

Chapter One

~~ ** ~~ ** ~~ ** ~~

"Club Destiny." Luke didn't bother trying to hide the gruff irritation in his voice when he clicked the answer button on his cell phone and all but slammed it against his ear. The damn thing had been ringing nonstop for the last two hours, so he'd stopped bothering to look at the screen before he answered.

"Hey, bro. What's going on?" Logan, Luke's nothing-if-not-persistent twin brother greeted back, seemingly immune to Luke's umbrage.

Flying under the radar for the last two months had taken some creative manipulation, but Luke had pulled it off, making a full-fledged effort to work on some of his own personal issues. Nonetheless, said personal issues were not resolved, but he found himself right back in the thick of things once again. He shouldn't be surprised that his brother was calling, and he wasn't really, he just wasn't in the mood to talk to him considering the ass chewing he was expecting.

"Not a damn thing. What about you?" He barked back, walking through the main floor of his club on the way to his office.

He'd spent the better part of the morning with Club Destiny's head bar manager, going through their weekly order, and trying his damnedest to get back into the groove. Between that and answering the phone, he hadn't had a minute to himself. Which, in his current state, was probably not a bad thing.

"Glad you could make it back." Logan said, and Luke heard his brother's sarcasm, as well as his frustration, but at the moment, he didn't give a damn.

"What do you want?" Luke made it to his second floor office and slammed the door behind him.

Thankfully there were only a handful of people at the club that early in the day since they weren't open to the general public yet. Only members were allowed in during the morning hours, and they all knew to give him a wide berth on a good day. Unfortunately for them, today wasn't a good day.

Even with the few familiar faces he'd seen that morning, Luke's only desire was to be left alone. Although he'd managed to abandon his responsibilities, as well as any of his personal relationships for the last eight weeks, Luke still wasn't in the mood to be around anyone, and he wasn't keen on the idea of talking to his brother either.

"What the hell's wrong with you?" His brother never did have a problem calling him to the carpet so to speak, and apparently, Logan wasn't in much of a better mood than he was.

Which was surprising with all that had apparently happened to Logan during the time that Luke had been away. The man was a husband now, for Christ sake. That alone should make his brother much more pleasant than he currently was.

With a silent groan, Luke flopped down into the high back executive chair that he managed to occupy for at least a few hours every day. Glancing around the immaculate office, gleaming with hardwood and soft, iridescent lighting, he tried to remember what made him find comfort in the place.

Oh wait. He didn't.

The oversized mahogany desk, the full size, distressed leather sofa, and the intricate, *way* overpriced designer rug had been someone's idea of soothing. Instead, the result was just fucking ugly. And the confined feeling that overcame him when he walked in didn't help either. Without windows, the not so small space seemed more like a broom closet than an office.

Even after spending thousands of dollars on some highly recommended interior designer, Luke hadn't felt comfortable in the space. Which explained why he spent most of his time down in the club or caught up on the mountains of endless paperwork from home.

Despite his discomfort with enclosed spaces, the club as a whole offered him a sense of peace that was absent from his personal life, thanks to his own demons that managed to haunt him day and night like a bad case of the flu. Rational decisions weren't generally on Luke's short list of things to do, so purchasing the club ranked right up there with one of the best he could come up with in quite some time.

Though he often wondered if the club actually intensified those demons.

Remembering that he still held the phone to his ear, and his brother wasn't going to wait patiently for long, Luke answered. "Just trying to get some shit done around here." *And not succeeding worth a damn.*

Luke almost felt guilty for directing his annoyance at his brother, knowing the other man had spent the last two months trying to juggle his own responsibilities, including a full time job and apparently a new wife, along with covering for Luke's absence at the club. Yes, the wife part had been a surprise because when Luke had left town, Logan and Samantha were only dating. When he came back... *Bam!* – new sister-in-law.

For some unexplained reason, just the thought of Samantha had Luke's body going instantly hard. Most likely that was due to the fact that he'd known Sam intimately, on more than one occasion, thanks to the few times Logan had invited him to be the third. The remembered feel of Sam against him, or her hot, sweet mouth on him, had Luke almost longing for another encounter with her. *Almost* being the key word.

Since his personal demons had begun making a daily visit, Luke had sworn off those little sexcapades.

Granted, Luke liked Sam. And as far as Logan went, she was a perfect match for him.

The fact that they had gotten married shouldn't surprise him as much as it did. Or perhaps the fact that his identical twin brother hadn't bothered to mention that little tidbit of information prior to Luke taking some time off was what kept throwing him off. Either way, he tried not to think about it too much. Especially knowing that what they had shared before could never be again, especially after that last night...

Luke brushed off the thought. He didn't have time to dwell on what couldn't be.

"I'm glad you're back, Luke, but we need to talk." Though Logan's tone was slightly less frustrated than before, Luke easily picked up on the insistence his twin had thrown in for good measure. Luke hated when his brother did that shit. He'd much rather face the anger than to have to face the fact that he had let his brother down.

"Then talk." Luke stated, leaning back in his chair, thinking twice about propping his size 15 boots up on the polished wood top.

He could almost predict what Logan wanted to talk about after all their twin bond was strong, and for most of their lives, they could finish each other's sentences, sometimes even knew what the other was going to say before they said anything at all. And now wasn't much different.

"I'll drop by around lunchtime. Don't disappear on me." Logan stated flatly before the line disconnected.

"Sonuvabitch." Luke mumbled to no one in particular. He might deserve to have Logan show up on his doorstep and read him the riot act, but it didn't mean he was going to be happy about it.

Luke hit the switch to turn on his computer screen so he could scan through his recent emails. While he had been away, he'd managed to stay on top of things as best he could. He couldn't abandon his responsibilities altogether, though he'd been so fucked up in the head that he had wanted to. Even now he had a hard time keeping his focus. So many things had happened in the last couple of months, Luke wasn't sure he knew which way was up anymore.

As much as he wanted to blame everything on what had happened that last night with Logan and Samantha, Luke knew he couldn't do that. Sam might've come into Logan's life, and in turn Luke's, but the woman hadn't done anything specific that would have thrown Luke's life off course the way it had been. No, he only had himself to blame for that, but his own denial wouldn't allow him to admit that either.

"Fuck." Luke ground out as he pushed out of his chair, nearly sending the damn thing over backward. He had too much shit to do to sit around pondering the reasons why he felt so off kilter lately.

He should just leave again, take another extended vacation and get away by himself. Not that it would do him any good. After all, he'd spent the better part of two months doing exactly that and look where it had gotten him.

Not a damn place.

Resigning himself to staying at the club and attempting to take care of business, Luke grabbed an invoice off of his desk and headed back downstairs to talk to Kane Steele, his bar manager. According to their earlier conversation, it appeared that there were some issues with the deliveries while Luke had been away.

Either that or someone was fucking with him and stealing his inventory. Luke didn't even want to contemplate that happening; Heaven help the asshole who would be brave enough to steal from him in the first place.

Sierra Sellers wasn't all that enthusiastic with the idea of being set up, regardless of how hot and mysterious – her mother's words, not hers – the man might be. Apparently her mother was under the impression that Sierra needed a date, and rather than asking her if she were capable of finding one on her own, Veronica Sellers had chosen to make her own arrangements. Those arrangements had led to Sierra piling into the backseat of Logan McCoy's supercharged Cadillac CTS while he and his wife talked quietly in the front seats.

After a very brief, very one sided conversation with her mother, Sierra had resigned herself to this outing. Very reluctantly she might add. Veronica's argument consisted of the words "new to Dallas", followed by "essential to network", with the cherry on top of the conversational sundae being "get your business established".

So, no, Sierra hadn't come up with a strong enough excuse not to go along with her mother's logic, though she still didn't understand how a date was going to help her in that regard.

When Veronica had mentioned that XTX – the company her mother worked for – was holding their annual vendors conference in just two days, Sierra hadn't thought anything of it. Why would she? XTX didn't have anything to do with the interior design company that Sierra had yet to even name.

Only when Veronica mentioned that the conference was in Las Vegas had Sierra's ears even perked up. And here she was on the next leg of this journey that she only hoped would turn out the way her mother intended.

And yes, she was incredibly nervous, despite her reluctance and despite the fact that she felt as though she were being led to an execution. Even armed with a few details about the man she was going to meet, Sierra wasn't feeling all warm and fuzzy about the outcome. The positive side of this endeavor was that she at least knew what the man looked like. Or at least she thought she did.

According to both her mother and Samantha, she was off to meet Logan's identical twin brother. That had immediately piqued her interest because hell, she had to admit, Logan McCoy was smoking hot. Not that she would share that little tidbit of information with anyone, especially the man's wife whom she had become close to over the course of the last few weeks.

But realistically, how similar could the two of them actually be? They were grown men for goodness sake, and surely their personalities would set them worlds apart in appearance. So when Sam and Veronica had reiterated the fact that they were identical, Sierra had mentally rolled her eyes and resigned herself to finding out on her own.

Maybe her mother's physical descriptions were accurate. Although Sierra liked Logan enough, she still wasn't all that enthusiastic about the idea of being set up with a man – gorgeous or not. The one positive that she could manage to conjure up from this entire screwed up ordeal was that she and Sam had actually become good friends. Since the woman was the epitome of what Sierra had worked her entire life to become, she knew she would ultimately win in this deal.

At twenty nine years old, Sierra still had some growing to do when it came to establishing herself in business, but after meeting Sam, she knew she'd found a role model who could undoubtedly teach her some things along the way. And when said role model had ganged up on her with the help of Veronica and another woman they worked with at XTX, insisting that Sierra actually meet Luke McCoy, she had found herself outvoted.

Both Veronica and the other woman, Deanna had spoken very highly of Luke, but something had set her sensors off when Sam had talked about him. If Sierra wasn't mistaken there was something much more intimate about the way Sam spoke of her brother-in-law. Just in case she was imagining things, Sierra hadn't bothered to ask. Not that it was any of her business anyway.

Now, two days later, she was on her way to meet the man, though she got the impression that he had no idea he was being set up.

"You said we were going to a club?" Sierra asked, interrupting the loving couple holding hands in the front seat. "Isn't it a little early in the day?"

"It's a club, but it isn't what you're thinking." Sam offered. "Well, at least not entirely."

Sierra noticed the subtle way Logan squeezed his wife's hand.

What other kind of clubs were there? Besides the ones that offered drinks to people who congregated to laugh, drink and have a good time?

Oh!

Her mind struggled with the possibility before shrugging off the comment. Glancing at her watch, Sierra added, "I didn't realize clubs were open this early."

Eleven thirty on a Tuesday and Sierra was on her way to meet a mystery man who, despite the fact that they didn't know each other at all, would likely accompany her to a four day business conference to be held in Las Vegas.

The Entertainment Capital of the World.

Sin City.

And one of Sierra's favorite vacation destinations.

She could certainly get down with going to Las Vegas, no matter whom she was going with. She was quite fond of the city, having gone numerous times for girl's only getaways. Never once had she come back disappointed. Going for business, now that would be a first, but no more so than going with a man. Any man.

What would they do if they didn't get along? How was she supposed to suffer through four long days in the party capital of the world with someone she had nothing in common with?

Granted, she was jumping ahead of herself. She hadn't even met him yet. The one upside to it all, if he looked anything like Logan McCoy, at least she was in for a visual treat.

Logan maneuvered the car into an underground parking garage, and Sierra felt the butterflies take flight in her stomach.

Glancing down, she noticed that she was wringing her hands in her lap, a sheer sign of the tension coursing through her veins. She chalked it up to the fact that she suspected Luke had no idea she was coming or anything else that was in store for him, in the coming days. She'd gathered that from the conversation she'd overhead – ok, more like eavesdropped on – earlier between Logan and Sam. When Logan mentioned that Luke didn't seem to be in the best of moods, she'd momentarily questioned her sanity.

Not that she really cared what kind of mood he was in, as long as he could manage to be polite and courteous for four days, only a few hours at a time while they were in Vegas.

Moments later, Sierra was climbing out of the back seat, coming to join Samantha standing at the side of the car.

"Brace yourself." Sam smiled brightly, looking almost playful.

"Is there something I should know before we go in?" Sierra asked, for the second time questioning what she was walking into.

"Not specifically. Let's just say that Logan's brother is the *darker* twin."

"Darker?" Confusion set in, and Sierra tried to comprehend what Sam was saying.

"You know, mysterious. Ominous." Sam laughed as she took Logan's hand.

Great. Just what Sierra needed. Her mind immediately conjured up a version of Logan McCoy; only this one had a permanent scowl, making him look sinister. She smiled to herself.

With a deep breath, she stood up straighter, adjusted her short skirt, and steeled herself for whatever was to come.

How bad could it be?